This Would Be Paradise

By N. D. Iverson

Man can now fly in the air like a bird,
Swim under the ocean like a fish,
He can burrow into the ground like a mole.
Now if only he could walk the earth like a man,
This would be paradise.
-Tommy Douglas

Chapter 1

I groaned and rolled over on the well-used, sagging hotel bed. Thoughts about all the people who slept right where I was laying made my skin crawl like imaginary bedbugs running amok. The sun had managed to peek through the ratty curtains of my once-clean hotel room, disturbing my alcohol induced stupor. I tried to swallow, but my mouth seemed drier than the Nevada desert. Cracking a tired eye open, I found the other twin bed empty.

Zoe, my dumbass friend must have stumbled home with a guy we met last night, while I managed to drag myself back to the room. *What was his name again? Mark? Matt?* I should probably learn to get that straight just in case I had to testify in court when she eventually disappeared after a nightly escapade gone wrong, and then turned up in a dumpster behind Denny's.

The clock read 12:35 PM and I knew Zoe would be staggering back soon, with yet another story to tell. Then in response I would give her the spiel again; the one that started with, "This is how you end up dead in a ditch, spread out in various plastic bags."

"'Let's go to Mardi Gras,' she said. 'It will be fun,' she said," I mocked aloud and then began coughing profusely.

My throat was on fire; the aftermath of a night of drinking, screaming, and taking part in the celebration. I got up in search of a water bottle, finding a sealed one on the messy dresser. In one gulp I downed half the bottle, and then finished it with the next. After throwing it into the garbage can already overflowing with empty bottles, I sauntered into the bathroom.

After splashing some water on my face, I realized I was going to need something stronger. I needed coffee. The hotel was overrun with fellow Mardi Gras partiers, which seemed to be an excuse for the cleaning staff to slack off. Which translated to no coffee. If I wanted a cup, I would have to venture all the way down to the breakfast area. This was not a pleasant prospect.

I glared at my reflection, the blue irises standing out against my red-rimmed eyes. I looked like I belonged in a Judd Apatow movie. I rummaged through my makeup bag looking for some eye drops and lucked out. After a few attempts, I finally managed to get some in my eyes, not just all over my face.

I walked over to the night stand, wiping at my moist cheeks and tried the front desk to see if they could bring me the coffee packets they were supposed to supply. Laziness had always been a problem for me and, as always, I was going to see if I could try the easy route first. It rang ten times with no answer before I hung up. The service here was awful. I tried again, but still no answer. Looks like I'd have to go down to the lobby after all.

I dug to the bottom of my suitcase for some clean clothes and tied my blonde hair up. I wasn't winning any Southern beauty pageants today, but no one was expected to look good with a hangover anyways. I shoved the key card into my pocket; patting it just to be sure it was in there. With the terrible service here I could only imagine what an ordeal it would be if I needed them to unlock my room.

The door latched shut, as I stepped out into the hallway. Noises were coming from somewhere in the hotel, but oddly the hallway was empty of people. As I passed one of the off-white doors, a loud banging sound from behind it caused me to jump clear across the hallway. Apparently some people were still partying. I placed a hand over my heart, feeling the rapid staccato my heart was beating; that was one thing I really didn't need when hungover.

Various bits of luggage and old room service trays lined the hall, making me regret my choice of hotel yet again. The smell of stale and rotting food hung in the air, no doubt drawing in bugs or worse, mice. The florescent lights burned my tired eyes, and I found myself squinting at the worn green carpet as I made my way to the elevator. We were only on the third floor, but like hell I was taking the stairs.

With the main floor button glowing, I leaned against the elevator wall as the steel doors closed. Thankfully, there was no one else in the elevator and better yet, no god awful elevator music to listen to. We shouldn't have been here in the first place, blowing the last of our student loans for a graduation celebration. Instead of partying, we should be out job hunting, armed with our fancy new Art degrees and wide-eyed obliviousness. My dad's words came back to me, like they always did whenever I thought about this, "You know how many people in our night stocking crew have Art degrees? All of them."

The doors opened with a buzzing sound. The main lobby was devoid of people; even the receptionist behind the front desk was gone. Usually there was at least one person standing there with the phone glued to an ear. *Did I sleep through a fire alarm or something?*

I slowly made my way to the buffet area, looking around for a sign of life. Everything was set up but looked like it hadn't been touched. Strange, considering it was already afternoon. Normally stale cereal and that one scary looking sausage that seemed to have been there all week would be all that was left by now.

I poured myself some coffee from the giant stainless steel percolator, watching the steam waft up from the foam cup. The smell alone helped invigorate my dulled senses. Sipping the hot liquid, I started to look around to figure out what was going on and maybe see about some maid service. We weren't messy people, but somehow our hotel rooms always managed to look like a disaster zone – overflowing garbage, towels on the ground, running out of the mini-shampoo bottles sized for the head of an infant.

All the tables in the dining area were open, no one sitting around enjoying the mediocre hotel-provided food. I felt my hackles rise. Usually there was at least one person or group in here at all times. A noise that sounded like someone eating caught my attention and I stepped over to the booths that lined the wall.

"Hello?" I called out as I rounded the tall booths.

The sight that greeted me was not what I had expected. A woman covered in what appeared to be blood, was kneeling over a larger mass on one side of the booth. Her shirt was torn down the front revealing her daisy spotted bra and deep scratch marks on her chest. She snarled at me, flecks of whatever she'd been eating spraying from her red stained lips. I took a big step back.

She slowly got up from the booth, all her attention now focused on me like I had just insulted her outfit. I could see the thing she was on before much more clearly now. *Holy shit, holy shit, holy shit!* It was a man. There was a gaping hole in the body cavity, knotted intestines dangled down the side. I retched at the sight. *Did I unknowingly step onto the set of a horror movie?*

The woman had managed to get herself out of the booth, slipping a little on the blood coated floor. The coffee fell from my hand, as she started toward me, her face contorted into a feral mask. I took off running back the way I'd come, my earlier fatigue forgotten as adrenaline pumped through my veins.

The crazy woman didn't have any weapons on her that I'd seen, but I still didn't want her to catch me. A person can do a lot of damage with just their teeth, exhibit "A" being that man turned into a live game of Operation. The woman was snarling and snapping as she chased me across the lobby. She hadn't said an actual word since I found her, just noises. I had never regretted not working on my cardio until now.

I made the mistake of looking back, which caused me to slow my stride, and the woman lunged at me. Her hands caught my ankles, and I went down with her. As I thrashed wildly, she managed to crawl her way up my body. She smelt the way our garbage can did in the summer heat, and if I wasn't so busy trying to keep her off of me, I might have thrown up. My shirt had ridden up from all the movement and I screamed in pain as her nails raked up my bare side.

Desperate, I grabbed her hair and yanked her to the side. She toppled over as her balance was thrown off. With my legs free of her weight, I kicked my right foot out as hard as I could. The sole of my shoe connected with her head, rolling her a few feet away from me. Clutching my bleeding side, I started running again not bothering to see if she got back up.

I ran straight past the elevator doors to the stairs entrance. I pushed on the metal bar latch, bursting through the door and bounded up the stairs two at a time. *Looks like I'm taking the stairs this time.* The lunatic who didn't even seem fazed by my kick to her head, crashed into the door, her full weight causing the bar latch to open. I spared a glance over the railing and saw her sprawled out on the bottom of the stairs like a drunken teenage girl at a house party. The momentum from going through the door must have caused her to trip. Her head whipped up toward me, and she snarled, clawing at the air, as if that would reach me. *What was wrong with this lady?*

I didn't waste any more time as I ran up to the entrance of the third floor. Once I was through, I booked it down the hallway dodging the various trays and pieces of luggage. Unlike in most horror movies, I didn't have to fumble with the lock as the card slid in and unlocked the door on the first try. A pair of hands grabbed me, as soon as I entered, and I let out a scream.

"Calm the fuck down, Bailey!" Zoe's surprised voice registered in my addled brain.

My shoulders slumped in relief as my adrenaline drained away, leaving me shaky and heaving. I looked up into the set of thinner, dark eyes of my close friend, Zoe, that had been inherited from her Japanese mother. She led me to one of the beds, and I dropped like a stone as the old mattress groaned. Zoe must have just gotten back to the room while I was downstairs being assaulted by a mental patient. She couldn't have timed it any better.

"Are you okay?" Zoe asked, her thin, dark eyes searching for injury. "Oh my god, you're bleeding!"

Zoe lifted up my shirt and gasped at the bloody nail marks that adorned my right side. After running to the bathroom, she re-emerged with a towel and handed it to me. I placed the white, scratchy towel on the wound and winced.

"The bleeding has to stop before we can treat that," Zoe said. "I'm going to call the front desk and see if they have someone who is first-aid qualified."

"Don't bother. There's no one down there. Well, no one helpful."

"What do you mean?" Zoe asked, the receiver against her ear. She gave me an odd look and mashed the buttons. "No one is answering," she muttered.

"Like I said, they aren't going to be much help." I applied more pressure to the wound. The pain was getting worse, so I got up and walked stiffly to the washroom to wet the towel with cold water. The freezing cloth felt wonderful against my burning side, and I sighed in relief as I sat down on the side of the tub. I kicked away the pile of dirty towels on the floor. I will be writing this hotel a nasty review when we leave.

"So what happened?" Zoe asked appearing in the doorway with her arms crossed.

"I don't even know. Some crazy woman attacked me in the dining area." I didn't mention the fact that it looked like the insane lady had cracked open another guy like a lobster dinner. Somehow, I didn't think Zoe would believe me; I still couldn't believe it myself.

"Where the hell was everyone else when this was happening?"

"Zoe, there's no one down there, not even at the front desk," I said, monotone. It all felt so surreal, like maybe I had just imagined the whole thing, dehydration from all the alcohol maybe.

"Should I call 911?"

A flash of anger shot through me. It was like she wasn't hearing a thing I had said. "I don't fucking know, Zoe!" I yelled. She glared at me, and I felt a tinge of guilt for freaking out on her. I sighed. "Sorry. Maybe I should go to the hospital; that woman looked like she was sick or something. I might need a shot."

The bleeding had finally subsided, so I loaded on some Polysporin. The Band-Aids we had didn't cover the whole length of the scratches, so I stuck on as many as it took to cover the three angry marks. *Oh god, what if she gave me something?*

I looked into the mirror. Other than being pale, which was a regular occurrence, I didn't look sick. Not that I'd be able to tell so soon, I'll need a blood test to be sure. The pain in my side was the only symptom I could feel. But then again, I wasn't a doctor.

I left the bathroom and sat down on the side of the bed near the side table.

"What are you doing?" Zoe asked, following me.

"I'm going to give my mom a call and see what she suggests." I dug out the long distance card from my suitcase and started punching in the three hundred numbers required.

I've always hated going to the doctors, let alone hospitals, so I lucked out with my mom. She was a doctor and was the one to treat me and prescribe my medicine. Although I wasn't entirely certain it was legal, it wasn't like she was prescribing me pot or anything. The call finally connected and started ringing. With each ring, I held the phone tighter and tighter. New Orleans was only two hours ahead of British Columbia; someone in the house should be up by now.

I hung up and tried again only to get the same result. My heart rate started to pick up as panic set in. I jumped up and grabbed the television remote, turning the flat screen on.

"What are you doing? TV? Really?" Zoe shook her head. "We should be heading out to the hospital!"

I ignored her as I flipped through the channels until reaching a local news station. A few of the channels were out with *Technical Difficulties* displayed across the screen. The anchor woman looked slightly hysterical as she kept doing her duty and read the news prompt: "There appears to be an outbreak of a viral epidemic. Some experts say it's a new strain of the flu. We advise everyone to stay indoors and, if you come in contact with an infected individual, seek immediate medical assistance. Violent behavior has been reported as a symptom of the virus; therefore, victims should be avoided at all costs. The military have been dispatched in all major cities to help contain the violent individuals."

"Holy shit," Zoe said as she absentmindedly sat down on the bed corner.

The report echoed through my head. *Am I infected with this viral thing now? What kind of treatment is there for it?* I didn't feel like I was going to have some violent outburst like the woman from the lobby.

Zoe just stared at me wide eyed as the news continued: "Due to the unusually high number of cases, all mass transportation has been suspended until further notice to help contain the viral outbreak and to prevent the infection of mass numbers of people. Please arrange for other transportation or other living arrangements if you are away from home, as we do not know when the airports and trains will be back to their regular schedule."

"You're fucking kidding me," Zoe exhaled, rubbing her temples.

"Do you think it's like the H1N1 scare that happened a few years ago?" I asked, trying to convince myself that everything was going to be okay.

"I don't know," she muttered scrolling on her smart phone. "It looks like our flight is cancelled."

With both of us being twenty-two, renting a car would be out of the question. Never mind the insane bill we would have racked up driving all the way back to B.C. *Shit*. This day could not get any worse.

We both jumped at the sudden onslaught of fists banging on our hotel room door.

I take that back.

Chapter 2

I stared at the door, not wanting to get up and see who or what it was. Zoe walked over to answer it, but I grabbed her arm as she passed by.

"Are you insane? That could be the crazy, sick woman," I hissed.

"I'm just going to look through the peephole," she answered, removing her arm from my grasp.

Zoe approached the door, peering through the small eyehole. Before I could say anything more, she ripped open the door. A disheveled guy in sweatpants and an unkempt beard burst into the room, shutting the door behind him.

"Mike, what the hell?" Zoe demanded of the scruffy man.

"Zoe," he huffed; a thin layer of sweat coated his pale skin.

I noticed his left leg was bleeding. The blood had seeped through his ripped sweatpants and had started to drip onto the carpet. *There goes our damage deposit.*

"Are you okay?" Zoe asked, taking a step back from Mike. His eyes were darting all over the place rapidly, like he was searching for someone.

"One of..." Mike took a deep breath. "...one of my buddies got sick, I think. He bit my leg!"

Zoe ran into the bathroom for our last clean towel and he placed it on his leg wound as he sat on one of the beds. Sitting seemed to calm him down; he didn't look as panicked as he did before.

"I'm Bailey by the way," I said, with a noncommittal wave.

"Mike."

I wanted to say, "Yeah I got that," but I held my tongue for once. I grabbed Zoe and ushered her into the bathroom.

"Uh, who's that?" I asked.

"He's the guy from last night." She at least had the good graces to look embarrassed. I rolled my eyes.

"Hey, you girls see the news?" Mike yelled from the other room.

"Yeah, there's some serious shit going on," Zoe said, leading us back to where Mike was sitting. "We were about to head to the hospital."

I glared at Zoe for telling him, undoubtedly he would want to come along.

"Mind if I go, too? I think I need to have this looked at," he motioned to the still bleeding wound that adorned his lower leg. *See, I knew it.*

"Well if we are going to do this, let's go," I sighed, grabbing my bag with all my documents in it.

The motion of putting the bag strap on my shoulder pulled my wound taut and I sucked in a breath at the fresh wave of pain that radiated from my side.

"You got bit, too?" Mike asked.

"Scratched, by some crazy woman downstairs," I answered through clenched teeth.

"Should we be going back down there then?" he asked, a scared look flashing across his face.

"How else do you suggest we get to the hospital?" I countered.

"Call for an ambulance?"

"No ambulance would come for a scratch and a bite," Zoe sighed, grabbing her own purse.

I had briefly thought of calling the police to report the attack, but I figured I would have to fill out something at the hospital, so I would just do it all there.

"We should call a taxi, though," I suggested, as the idea came to me.

Zoe nodded and flipped through the ratty phone book beside the room phone. She found a number and dialed. Mike and I just watched in silence as she held the receiver to her ear.

"You're fucking kidding me," Zoe gritted as she slammed it down. "No one is answering there either!"

All right, at this point the situation was starting to make me nervous. One thing after another kept happening; I was attacked by some crazy woman who appeared to have ripped open another man earlier, the news was going on about some virus, and flights had been cancelled. This was like something straight out of a B-List Hollywood horror movie and I was having a hard time believing it was all real.

Maybe I was still hungover, asleep. At that thought, hope bloomed in my chest. Then I remembered the radiating pain from my wound and I knew I wasn't imagining all of this. Unfortunately, I was living it and first things first, I needed to get my side looked at.

"Well, I guess we'll be walking so let's go," I said as I headed toward the door.

"Are you going to be able to walk?" Zoe asked Mike.

"I should be able to hobble there, it's only got to be like a ten-minute walk from here anyways," he said, heaving himself back to a standing position.

I opened the door a bit and peeked outside, looking down the hallway for signs of any sick people. The coast was clear, so I stepped outside with the other two following me. Mike was limping, slowing us down as we walked quietly to the elevator. I wasn't going back to the stairs again and this time it had nothing to do with my laziness. Plus, Mike wouldn't take the stairs too well either, he was going to slow us down enough as it was.

"Should we be taking the elevator?" Mike asked as I smashed the down button.

"The place isn't on fire."

The ride down was awkward; we were all looking anywhere else but at each other. *Oh look, a stain on the floor how interesting.* This is what I hated about elevators. They turned everyone into socially awkward weirdos. With a ding, the elevator opened up to the first floor, but none of us made a move to get out. I was about to say, "After you," when Zoe took the plunge and stepped out first. I glanced around trying to spot anyone or see if that crazy lady had escaped the stairwell.

"Wow, there really is no one down here," Zoe said quietly.

"What, did you think it was all an elaborate hoax?" I asked, and she glared at me. The pain continually throbbing along my side was making me even more unpleasant than I normally was when I woke up hungover.

We walked outside, and instantly I noticed all the activity outside the hotel. Cars were rushing and honking all over the road, people were running along the sidewalks, and sirens were going off all over the place. Since this was Mardi Gras, all the activity wasn't that unusual, but the atmosphere had taken on a panicked feel rather than one of letting loose. I was almost run down by some guy pushing an overflowing shopping cart he had stolen from a local Walmart, but I managed to dance around him as he sped by.

"Excuse you!" Zoe yelled after the guy, but he was long gone.

"So I don't think we will be able to get a taxi," I sighed as I started the walk to the hospital.

I could see the giant H sign from our hotel, but like everywhere in the city, all the buildings were farther away than they looked. With Mike slowing us down and all the craziness going on, the ten-minute walk would most likely be stretched out. We almost got mowed down while crossing the street and Mike barely hobbled out of the way in time.

"Jesus!" Mike yelled as he stumbled to find his footing.

"This is like the L.A. riots!" Zoe said.

"Zoe, you were like four when the L.A. riots happened." I shook my head.

"Well Bailey, there's this magical entity called 'The Internet' that gives you information for things that you weren't there to see happen in person," Zoe shot back.

"Anyways, it doesn't look like there's any looting going on yet," I said and as soon as the words left my mouth, one of the store front windows crashed in on the other side of the street.

Zoe shot me a smug look and I gritted my teeth. I gave a quick glance over to where the noise had come from and thankfully I didn't see anyone carrying off a TV set, but people were filing in through the open store front window. Jay's Pharmacy didn't stand a chance. Looking up, I could see that we were closer to the hospital, but a lot of the traffic seemed to be heading that way so I took that to mean I wouldn't be getting treated anytime soon. *Maybe I should have hit up that pharmacy...*

"How much longer do you think it will be?" Mike asked, pain dripping from his voice.

"I think we're pretty close?" Zoe offered.

An ambulance whizzed past us with its sirens blaring and tires squealing. I heard a scream from behind us, and we wheeled around to see what happened. A woman had been tackled by someone who looked like they were infected with whatever the crazy woman from the hotel had. The guy launched himself on top of her, *tearing* into her, causing blood to spray everywhere and pool around her. Her muffled screams soon stopped and new screams of the people who witnessed the attack erupted. People scrambled to get away, and we were forced to run before we got trampled by the panicked group now heading in our direction.

"Holy shit!" Mike yelled as he tried to keep up with us despite his injured leg.

Zoe sent me a look that could only be summed up as, "What the hell did we just witness?"

For that, I had no answer. It did help shine some light on what happened to me in the hotel lobby. I had come so close to ending up like that poor woman back there, the thought made a shiver run down my spine. I had no desire to end up a human chew-toy.

Panting with exertion, we had finally made it to the hospital thanks to the group on our heels forcing us to run. My side was burning anew from the heavy breaths that were wracking my lungs and chest. Mike seemed to have it worse, he was now wincing with every step he took and his skin had taken on an ashen color making him look sickly. He reminded me of the woman who attacked me in the breakfast room. I shuffled to the other side of Zoe, as far away from him as I could go without looking suspicious.

I unconsciously touched my side and looked at my reflection in the glass windows surrounding the hospital. I didn't have the sickly appearance, so maybe a scratch didn't have the same effect that a bite did. There was only one-way to find out.

"Shit, we're going to be here for hours," I grumbled as we walked into the crowded lobby.

We had to squeeze our way through the masses just to get to the front desk line. People were yelling and crying all over the place. Some people had bloody rags pressed to their wounds, dripping blood all over the place. This had to be the most unsanitary hospital I had ever seen. Others were trying to calm down the hysteric patients, not having much luck. Finally, we had gotten through the line and had our turn at the desk.

"Number of people and emergency," the frazzled receptionist stated.

"Uh, two injured with a bite and deep scratches," I said adding an extra bit of pain into my voice hoping she would not just send us away.

"We're only taking emergencies at the moment due to the high volume of incidents," she stated.

"We were bit and scratched by someone who has that sickness or whatever it is," I reasoned.

Her eyes flashed to mine. She knew something we didn't.

"Fourth floor, take a left at the elevators."

I was about to ask her why, when she yelled, "Next!" and we were *effectively* dealt with. I motioned for the stairs, and Mike grimaced, but it looked like the two elevators would be busy for a while judging by the crowd waiting to get on to them. The door to the stairs was held open due to the steady stream of people going up and down not wanting to wait for the elevator.

"It's only the fourth floor," I shrugged after Mike said he wouldn't be able to take them.

My attitude toward stairs had changed abruptly in the last twenty-four hours; not that taking the stairs appealed to me, just that they would be quicker. We squeezed into the cramped flow of traffic heading up the stairs, with Mike being prodded on by the people behind him. Now came the tricky part of being able to stop long enough to get through the door we needed. I managed to open it enough so that I could get through, much to the dismay of the very vocal people behind us. I flashed them the middle finger for their troubles.

Unfortunately, the fourth floor was just as crowded as the downstairs and even more alarming was the fact that some doctors were coming in and out of certain rooms in bulky biohazard suits. Every seat was taken up with sickly looking people, and pretty much every square inch of the walls were lined with people just waiting to be treated. Going past the elevators, we found yet another desk to approach and told them what happened.

"Take a seat, and we'll call you when it's your turn," the nurse said from behind her glass wall, taking one last look at my Canadian driver's license before she handed it back.

"Let's see if there's any space by the water fountains," I said, leading Zoe and Mike away.

Once we found enough space to claim as our own, Mike plunked down looking worse than ever. It seemed like he wasn't able to catch his breath, even though we had more than enough time to do so while standing in line at the desk. Zoe plunked down beside him, then I gingerly sat down on the other side of her, my side protesting the whole way. We sat there for a good hour watching person by person being called, new people taking their vacated chairs and spots.

What I didn't start to notice until just then, was the fact that we never saw them leave through the lobby area. It didn't look like there was another way off this floor other than the area we came in through. The biohazard men were mainly sticking to the rooms at the end of the hall, which only the worse looking patients were being ushered to. It all seemed very suspicious, made more so by the fact that the staff refused to answer anyone's questions.

"Girls, I think it's getting worse," Mike said. We turned to him before slowly scooting away.

He started to cough violently with his back hunched over. His messy hair obscured his face, but I could see the steady stream of blood dripping from his mouth onto the dirty titles. When he finally looked up, his teeth were stained red and the vessels in his eyes seemed to have taken over the whites. He coughed and blood misted into the air.

"Holy shit!" Zoe and I jumped up as he started to go into convulsions. "Help!" she screamed in panic.

I just stood there, not having a clue what to do and hoped I wasn't next.

Chapter 3

Two men in hazmat suits rushed over with a gurney, squishing through the sea of people just to get to us. It took two doctors to restrain Mike enough to get him onto it. I was no doctor, but I was pretty sure you weren't supposed to try to move someone while they were having a seizure.

"Hey!" I yelled to the suited men. "Should you be moving him right now?"

They completely ignored me as they strapped Mike down and shoved us out of the way, carting him off to one of the rooms down the hall.

"Hey!" I yelled again, but it was to no avail.

Mike was still thrashing around when they opened up one of the doors and tried to push the gurney in. But before they could, another patient rushed out of the room snarling and clawing at them. The doctors lost their grip on Mike, and he was pushed up against the wall as they tried to subdue the crazy patient. The deranged man had waxy, grey skin and his eyes were beyond bloodshot, almost as if all the vessels in his eyes had burst. His jaw dripped with red, as did his clothes and hands.

One of the doctors howled in pain as the man's teeth sunk into his arm. *I guess those suits weren't bite-proof.* The suited doctor tried to pry the lunatic off, but he was stuck on there good, and it didn't look like he was going to let go anytime soon. The other doctor stood still for what seemed like forever before he took off running in the opposite direction. That was when all hell started to break loose. All the patients around us started to panic, and screams soon erupted all over the waiting area.

"Bailey!" Zoe yelled, as she was shoved out of the way when people started to dart all over the place.

I tried hard to keep track of her, but was soon lost in the crowd of scared people trying to get off the floor. I found myself being ushered against my will toward the hallway, where the deranged patent was now fully on top of the suited doctor. His blood ran down the sides of his bright yellow suit, pooling under him.

The crazed man on top of the doctor snapped his head up, chewing and snarling at the same time. Red stained pieces of the doctor's skin and hazmat gear were sprayed all over the place. The sick man scrambled over the doctor's unmoving body and lunged at the group of us who were being pushed toward him. I felt panic grip my body as the man started to rush us. People screamed, arms and limbs were bumping into me from all directions, then someone was shoved callously right at the approaching crazy patient.

"Help!" the woman shrieked. For a reason that I could not explain, I reached out and tried to pull her back.

But it was too late. The man latched onto her like a rabid dog and soon her screams turned into gurgling then stopped all together, as the blood poured from the bite wound in her neck. The doctor who had been viciously attacked first, started to sit up slowly and I knew that meant it was time to run. Putting the terrified face of that woman out of my mind, I tried to shove my way back through the crowd toward the stairs. I found that if I stuck close to the wall, I was better able to move through the crowd.

I frantically looked around for Zoe, but I couldn't see her over the mass amounts of people. Her straight, black hair was camouflaged among the horde of heads, even though she stood over 5'10. She managed to make me look short at 5'5.

"Zoe!" I yelled as hard as I could over the chaos, but if she heard me I got no reply.

I had to make my choice fast. Either I kept trying to search for Zoe in here and possibly get trampled to death or try to get out and hope Zoe did the same. Soon that choice was made for me as the doctor in the bulky bio-hazard suit, joined in the fray, attacking people. His teeth were rendered useless as the face shield protected the unfortunate individual he had grabbed. It looked like the woman who had her neck bitten was starting to convulse on the ground as the virus wracked her body. I don't know how that was even possible. At this point, more of her blood was coating the linoleum than pumping in her veins, if her heart was even still working.

I took one last look back and wished I hadn't. One of the patients in the waiting room must have had a gun – this was America after all – and shot the crazed sick man. The loud sound from the gun caused everyone to duck and scream anew. The crazed man was shot point blank in the shoulder, causing him to whip around from the impact sending a spray of dark blood all over the wall behind him. I watched in mute horror as the sick man pulled himself back to his feet, his left arm barely hanging on. The bullet had punched a wide hole in his shoulder, and the tendons now looked like wiggling ground-up meat. Still snarling, he walked unsteadily toward the shocked gunslinger. The brief thought of why no police were here yet crossed my mind.

The sick man lunged at the guy holding the handgun, and soon a barrage of bullets impaled him. Not until one of the bullets hit the sick man in between the eyes, did he stop his assault. The body slumped to the ground finally unmoving and didn't get back up. The man lowered his emptied gun, the barrel smoking at his side. Panic rained all around and I stood frozen, too shocked to move. I had seen a lot since I woke up this morning, but somehow seeing a man shoot another in the face was enough to hit home. Something was happening, something big. I knew right in that moment life would never be the same.

"Bailey!" I heard my name screamed over the noise, but I didn't move until fingers wrapped around my wrist. I barely registered the tugging at my arm. "Bailey we have to leave!" Zoe shouted, trying to pull me along.

I stumbled behind, Zoe dragging me by my arm, still in a daze from everything. My mind was trying to play catch up to all that I had witnessed. I could no longer shrug this off as another episode of H1N1, nor could this be a horribly vivid dream. The stairs were even worse going down now that everyone was trying to flee the fourth floor. A man was shoved down, taking a bunch of people with him, but no one stopped to help. Instead, they just tried to jump over the pile of bodies in their attempt to get out. It was every man for himself.

Zoe continually gave glances back to make sure that it was still my arm she was grabbing. My legs managed to work even though I was not really there, it seemed. I was turning into one of those people who froze up and shut down in emergencies. *They were always the first to go...* At that thought my mind tried to snap itself back into place, self-preservation taking over. Like hell I would be one of the first knocked off.

We managed to overtake the stairs as one massive group, bursting out onto the first floor. People jumped up from their chairs and dodged out of the way, as we all poured out into the lobby in an attempt to escape the hospital. A shrill alarm went off, the emergency lights blinking.

Why did we even come here in the first place? If this infection was spreading, then the hospital is where the sick would go. I wished I had clued into this earlier. But, then we would have been stuck with Mike when the virus took over and did whatever it did to him. Guilt wasn't something I was accustomed to feeling, but I felt a twinge of it at the moment knowing we left Mike behind. I tried to justify it to myself by saying he was doomed either way, which was unfortunately true. *Was I next?* I wasn't bitten, just scratched. I had lasted this long when it looked like it over took all the others quickly by comparison.

Soon, the people in the lobby started to join our massive group and ran for the exit as well. It must have been a sight to see; hundreds of people pouring out of the hospital doors, running onto the roads and sidewalks. Car tires were squealing as people were pushed out into the flow of traffic. Zoe had managed to steer us back toward the direction of the hotel and we took off in a sprint, no longer slowed down by Mike. After what seemed like hours, we finally stopped running to catch our breath and give my side a break.

"Zoe," I huffed and pointed to the corner store.

"It's going to be just as bad in there."

"I know, but I'm going to *need* some antiseptic or something for my scratches."

Zoe gave the store a skeptical glance, but nodded. We jogged over to the entrance, the automatic doors opening for us. The inside was pandemonium; people were grabbing everything they could. I made a dash for the first aid section, scanning the shelves around the people looking for anything I could use. I managed to grab a couple bottles of spray antiseptic and gauze. I hadn't realized just how hungry I was until I saw the hanging strip of beef jerky packages, so I grabbed a couple of those as well. And a bottle of Flintstones vitamins just to be on the safe side.

I jumped in the back of the long line, with Zoe joining me with her arms full of stuff. I had to continually elbow people out of my way, not unlike shopping on Boxing Day. We handed the cashier some money when got up to the till, not even bothering with our change as we ran out of the congested building. I stuffed my haul into my pack as we continued back toward the hotel.

"What do we do?" Zoe asked quietly after we had been walking briskly in silence for a few minutes.

"I have no idea," I shrugged. "Not something we can prepare for you know?"

And I used to laugh at my Dad and brother for watching those crazy survivalist, doomsday TV shows. If I was in a laughing mood, I would have laughed at the irony.

"We need to get back home," Zoe said.

"We would basically have to cross the entire U.S. to get home," I groaned at the thought of the daunting task. "With no airplanes or trains, unless we steal a car, that's out of the question as well."

We fell back into a silent trot the rest of the journey back to the hotel. The streets hadn't improved at all. An ambulance had crashed into the front of one of the stores; its siren still going off as it lay, still embedded in the wall. One guy was running down the streets yelling about zombies and that was probably the sanest thing I had seen all day.

The hotel lobby was empty, but we booked it to the elevator anyways. Our hallway was still deserted except for the mess, luckily no sick people. Once we stepped into the quiet room, I finally noticed the ringing in my ears. I sat down and took a bite of my beef jerky just as my stomach started to growl. I offered some to Zoe, who gave me a bottle of water in return. We sat there eating and contemplating.

"Do you think you're going to catch it?" Zoe asked me with concern in her eyes.

"I really hope not," I said taking a drink of my water. "I don't feel sick or anything."

Zoe eyed me more carefully, nodding when she convinced herself it must be true.

"You don't look sick, just pale," she said. "But you're always pale."

We sat for hours flipping through the channels for any useful information, but all we could gather was that main transportation had seized and that emergency centers were being set up in the Superdome and nearby schools.

"Should we try for the arena tomorrow?" Zoe asked, pointing to the onscreen picture of the giant football field.

It sounded all well and good, but having that many people crammed into an area like that would probably have the same results as the hospital. *But what other choice do we have?*

"I think the school would be the best option, since it would be less crowded," I said finally, and Zoe nodded.

I gathered up the sheets and pillows on my bed and carried them off to the bathroom.

"What are you doing?"

"I'm going to sleep in the bathtub just in case I do get sick or whatever it is," I said dropping the sheets into the dry tub. "I can lock the door so I won't be able to attack you or anything."

Zoe stared at me, fear plain as day on her face. She gulped and nodded as she gave me a hug, her eyes a little glassy. I shut the door and latched the lock getting ready to try to sleep. I didn't feel sick, but who knows how this thing went. I changed out my bandages and sprayed on some of the antiseptic, which felt akin to pouring acid in the wounds.

Is now the time my brief life is supposed to flash before my eyes in a moment of self-recollection? If so, I really hope it was the good highlight reel, not the one that included me chasing my shoe down the hallway steps during the break between classes in grade school or the time I kicked a rock that turned out not to be a rock, but a very upset raccoon.

If I was wishing for things, I might as well wish to not catch this sickness. I wasn't ready to die. Tears started to threaten at the thought, but I held them back. Crying would do me no good.

From behind the door Zoe said, "What do I do if I need to pee?"

I wiped at my moist eyes as I lowered myself into the makeshift bed, my thoughts returning to something less morbid.

"Should have thought of that before."

Chapter 4

The first thing my mind registered was the stiffness and lack of cooperation in my limbs. Images from the previous day roared through my head, forcing me from my dreamless sleep.

I'm alive.

My eyes flashed opened and I tried to move, but soon realized I was confined in a small, hard area. Right, I was in the bathtub. I sat up only to smack my head on the faucet. *Why the hell did I sleep with my head on this side?*

Rubbing the sore spot on my head, I climbed over the tub wall. My limbs protested as I was finally able to stretch out. I used to sleep in the bathtub when I was sick as a kid, but didn't remember it being so uncomfortable.

I lifted up my shirt to inspect my wounds and surprisingly they didn't look worse like I thought they would. Whatever was in that antiseptic spray actually worked; for once the stinging was worth it. So I applied some more, wincing at the burning sensation before I taped the gauze over the wound.

"You still alive in there?" Zoe asked hesitantly as she tapped on the door.

I debated making a groaning sound in lieu of answering, but even I wasn't that cruel. "Still kicking, though my side is killing me," I admitted, opening the door.

Zoe gave me a brief hug, which added unwanted pressure to my pained side, so I politely shoved her off. Relief was plastered on her face, but her red rimmed eyes hinted that she had been crying.

"I'm glad," she smiled.

"That makes two of us."

"So does this mean you're immune?" Zoe asked following me back out to the beds.

"You're asking the wrong person," I shrugged. "Maybe it only gets passed on through saliva."

I turned on the news to see if anything had changed, and after watching for a bit I realized that they were showing the exact same newscast that was on the day before. The same reporter, the same clothes, the exact same words and expressions. Could they even do that?

"So are we heading for that emergency shelter?" Zoe asked.

"You think we should?" I asked turning from the television screen.

Zoe nodded. We didn't stand much of a chance just waiting in the hotel room. The school would have supplies, guards, and maybe even transportation out of the city. We jumped into motion stuffing our bags with all that we had packed. I was glad I had brought my huge camping backpack even though I have never camped a day in my life; it just had all the storage I needed. And it came with a free compass, which was still wrapped in its original packaging in one of the various pockets. I hefted it onto my back to test the weight, and I almost toppled over from the added pounds.

"Do you think we can bring our suitcases?" I asked, looking longingly at my stuff that I really did not want to leave behind.

"Sure, why not?" Zoe shrugged. "But you're wheeling your own damn suitcase."

"Oh come on, I'm injured," I whined.

Zoe just shook her head.

We packed in silence for a little before Zoe spoke up. "I feel guilty that we left Mike yesterday," she said quietly.

"I admit I feel a tad bit guilty too, but what could have we done differently?"

"I don't know, something."

"Like what? Run over to his gurney and have him attack us as we unstrapped him?"

She flinched. Mike had gotten whatever virus this was and would have eventually turned on us. None of the sick people we had encountered had seemed in their right mind; in fact, they didn't seem to understand anything at all. Of all the infected people we saw yesterday, none of them spoke so much as a single word. Just snarls. And even a swift kick to the head didn't seem to slow them down. We needed some sort of protection, like a gun, not that either of us knew how to shoot one.

"What do we do if we run into more of the sick people?" Zoe asked as she tied up her shoes. I noticed she fumbled with the laces, her hands shaking.

"Go Babe Ruth on their asses?" I joked to tried to ease the tension.

"And where would we get the bats, pray tell?"

"Walmart, sporting goods stores, pawn shops, take your pick," I guessed running through all the likely suspects.

"We could add nails to them, too."

"What kind of badass weapon would be complete without nails?"

I guess making light of the situation was a coping mechanism of sorts; it helped to take our mind off of the horrors of the past day, if only by a little bit. A gun would be our best choice but who would sell a gun to an unregistered, twenty-two-year-old girl who had never even held one before? I've played shooter games on Xbox, but that was all the experience I had in that department.

The mention of homemade explosives was tossed into the game of weapon roulette we seemed to be playing. My knowledge in that area was limited to putting a rag in a bottle of booze and setting it on fire, not that I had ever attempted that before. Knowing my luck, I'd set myself on fire instead.

We joked about the different methods of protection, but it felt forced. We were purposely avoiding what we wanted to say. Zoe stilled her mad packing, which was normally at lot more organized and looked me in the eyes.

"Bailey, aren't you freaked out?" Zoe scrutinized me the way one would for a particularly hard version of the daily crossword.

"No, I'm perfectly at ease. Just another day in New Orleans."

"You don't have to be such a sarcastic bitch all the time," Zoe scowled.

"What do you want me to say? That I'm freaked out because we're trapped here, practically a whole country away from home?" My unease was starting to leak into my voice. "Or worried that I seem to be considering building an arsenal like the Unabomber? Or that we seem to be living a high-definition version of *Dawn of the Dead*?"

Zoe arched a brow as I stopped to take a breath. "Feel better?"

I sighed and plopped down on the bed, finally allowing my mind to process the last twenty-four hours. We were living the start of every zombie movie ever, and I chuckled at the thought. The laughter spread through me like an electrical current and soon I was clutching my sides as the peals of laughter just wouldn't stop. Zoe gave me the look that meant she was contemplating my sanity. I had seen this look a few times throughout our years of friendship.

"You always laugh at the worse times," she muttered. "So this must be serious."

I wiped the unwarranted tears from my eyes and felt marginally better, like I had just undergone a twenty-second therapy session. But the hysterics came at a price. My side was starting to burn again from the sudden movement, and I held my breath, my usual reaction to pain. Once the throbbing started to subside, I turned back to our task at hand.

"So, just how screwed are we?" Zoe asked her voice uneven.

"Truthfully, I don't know."

I looked away, but not before I spotted the tear slipping down her cheek. I was not one for comforting nor did I have the capacity for it at the moment, so I just kept going on like I hadn't noticed. Zoe sniffed and wiped at her eyes. I scanned the room for the Kleenex box and grabbed a tissue. She took it without hesitation.

"I wish I could deal with things the way you do," she admitted.

I was rather shocked at her declaration, "Trust me; I'm just trying to keep it together."

Zoe was the nice girl who got along with everybody, why would she want to be like me? I was the girl who made sarcastic remarks and managed to make more enemies than friends. If anything, I envied her ability to make friends and trust so easily. I shook my head, realizing now was not the time to go down that road.

With our bags packed, we took one last look around the room to see if we missed anything. It felt like we had taken everything that wasn't bolted down. I peeked out the door and motioned for Zoe to follow when I didn't see anyone in the hallway. Well, at least I wasn't going to miss this place. I had to maneuver my suitcase through the mess that was the hallway, so that it wouldn't tip over. I could hear noises coming from behind a couple of the doors, someone even rammed up against one from the other side. I looked at Zoe and she gave me a frightened look in return.

"Ah, hello?" I asked as I approached the door labeled 315.

Instead of an answer, snarling erupted from the other side and whoever was in there started to hammer and bang against the door.

"Holy shit, let's move," Zoe said grabbing my arm and trying to steer me toward the elevator.

Why couldn't the person open the door? Maybe the virus wrecked the brain so much that they couldn't even figure out how to use a door handle. They could still move, so motor functioning wasn't the issue. It was like once infected, the person turned into some mindless, violent predator only focused on attacking others. I was really trying to stay clear of the word *zombie* because it seemed so ridiculous, but it looked like Hollywood got it right for once.

We rode down the elevator for the last time and started on our long walk to the school. The streets were not as busy as the previous day, but the destruction and chaos were still evident. Stores were broken into and windows were smashed. Cars were all over the place, some just sitting in the middle of the road with their doors wide open but no one inside. It truly looked like a mass evacuation had gone on because no one would just leave their car sitting in the middle of the road abandoned. I had a rusty 2001 Honda Civic back home, and although it was a hunk of junk, I still wouldn't have just left it.

People were still scurrying around; smoke was rising from some of the buildings on the east side of the city. Luckily, the school we were trying to get to was south and a good distance away from the billowing smoke. Downside to that was that it was a fair walking distance from where we stood.

"We could not look more like tourists right now," Zoe sighed, as she rolled her suitcase behind her.

I chuckled, "Might as well have a 'Please Rob Me' sign plastered on our foreheads."

Our joking cut off abruptly as we spotted a body lying in the street, next to one of the abandoned vehicles. There was bloody stain all around the unmoving corpse, and I could smell the rotting stench from the sidewalk. A flash of color in my peripheral caught my attention and I turned to witness a crazed man chasing a woman around the corner. At that, we started to walk faster.

After a few minutes of hiking, we noticed a crowd of people standing around on the sidewalk. When we got closer I saw the bus stop sign sticking up over the crowd.

"Aren't the buses canceled?" I stopped and asked one of the people waiting.

"There was an emergency broadcast sayin' that the buses are in use only for transportation to the shelters," one lady answered, looking about her nervously.

Zoe and I shared a look then parked ourselves, and our bags, in the queue line to wait for the bus. All the people in line seemed to be in a daze, one child was quietly sobbing into her mother's jacket, while others were whipping their heads around for any signs of sick people. Just as I was starting to get antsy, the bus roared around the corner, and everyone started to grab their bags in anticipation. Through the windows I could tell the bus was not completely full, which was good since there were at least a dozen of us.

"I don't have any change," I said to the driver as we boarded the bus.

"We're not charging anyone since this is to go to the emergency shelters," he replied, looking at me like I was retarded. I thought it was a valid thing to say.

There was no sitting room, so Zoe and I had to stand which, admittedly, was still better than walking all that way through the chaos. The bus driver announced that we would be going to the high school located on the south side of the city, and that if we wished to go to the Superdome, then we would have to wait until the next batch of people were picked up.

"God, I hate buses," Zoe muttered as she looked around in disdain.

"Why, Francis? Why must you hate everything?" I joked and she cracked a smile.

Ironically, it was usually the other way around; I was the one hating everything. Zoe still calls me Daria as a joke every once and a while. The bus took a sharp corner, and I was thrown into the person behind me, my elbow connecting with their nose.

"Oh god! I'm so sorry!" I quickly apologized as I scrambled to get off the person's lap.

I got a nasally response, "It's all right; at least your giant suitcase didn't come with you."

The person I happened to smash into turned out to be a decent-looking guy with blond, shaggy hair and a grin plastered on his face, despite the fact that he was now holding his injured nose. His broad shoulders were framed nicely in his dark brown leather jacket. I found myself grinning back in return as I sat back up.

"Yeah, it probably would have done even more damage," I said apologetically.

"What do you have in there?" he asked, eyeing the suitcase warily.

"Oh you know, everything."

"I'm Darren, by the way," he flashed his white teeth as he smiled; scrunching his nose, making sure that it was not seriously injured. At least I hadn't made it bleed.

"Bailey, and this is Zoe," I said pointing my thumb at her.

She wiggled her way over, the prospect of a good looking guy too much to pass up.

"Bailey, that's a nice name," Darren said, pulling a line from every pick-up line ever.

"Well, my mom's a raging alcoholic so..." I struggled to keep myself from laughing at the look of shock that over took his face and ruining the joke.

"You're kidding right?"

"Don't mind her, she's always like that," Zoe barged in, saving the poor guy. He laughed a little in relief.

"Which shelter are you guys heading to?"

"The high school," Zoe answered.

"Me too," Darren said. "Seems like a better choice than the Superdome."

"So, you here for Mardi Gras, too?" I asked.

"Yes I am, not that there will be any more partying going on."

"By yourself?" I prodded.

His face faltered a little bit. "No, I got separated from my group last night and haven't been able to meet up with them." His reply sounded off to me somehow.

"They probably headed to one of the emergency shelters too," Zoe beamed at him, as I resisted the urge to roll my eyes.

Here we were in the middle of some viral outbreak, and Zoe was flirting up a storm. Well, at least she was good at it. The more we talked to Darren, the more I faltered in between believing him and feeling that something was off with him. I suppose I could have just as easily been separated from Zoe at the hospital, so maybe his tale of losing his friends was the truth.

"So zombies, huh?" Darren offered when our conversation hit a lull.

"That sounds so ridiculous," I sighed.

"How else can you explain it?" Darren countered.

"Maybe mad cow disease has made a comeback and this time got passed on to humans?" I mused.

"Maybe, but I saw a girl *bite* and *chew* on another yesterday. You saying mad cow turns people into cannibals?" Darren asked.

"Hey, I never said I was a scientist," I put my hands in the air in mock surrender. "It's just that the word zombie seems absurd."

"They're only zombies if they're dead," Zoe pointed out. "Are the sick people dead?" None of us had an answer to that.

I thought back to when the doctor and woman bled out in the hospital then started to move around again once I thought they were dead. So far, it seemed George Romero had it right, except for the movies that came after *Dawn of the Dead*; now those were just terrible.

The bus came to a halt outside the school. It was surrounded by police cars and emergency response teams, like a medieval army defending a castle. As we filed out of the bus we were directed into the building by people in generic reflective vests. I felt Zoe grab onto the back of my shirt so that we didn't get separated and Darren followed close behind.

"How many?" a man at the entrance asked holding up his clipboard.

"Two," I answered.

"Make that three," Zoe corrected.

Great, another stray.

"Anyone in your party sick?" he asked with a serious, no-nonsense face.

"Nope," I answered calmly even though I was sweating on the inside. What if they found out I was scratched? Would I even get a chance to explain that I didn't catch the sickness?

"Go on through the main doors," the man said ticking off something on his clipboard.

I followed the parade of people in front of me leading to the main doors. Before we got through, we heard a bunch of shouting back at the man with the clipboard.

"What do you mean he can't come in?" a hysteric woman was yelling, motioning to her son.

Standing beside her, the small boy must have been no more than ten years old. His face was ashen and grey, his eyes almost sunken in. Rattling coughs were shaking his body.

"Sorry, no one who is sick is allowed into the shelter. It's to protect the others inside and prevent further spread of the virus," the man tried to reason.

Other emergency workers were called over to usher the distraught woman and her sick son off the premises. I felt bad for them, but at the same time I was relieved they weren't going to be sharing any enclosed space with us. Like me, I'm sure there were a few people who hid their wounds from the emergency staff. I knew I was okay, but would the others be? No one looked sick at the moment, but I knew that could all change in a heartbeat. All it took was one to start attacking others for it to spread around like the flu during flu season in an office.

Great. Suddenly I didn't feel so sure about going to the school.

Chapter 5

We had found our way over to a corner with a few cots and claimed it as our own. As I slid my backpack off my shoulders – much to my back's relief – I looked around the area we had been ushered to. The main gym had been full so they started putting people in this multipurpose lunch room, which is where we were currently located. The cheap fluorescent lights made everything appear clinical, and I wondered how long they expected us to stay in here for.

All the families and groups of people mainly stayed to their own area, no one was in the mood to socialize. It was extremely loud in the cramped area with kids screaming all over the place. It reminded me of going to the mall on a weekend; I hated malls for that same reason.

"We should have just stayed at the hotel," I said as a screaming herd of kids ran by. "At least it would have been quiet."

"Yeah, but at least we have supplies and protection here," Zoe pointed out.

That was true, but being around this many people was nerve-wracking in the best of situations. I was never a people person.

Darren raised an eyebrow at me. "You keep looking at people like that, you're going to freak them out."

"So? I don't want to be attacked in the middle of the night. Not that I will be able to sleep in this anyways."

"I'd be more worried about getting robbed," Darren said.

"Thanks, now I really won't sleep," I muttered.

A table was set up that had an emergency worker handing out wrapped sandwiches to people. Darren and I went to get in the line before the crowd of people amassed over to it whilst Zoe stayed behind to watch our stuff and hold our claimed territory.

We grabbed our sandwiches, taking an extra one for Zoe and headed back to our corner. I took a bite and chewed, grateful for some real food. We sat in silence as we ate, just looking around. Cots and people were everywhere; the space was extremely loud as a result. I had hoped that maybe we could sneak off into a classroom to escape the noise that would no doubt carry on throughout the night. Why did I always seem to make these types of decisions and end up instantly regretting them? *Kind of explains the Art degree.*

I pulled out my smartphone and tried dialing my parents again. Screw the long distance charges. Once again no one picked up. I tried my brother's number last, and an operator recording played through the ear piece letting me know that there was an unprecedented overload of their system and that calling services may not work. I hung up and stared at the screen, the goofy face of my little brother peering back at me. He always hated that contact picture, which is why I still had it.

"No one answering?" Zoe asked.

"No, and I got some weird operator overload message," I frowned.

Zoe pulled out her own phone and tried her parents as well, but it was just as fruitful as my attempt had been. She shook her head.

"This is ridiculous. In an emergency they should be focusing on keeping the phone lines up as long as possible."

"Who's *they*?" I raised an eyebrow.

"I don't know, the government?"

"I think they might have a little bit on their plate at the moment," Darren butted in.

I had finally noticed all the police presence stationed throughout the large room. None of them seemed to be helping, just looking around with a stern eye with their hands on their holstered guns. I found that odd. It was almost like they were just waiting for someone to turn. One officer went around to the others, saying something to all of them and then put the megaphone he had in his hand to his mouth.

"Everyone quiet down please. In a few minutes we are going to play a broadcast from the national news due to the numerous requests for information." His amplified voice boomed over the room causing the noise level to fall to near silence.

"Do you think it will be real?" Zoe asked.

I turned to her, confused. "What do you mean?"

"Well, if they are just playing it over the intercom it could be anyone," Zoe pointed out as if it was obvious. "You know to placate people and not cause panic."

"For once you could be right," I said and Zoe punched me in the shoulder.

I rubbed my sore arm as Darren chuckled at us. My sarcasm aside, Zoe could be right. Isn't that what the government did in emergencies? Lie to the public and then justify it by saying they did it so as not to cause panic? A few minutes later, the intercom crackled to life, a feminine but stern voice carrying through the now muted noise:

"...the President has declared a state of emergency. We advise all citizens to avoid contact with the infected individuals. Emergency teams have been sent to all major cities to deal with the situation and will span out to rural areas soon. If an infected person is spotted, please call the local law enforcement and do not engage them. We repeat, do not engage them. If an emergency shelter has been put up in your community, please proceed there immediately. Again, avoid all contact with the infected and..."

The recording cut out and all that was left playing was the hiss of the radio frequency. Then the lights went out with a flash, darkness blanketing the room. People started screaming and the sound of shoes hitting the linoleum reigned in the small space.

"People! Please do not panic, we have everything under control. We are working on getting the backup generator running right now," announced the policeman with the megaphone.

All three of us jumped up as people started to move all around us. I was knocked from behind as a man shoved his way through the people, but I managed to catch myself before I hit the ground.

"Bailey, you all right?" Zoe asked from right beside me. It must have been her arm I grabbed while flailing.

"Yeah, some panicking jackass just bumped into me," I grumbled as I rubbed my still sore shoulder. I don't think I could afford any more injuries with the hospitals being useless.

My eyes were swamped with light as the emergency lights came on, like a flare in the night sky. People started to calm down, or at least stop running around screaming like idiots.

"Well power outages aren't a good sign," Darren muttered and I wasn't even sure he was talking to us.

"None of this is a good sign."

The broadcast was not what I had expected. What did a state of emergency even mean? The planes and trains had already been down the day before so what else happened?

"So now we're supposed to call the sick people *infected*?" Zoe asked.

"What else would you call them?" Darren replied. "Zombies?"

"I don't think any self-respecting newscast would use that word," I said.

"Fair enough," Darren shrugged.

"They are zombies, though," a small voice said from behind us.

I turned around to see a little girl who must have been no more than ten years old. "And how would you know that?" I asked, arching an eyebrow at the strange kid.

She was dressed in those little kid jeans and a T-shirt that had Scooby-Doo on the front. I half expected to see light up runners on her feet, but she just had a pair of old Nikes. Her brown eyes matched her mousy brown hair that was up pulled up into a scrunchie. I was not aware they had even made any of those past the nineties. "'Cause I've seen all the zombie movies." Her voice was tinged with a country twang that made me crack a grin. I guess we were in the South after all.

"Which ones?" Zoe asked kneeling down to the kid's level.

"*Night of the Living Dead*, *Dawn of the Dead*, that zombie TV show," she listed off.

"Wow, you've just about seen them all," I grinned, and she narrowed her eyes at me.

She was about to say something else when a deep voice yelled out, "Chloe!" The little girl looked panicked for a second and then a guy, somewhere in his mid-twenties, burst through the crowd to her.

"Chloe, what the heck did I tell you about runnin' off like that?" his country twang accent much more prominent.

Great, more Southerners. They seemed like they were related, both had similar features like the brown hair, but unlike the girl's, his eyes were blue. His hair was cut short, very all-American boy style. His T-shirt was faded with many washes, the words *New Orleans Saints* almost worn off.

Although I had to admit, country boy was put together nicely, for lack of a better term. The shirt was on the tighter side, showcasing his athletic physique and muscled arms. I was willing to bet good money – if I had any, that is – he had a farmer's tan under that shirt.

"I'm sorry." The way she said it sounded like she was not sorry at all.

We all grinned at her insolent, childish tone.

"Sorry, hope she wasn't botherin' you," he grinned, flashing his straight teeth. "I'm Ethan by the way, and this little kid is Chloe."

"Little kid!" Chloe said indignantly. "I'm nine and a half."

Why did kids always insist on adding 'and a half' at the end? It sure didn't help her cause.

"Naw, she was just telling us about all the zombie movies she's seen," I said, stamping down the urge to use my poor excuse for a southern accent.

Ethan rolled his eyes at Chloe, "How many times do I have to tell you to stop talkin' about the dang zombies?"

I inwardly grinned at his use of censored swear words.

"What're your names?" Chloe asked.

"I'm Bailey, this is my friend Zoe, and this guy is Darren," I said.

"Where are you from?" Chloe prodded.

"Me and Zoe are from Canada. Not sure about Darren here," I answered.

"Wisconsin," Darren added, not sounding enthused about that at all.

"If you're from Canada what're you doin' here?" Chloe asked bluntly.

"Chloe," Ethan sighed.

Zoe chuckled and answered for us, "We were here for Mardi Gras."

"My dad said Mardi Gras is for drunk college students," Chloe said, cocking out her hip.

"Well he's not wrong," I laughed before Ethan could chastise her for saying anything.

"True that," Darren grinned, before he sat back down on his cot.

The full lights came back on and I could hear the sigh of relief from the people in the multipurpose room.

"Can we stay by you guys?" Chloe asked, looking up at us expectantly.

"Sure, pull up a cot," Zoe smiled and I narrowed my eyes.

I had a nagging suspicion Zoe was the type to bring home stray cats as a kid. Chloe clapped excitedly and ran off to grab her things with Ethan in tow. I gave Zoe a look.

"Shut up," she said.

"I didn't say anything," I grinned.

"I know you well enough that you don't have too," Zoe said plunking down on her cot.

"Touché." I lugged my suitcase over to the side so they would have room for their cots.

A few minutes later, Chloe came bounding over with her rather large backpack and I wondered how her tiny body was able to hold it up without falling over. Ethan was a few steps behind her with the cots folded under his arms. Chloe took the cot beside me flinging her backpack down and Ethan set his up beside hers. For the next hour, we were barraged with questions from Chloe, ranging from what was our favorite food to did we live in igloos.

"Sorry about her," Ethan said apologetically to me when Zoe became the recipient of the new round of questions.

"No problem, kind of takes your mind off everything." I shrugged.

I wasn't great with kids having not been around them a whole lot throughout my life. I had a brother who was two years younger, but we basically fought the whole time. I still remember when he hit me with his hockey stick, so I chased him around to get my revenge, and he ran straight into his own door frame, giving him a huge black eye. Of course, he ran to our mother saying it was me, and I was grounded for a week. *You know, come to think of it, I don't think I like kids.*

"So you're here for Mardi Gras?" Ethan asked.

"Yeah, celebrating finishing our degrees."

"Congrats," he said mildly impressed.

"Don't be too impressed," I snorted. "It's a 'would you like fries with that?' degree."

"Still it's somethin'."

"So is Chloe your sister?" I asked, hoping I was guessing right.

Ethan chuckled, "Do I look old enough to have a daughter her age?"

"Hey you never know. Sixteen and pregnant is no longer scandalous; in fact, it seems to be a trend."

"Well to answer you, yes she is my sister." Ethan leaned back on his cot.

"Where are your parents if you don't mind me asking?" I asked.

"Mexico," he answered. "My dad and step mom always go there for two weeks 'round this time. I tried gettin' 'em on the phone, but no luck. Looks like they'll be there for a while now."

"Yeah, Zoe and I are stuck too. Our plane was cancelled, and trains aren't an option now either." I frowned as my words sunk in.

We really were stuck unless we could commandeer a car along the way and drive back to B.C. Which seemed daunting as well. *How hard could it be to hotwire a car?*

"Well you're welcome to stay with us for the time bein'," Ethan offered.

"I wasn't aware you owned the school." I smirked and watched as Ethan rolled his eyes.

"No, I mean we can't stay here forever. My family has a huntin' cabin 'bout three hours west of here."

"Well how nice of you. Is that the famed Southern hospitality I've heard so much about?" I grinned.

"Yes ma'am," Ethan smiled, purposely exaggerating his Southern accent.

"How come you didn't just head there in the first place?"

Ethan ran his hand through his hair. "Well for one, the school was closer. And I wanted to see just how bad the situation was before I headed out by myself with Chloe."

"Did you get your answer?"

"Unfortunately."

"What's a poutine?" Chloe's questioning voice carried over to us, but the last thing we felt like doing was laughing.

Chapter 6

I rolled over for the millionth time tonight, as I tried to get comfortable on the cot, which was proving impossible. What the hell did they make these things from? The collective hate of customer service workers? Zoe was snoring away beside me and I punched her in the arm to get her to stop. She spluttered for a few seconds then rolled over and resumed her snoring, which harmonized with the other people snoring all over the room. *Geez, they could start a band.* I sighed, knowing I wouldn't get more than a few hours of sleep tonight if I was lucky. Being a light sleeper ensured this.

"Can't sleep?" Darren whispered from his cot.

I was going to give him a look that said *You don't say?* but realized it would be lost on him in the darkness of the room. "What gave it away?" I instead whispered back sarcastically.

He chuckled. "You a light sleeper, too?"

"Yep."

"I'm not, but you two are keepin' me up," Chloe said sleepily from her own cot.

"Sorry," both Darren and I apologized before resigning to our fate of getting no sleep.

It seemed like I had been out for only a few minutes rather than the hours it actually had been, when the shrill sound of a screaming woman woke me from my light sleep. I sat up quickly, the change in altitude causing my head to spin.

No sooner could I get the sound, "Wah?" out of mouth before Zoe started to yell at me. "Grab your bag, we have to go!"

Everyone was springing into action, and more screams erupted. The police that were stationed in the lunch room were running around panicked, waving their guns in the air. *I'm pretty sure that wasn't in the police training guidelines.* I jumped up and pulled my backpack onto my shoulder. I went to grab my rolling suitcase, but Zoe stilled my arm.

"We'll never get out of here with our suitcases."

I looked longingly at my zebra striped suitcase already missing it and its contents, but I knew Zoe was right. I nodded and glanced around to see the others all geared up with their backpacks on and ready to run.

"What's going on?" Chloe asked, her eyes wide as she surveyed the chaos.

"We just gotta get outta here, that's all," Ethan said calmly to her, placing his hand on her head gently.

A gun fired somewhere in the school causing people to duck and scream, which seemed to be the knee-jerk reaction to a gun shot.

"Guns are never a good sign," Darren said flatly.

I was too focused on trying to find a path through the madness to roll my eyes at his redundant statement.

"We need to get somewhere out in the open; being in a crowd like this makes us an easy target," I said while scanning the three exits out of the room.

"An easy target for what?" Zoe asked.

"The infected people, a stray bullet, et cetera," I listed off.

"She's right." Ethan nodded, and I was glad someone else was thinking at the moment.

"How about the main doors?" Zoe asked pointing to the biggest exit.

"All right, let's go and meet up in the parking lot across the street if we get split up," I said on the spot and we started to move toward the exit.

I took lead with the others in tow; Ethan had his hand wrapped tightly around one of Chloe's. We were pushing our way through the throng of people when they all started to push us back the way we had come.

"What the hell?" I muttered, and then I heard it.

The groaning and snarling that accompanied the infected. People were screaming bloody murder as a group of infected people stumbled through the large exit doors, latching onto the unfortunate souls that were within reach.

"Infected! Go back!" I yelled, and we turned around to try and reach the exit that was on the other side of the room.

I was now trailing behind the others with Zoe leading us out. I looked back to see a bunch of people go down with the infected and the remaining police men were trying to take aim, but were finding it hard with all the live bodies in the way. As one infected lunged at a cop, he fired a couple of rounds into the sick man's chest, but all it did was put the infected on his ass. It slowly got itself up from the cold linoleum like a toddler learning to stand up, much to the shock of the cop who was gaping at the scene before him. No living person could have taken that many bullets to the chest and still be breathing let alone up and moving around.

Dark blood trailed down the infected man's shirt, dripping onto the floor, as he lunged for the policeman again. I had a sickening feeling I knew exactly where this was going, but luckily the cop's partner took aim and shot the infected in the side of the head, sending a pulpy mess into the air. The body fell down sideways from the impact and both policemen just stared at the corpse as if waiting for it to get back up again. But it remained still, the oily blood pooling out around its head in a morbid halo.

"Come on." I felt Ethan's fingers dig into my wrist as he pulled me forward.

Chloe had gone silent, her eyes wide with fear as she clung to Ethan's hand. I pulled my arm free from his grasp as I picked up the pace, leaving the grotesque scene behind me. Zoe waved at the entrance, indicating it was clear. We burst into the hallway lined with rusty lockers, the other people from the lunch room right behind us. Since the school only had one floor, we didn't have to worry about stairs, just navigating the narrowed hallways.

We followed Zoe, trusting that she knew where she was going. I didn't pay any attention to which turns and hallways we used to get to the multipurpose room when we had entered the school, but Zoe always managed to notice those things. In fact, I couldn't even tell you what direction we were running in; to me straight forward was always north.

We reached the end of the hallway only to be faced with the choice of left or right, and unfortunately neither direction gave a hint as to where a door was located. The corridors were empty of people; there weren't even any rent-a-cops roaming the halls like I had seen them do yesterday.

"Left!"

"No right!"

We heard screaming from the crowd behind us, not being helpful at all. I looked at Zoe and clearly she had no idea which direction to head.

"Right," Ethan said as he took the lead.

Our little group followed him plus a few more of the people behind us, while the other half of the group went left. I hope I didn't live to regret this or worse, didn't survive long enough to regret this. Further down the corridor I could see blood smeared on the lockers and a few unmoving bodies on the dirty floor. People gasped, and Ethan hauled Chloe closer to him trying to steer her sight away from the horrifying mess. We took a sharp left, and were greeted with the sight of the light reflecting on the linoleum floors from the entrance doors.

As we were about to round the last corner and reach the entrance doors, I heard the snarling and banging before I saw them. A horde of the infected were pounding and clawing at the doors trying to get outside. From the looks of it, they were once people who had sought refuge in here. Some still had on backpacks and bags, while others were wearing their pajamas.

As a group, we stopped in our tracks looking at the obstacle that blocked our escape. One of the infected turned, somehow sensing we were there, and started toward us. The others soon followed, but before we could turn to run back the way we came, the two cops from the lunch room were shooting off rounds into the approaching group of infected. They must have been in the group that had followed us.

The loud gunshots reverberated off the concrete walls, and I had to cover my ears in an attempt to block out the sound. The bullets hit a few targets right between the eyes, causing the bodies to sink to the ground in a heap. Others tripped over the fallen, struggling to get upright once again.

"Let's go back – I think I saw an emergency exit along that last hallway!" Darren yelled right beside me and I could barely make out his words from all the noise and the ringing in my ears.

I nodded and yanked Ethan's arm to get him to follow. Zoe was already looking back around the corner we had come from. Some of the people had run backwards while others stood transfixed by the scene at the doors. We ran back down the corridor that had the two dead people fallen on the floor. As we passed their slumped forms, one corpse started to stir.

"Keep moving!" I yelled as Zoe stopped in front to stare.

One reached its mangled hand up toward us, and Darren stomped down on it as hard as he could. The infected didn't cry out or scream like a normal person would have at the pain; instead it snarled and tried to reach us with its other hand. We all knew what Darren was going to do next as he raised his boot clad foot high above the infected person's head.

Ethan grabbed Chloe and pushed her face into his chest so that she didn't see. I almost wished I could have done that as I watched Darren's boot come down and the infected man's head explode like an over-ripened watermelon. It made a sickening sound of bone and cartilage snapping as blood and brain matter splattered all over the floor. Zoe gagged, as Darren shook off his messy boot, and Ethan gulped audibly as Chloe clung to his shirt.

I wasn't sure how I was supposed to react; my emotions were almost dulled as a result of the last couple of days. To be honest, I was more disturbed by the way that Darren had taken no time at all to think about stomping the thing's head. The fact that he seemed more concerned about the mess on his boot, than what he just did to a person, worried me. Still, I was the first to recover.

"Come on, we can't stop."

I took the lead, stepping over the mess trying to avoid getting any of it on my own shoes. The other body remained still and judging from the condition of the corpse, I had a feeling she wouldn't be getting up anytime soon. Her legs and arms were badly chewed up, muscle and tendons were exposed through the open wounds making it almost impossible for her to move properly if she ever woke up again.

I saw the word EXIT glowing and sighed in relief that Darren had been right about the door. I pushed on the latch, and a loud siren went off indicating that we had opened the door. I squinted against the morning sun that momentarily blinded me. When I could finally open my eyes fully, without the searing light snapping them shut, I looked upon a scene straight out of a horror movie.

The street was devoid of moving cars; all the ones on the road had been abandoned. Some stood with doors hanging wide open and blood-stained windows. The police and emergency crews that were originally stationed outside the school had either left their post, or worse. One of the tall buildings a few blocks away had massive flames shooting out of it. Helicopters were flying overhead, and I could hear the sound of rapid gunfire coming from somewhere pretty close. I was no gun expert, but I was sure that was the sound of assault rifles not just measly hand guns.

"Where do we go?" Zoe asked panicked, running her hand through her hair violently.

We all spun around looking for answers. I suddenly remembered mine and Zoe's joking banter about weapons. As much as it was meant for taking our minds off everything, it was also true. We needed weapons of some kind and we needed them now. My mind ran through the possible stores that would have anything like that.

"You remember that outdoor sports store we passed on our way back to the hotel the other night?" I asked Zoe.

She nodded, "Weapons?"

"That's what I was thinking."

"So you're suggesting we run further into the city instead of away from it?" Darren asked skeptically.

"Well how else do you suggest we find any weapons?" I asked sharply, the stress starting to get to me.

"Along the way, out of the city," Darren said as if it was a sure-fire plan.

"There is no guarantee we will find something along the way," Zoe reasoned.

"There's no guarantee we will find anything at that store. For all we know, it's already been looted or worse, and we'd be trapped in the thick of everything," Darren said throwing his arms in the air.

As much as he was being a dick about it, Darren was right. But there were no guarantees for any plan at the moment.

"He's right. We can't head further into the city. There'll probably be more sick people congregatin' there," Ethan's Southern accent became more pronounced. "There's a huntin' store further near the city limits, I doubt it's been touched. We can stop there on the way to my cabin."

"Okay, well how do you suggest we get there?" I asked calmly.

Before Ethan could answer, Chloe piped up, "We brought Ethan's truck."

"Where are you parked?" Darren asked Ethan.

"The public parking lot behind the school."

"We would have to run around to the back and hop the fence to get there," Zoe said, looking off into the direction of the public parking lot.

"We don't have any other choice," Darren pointed out.

"All right," Zoe said after a beat, taking a step toward the back of the school. "Let's go then."

"One second," Ethan said, letting go of Chloe's hand.

He ran to a car that had been abandoned on the sidewalk and pulled open the driver's side door, hitting the latch to pop the trunk. He ran to the back and rummaged through the trunk, pulling out a tire iron.

"We need some sort of weapon," he explained as he ran back to us, testing the weight of the iron in his grip.

Chloe latched her little hand back onto Ethan's and we started heading around the school.

Chapter 7

We rounded the back corner of the school, open green space greeting us. As a group, we continued passing the trampled football field; the bleachers casting a shadow over the destroyed arena. I spotted movement underneath the bleachers and tapped Ethan on the shoulder, nodding toward the seats. We widened our berth from the bleachers as we moved around it, hoping to not catch the attention of whatever was lurking beneath them.

The grass quietly crunched under our feet, but I failed to notice the pop can, as my attention was so focused on the figure. All eyes whipped to me as the aluminum crumpled under my foot. I winced at the sound, my heart missing a beat. We stood frozen in our tracks as we watched the shuffling figure appear from under the benches, like a bear roused from its cave.

The man's arm hung limply, like it was hanging onto his shoulder by a thread, as he staggered toward us. His face looked like he had just been attacked by an animal, jagged cuts running from scalp to chin. We started to back up a few feet then full out sprinted away from the infected man. Ethan led us to the back wall of the fence that surrounded the school. The infected man ambled toward us; his one good arm rose up to grab whoever was closest. We outran him with ease thanks to the condition of his body.

When we reached the chain link fence, Ethan hoisted Chloe over first. Zoe and I scrambled over next. I landed on the other side hard, the scratches on my side pulling taut sending a wave of pain up my torso. I managed to catch myself on the metal links before I fell over. The fence rattled with all the movement and the infected man took this as a sign to speed up.

"Hurry!" Chloe screamed as she grabbed the fence, yelling intently at Ethan on the other side.

Darren and Ethan glanced back to see that the infected had managed to pick up speed. They quickly climbed over and joined us on the other side. Chloe immediately made a grab for Ethan's hand.

With his bloodstained fingers sticking through the chain links, the infected snapped at us, but he no longer posed a threat. He wasn't able to get over, so he just continually smacked the fence trying to get to us.

"He can't climb over right?" Chloe asked as she stared wide eyed at the infected.

"Naw," Ethan said. "But let's keep goin'."

I looked back at the man one last time as we headed toward the parking garage. It was as if he couldn't comprehend how to get to us. He either wasn't in good enough condition to climb over or didn't even think to climb over. Either way, it was of benefit to us. He just stood there rattling the fence and snarling as we got further away. I wondered how long he planned on standing there, but we were not about to stand around to find out.

The parking garage was a giant cement building about five floors high. I could see the gleam of the cars reflecting the sun through the openings. The booth at the entrance was without an operator, so we ducked underneath the yellow and blacked stripped bar to get inside.

"I'm parked on the third floor," Ethan said as he readjusted his backpack on his shoulders.

We followed him over to the door for the stairs and started up the cement steps. The stairwell was dark, barely lit by the tiny window slits. Relief washed over me as Ethan opened the third floor stairs and light poured in. We passed by parked vehicle after parked vehicle, until Ethan stopped at an older model Chevy Silverado. It was in good shape, no rusting anywhere on its black paint job. Clearly he took care of his truck.

"How much gas do you have?" Darren asked, throwing his backpack into the truck bed.

"At least three-quarters of the tank," Ethan answered throwing in his own backpack and then Chloe's beside Darren's.

"We should probably fill up and get extra gas before we leave the city," I suggested, internally debating if I wanted to throw my backpack with the rest or have it with me in the cab.

"We have gas stored at our cabin," Chloe said.

"Purple gas?" Zoe asked.

"Purple? No, it's red. But how'd you know it was dyed?" Chloe asked, and I eyed Zoe suspiciously.

She shrugged. "I grew up in the country."

"It's like I don't even know you." I feigned a look of horror.

"Shut up and get in," Zoe replied as she rolled her eyes at my comment.

We jumped into the truck with Zoe in the middle seat with Darren and I on either side of her in the back. There was a surprising amount of room considering the truck didn't have an extended cab. I looked out the back window longingly at my backpack, wishing I had decided to bring it in here with me. If I lost that, I really had nothing to my name. Ethan started the vehicle and Chloe buckled herself in. We made it down to the first floor only to be stopped by the yellow and black bar and with no one operating the booth, it just stood in our way.

"So, anyone here ever work in a parking garage booth?" I asked and of course everyone shook their head, even Chloe.

"Ram it?" Darren suggested but the look on Ethan's face said that was not an option.

"Do you think it will move up if we just lift it?" I wondered out loud.

"Only one-way to find out," Darren muttered as he climbed out of the truck.

He tested the bar first, and it gave way to Darren's strength. The bar rose higher as he walked from the free end to the part that connected with the booth. Slowly, Ethan inched past the bar and Darren let it drop as he ran to get back in.

We rode in tight-lipped silence as we tried to drive out of the city. No one dared to make a sound, too focused on scanning our surroundings. Vehicles were abandoned all over the road, their owners nowhere to be seen. Ethan had to maneuver around more than one big cluster of parked vehicles, which meant driving partway on the sidewalk.

"Ah, guys," Chloe said as she pointed at something through the windshield.

We all looked out to see what she was going on about. The bridge that we needed to cross to head out of the city was not only blocked with numerous vehicles, but a bunch of the infected were ambling around and corpses were strewn across the bridge. The diseased people were moving in between the cars like ants around a mound of fallen food.

Even if there hadn't been any sick people walking around, there was no way we would have been able to get across due to the various abandoned cars and trucks that were blocking every lane both ways. The bridge created a bottleneck where everyone tried to cross but no one made it over. The infected that were ambling around were most likely the former owners of those vehicles.

The sound of the Silverado's engine finally caught the attention of one of the infected and he started toward the noise. The other infected people noticed his movement and started to mindlessly followed instep behind him.

"Um, maybe you should back up, yeah?" I said, panic rising in me.

If the horde surrounded us, we would be screwed. Ethan threw the gearshift into reverse and slammed on the gas, sending us flying against the front seats. *Maybe I should learn to wear my seatbelt.* I had to say I was quite impressed with Ethan's driving skills, though; maybe all country boys could drive that well, who knows. I remembered the sorry state my bumper was in on my old Honda from backing into so many things.

He managed to both back up without hitting anything and turn us around so that the group of infected were behind us. I looked back to see them fading into the distance, as we drove away. The sight of a little boy no more than five mixed in with the horde made me freeze in my twisted position. His once strawberry-blond curls were matted with blood, and he was only wearing one of those little kid shoes that looked like miniature adult ones. His neck was a mess, the greasy blood dried all over his wound and shirt. I swallowed hard, as I forced myself to sit forward and will the image out of my head.

"All of the major city exit points are going to be like this," Darren said quietly. "Do you know any other way out of the city?"

Ethan thought about it for a minute, "Yeah, but it's backtrackin'."

"Would it involve going through downtown?" Zoe asked, her frantic eyes glued to the windshield.

"No, but it's a lot of back streets and then roads on the outskirts of town," he replied.

"Sounds better than running into that," I said motioning to the back window.

Everyone nodded in agreement.

An hour later we found ourselves on yet another city one-way. This place was littered with them, but the main roads were either blocked or overrun so we stuck to the crappy one-ways.

"You're goin' the wrong way," Chloe studiously pointed out.

"Not like it matters," Ethan sighed. "There are no people or police to stop us."

Chloe stared open mouthed at him in disbelief. Her almost ten-year-old mind couldn't comprehend breaking the law, but yet she seemed to be taking the whole zombie apocalypse thing very well. *Weird kid.*

"Look," Chloe pointed to a billboard sticking out between two buildings. It read *Bobby Joe's Gun Shop*, and I laughed out loud at the redneck store name.

"What's so funny?" Zoe asked, looking at me like I was crazy.

"Nothing." I looked back at the billboard, ignoring everyone's confused stares.

"That's where we're headin'," Ethan announced, taking the attention away from me.

Here we were, heading off to a gun store, and I had never even held a gun before. This was insanity, which showed just how dire our situation was. I started to bite at my nails, as I worried over that thought. Well, until I looked down in horror and realized my nails much have been covered in germs. I quickly dabbed at my tongue with the inside of my shirt.

"We're only 'bout an hour away if we keep on these one-ways," Ethan announced.

"I can't wait to have a weapon other than his tire iron," Darren said, pointing his thumb at Ethan's weapon of choice.

I wasn't sure giving Darren a gun or even a bat was a good idea; I hadn't decided if I trusted him or not. But who was I to say? I shouldn't be allowed to handle a weapon either.

"You guys know how to handle a gun?" Ethan asked, almost as if he could read my mind.

"Used to go to the gun range all the time," Darren said.

"I grew up country, used to shoot all the gophers that destroyed the yard," Zoe admitted.

Everyone looked at me.

"I used to play duck hunt all the time as a kid, does that count?" I offered up.

"So, no guns for you," Zoe muttered.

"Trust me; it's for *your* benefit that I stick to a bat."

Chloe rolled her eyes. "Geez, even I can shoot."

"Maybe you can teach her then." Ethan smirked at me via the rearview mirror.

Everyone chuckled at the look on my face.

"But seriously, you're not actually going to let a nine-year-old wield a gun right?" I asked, not sure if Ethan was joking or not.

Chapter 8

We pulled into the gun shop's parking lot, and by parking lot I mean gravel pit. The only vehicle in the parking lot was a small Mazda.

"Well at least this place doesn't look touched," Darren said as he peered out the window.

Ethan and Chloe hopped out and opened the cab doors to let us out as well.

"At least from the outside," Ethan said. "I'll go in first and scout the place out. Make sure it's empty."

"But–" Chloe grabbed his arm.

Ethan kneeled so he was talking to her face to face. "It's gonna be fine. You stay here and keep an eye on these folks, okay?" he said calmly, and she nodded.

"I'm going with you," Darren said, but Ethan shook his head.

"I want you out here in case one of those things comes roamin' by." Ethan handed Darren the tire iron. "You keep this one; I have a crowbar in the back." Ethan walked to the bed of the truck and rooted around until he found our only other weapon; the crowbar.

"I'll go with you," I said and even I felt surprised at my words. I wasn't one to voluntarily put myself into danger. Unless drunk, that is.

Ethan nodded and started toward the front door. I glanced at Zoe, who was giving me a look that I had a hard time placing. She was probably as shocked as I was that I volunteered. I had to run to catch up to Ethan, who was already at the front doors.

"Do you think we should just go in the front doors?" I asked, peering into the dark store.

It looked like they weren't even open.

"Let's see if there's a back door," Ethan suggested.

Gravel crunched under our feet, as we made our way around to the back. The grass was overgrown, but a worn footpath led us straight to the back door. It was outdated and had an intimidating deadbolt right above the handle. Ethan raised his crowbar to wedge the door open, but I grabbed his arm.

"What if this place has an alarm? We'll attract everything within miles."

Ethan seemed to think it over. "What if it doesn't?"

I made a face at his comeback.

"And if it does, let's just make sure we are gone before anythin' shows up."

"This is a gun store, they'd be stupid not to have an alarm," I pointed out.

"Exactly, this is a gun store. In the South. Who'd be stupid enough to rob 'em?" Ethan asked, proud of his reasoning.

"Fine, do what you want," I muttered as he jammed the crowbar in between the door and frame.

Within a few moments of Ethan grunting at the exertion, the door flew open, and the wooden frame splintered into the air. The dead bolt was still sticking out of the door, but now there was a giant hole in the frame where the bolt tore through. We held our breath as we waited for an alarm or infected person to greet us, but after counting to sixty, nothing happened.

"Well, looks like there's no alarm," Ethan said, slightly smug.

Hesitantly we walked into the building, me right behind Ethan. The old wooden floor creaked under our weight making my heart jump into my throat with every step. The air stunk of sulfur and bleach; what I had always assumed a cleaned up murder scene would smell like. The back entrance led straight into the employee only area, as evident by the employee lounge and office we passed.

Both rooms were devoid of people. The hallway ushered us to the sales floor, which was covered wall to wall in guns. Huge rifles and shotguns lined the walls and the display counters were packed with handguns, knives and ammo. Ethan shot me a huge grin, and I could only imagine this was like his version of a candy shop.

"We got lots to choose from," Ethan whispered, and I nodded as my eyes wandered back to the impressive displays.

There were oversized duffels hanging from a coat rack and I grabbed a couple, handing one to Ethan.

"Should we go grab the others?" I asked. "Or just grab what we can ourselves?"

"No, we can take more if we have more people to carry stuff," Ethan answered.

We summoned the others from the truck, handing them each a duffel bag to fill as they entered the gun shop.

"This is like Christmas," Darren grinned as he took in the sight.

"Geez, what kind of Christmas did you have at your house?" I commented.

Everyone else was shopping through the stock, even little Chloe, but I had no idea what to look for. I had never even shot a gun before. I went over to the knife display case only to find it locked.

"We need the display keys," I announced.

"Yeah, we also need the keys for these guns on the wall," Darren said as he pulled one only to have it yanked back due to the metal wire locking it in place.

He walked over to the knife display I was at and peered into the glass.

"Well, you don't really need a key for this."

Darren raised his coat clad-arm, and I instinctively moved my arm to shield my eyes, knowing full well what he was about to do. With brute force, his elbow connected with the glass display and shards erupted everywhere. Everyone stopped what they were doing at the crashing noise and stared.

"There," Darren said whilst he stretched out the arm he used as a club.

I wasn't sure what to say to that so I just nodded, "Thanks, but unless you plan on sawing through the gun holding wires with your teeth, Rambo, we still need a key."

Darren smiled at that, and I felt like I was looking into the maw of a lion. He was a little more dangerous than he let on. I would have to keep an eye on him.

I put down the duffel bag and walked back to the *Employees Only* area. The keys had to be in the office we passed. Slowly, I opened the door further and peered inside. The room was small; a nondescript desk with papers scattered all over taking up most of the room. On the wall beside the door was a small metal cabinet, and I was willing to bet that was where the keys were hanging.

Inside was a bunch of keys, each labelled with a numbered tag, and I groaned. We would have to test every one in every lock. I was about to grab them all when I noticed the last one was labelled Master Key. *Well that was lucky.* I grinned and shut the cabinet, twirling the key and tag around my finger.

"You find the keys?" Ethan asked as I entered the sales floor.

"I found *the* key."

Ethan held his hand up for the key, and I tossed it to him. I went back to the smashed knife cabinet, moving some of the larger glass shards off the merchandise. I leaned down to inspect the contents of the display case. Grabbing the largest knife I could find, I pulled it out and unsheathed it. The blade was perfectly sharpened and curved slightly. It looked like a combat knife. I sheathed the blade and threw it into the duffel.

After grabbing a couple more, I moved onto the handgun display, which had already been opened, and some guns placed on the display counter top. I eyed a few and picked them up to see how heavy they were.

"You'll probably want this one," Ethan said handing me a silver and black gun. "It's a Beretta 9mm. Nothin' fancy, but it's a police and military standard, a good long range pistol, and easy to find attachments and ammo for."

"Thanks," I said taking the pistol from him and giving it a good heft. "Seems like it's a good weight, not too heavy or light."

Ethan rummaged through the display and produced two matching metal tubes.

"And here are the suppressors for them," he said, dropping them in my bag.

I grabbed the other matching Beretta and added it to the bag. I also added extra empty magazines and a holster belt attachment that Ethan handed me.

"Well, Mr. Guns and Ammo, what other guns do you recommend?"

Ethan chuckled and led me over to the gun wall. "This here is a Blaser R8 professional rifle, lighter than a regular hunting rifle and holds more rounds," he rattled off, handing me the sleek, black weapon.

"I have to say this feels weird," I said raising the gun's scope to eye level. I could see the crossed lines and aimed my sight to the *Employees Only* sign.

"You need to rest the butt against your collarbone where your arm meets your torso," Ethan pointed out as he moved the rifle butt from my arm to near my collarbone.

It felt unnatural having it in that spot, but I guess it was for a reason.

"Unless you want a broken arm, I suggest keepin' it flush against that exact spot," he added.

"All right," I said kneeling down to add to my highly illegal collection. "Now on to the ammo."

We walked over to the shelves, which were jam-packed with small boxes, all marked with sizes and descriptions. I spotted the section that seemed to be labelled 9mm, remembering what Ethan had said about the Beretta's.

"See ya'll are learnin'," Chloe grinned as she threw a bunch of boxes into Ethan's duffel.

"Know-it-all."

Ethan showed me which ones to grab for my rifle and I added those to the mix. The bag was extremely heavy with all the guns and ammo now jingling around in there. By the time we were done and standing in the middle of the room, we had done a fair amount of damage to the stock.

"Should we leave money or an I.O.U or something?" Zoe asked as she slung her own over-flowing bag onto her shoulders.

"We could, but I'd bet they'd never collect," Darren replied. "Plus, you got the thousands of dollars to pay for all this?"

"Why yes I do, right here," Zoe said making a motioned like she was reaching into her pocket, but produced her middle finger instead of a wad of bills.

We all laughed, and Chloe gaped.

"I was told never to do that."

"You're still never to do that, you hear?" Ethan pointing an index finger at her and she nodded.

"Man this is something straight out of a Stallone movie," Darren grinned as he motioned to all of our stocked duffels. Maybe we shouldn't have let the potentially mentally unhinged guy gather such an arsenal. But that debate would have to wait.

"We should see what we can find in the back," I suggested.

Ethan and I started back toward the employee lounge, hopefully to find some food to pack with us. We opened all of the lockers and rummaged through. All I found were granola bars and an opened bag of chips. I shoved the granola bars into my duffel, but left the no doubt stale bag of chips.

"You find anything good?" I asked.

"Case of water," Ethan said pointing to the case of bottled water sitting in the corner by the fridge.

"Good find."

"You think we should take some of these paper plates and plastic utensils?" Ethan asked, gesturing to the bags sitting on top of the refrigerator.

"Couldn't hurt."

I walked over and grabbed the necks of the bags. Ethan leaned down to pick up the case of water when I heard the unmistakable sound of a gun being cocked right behind me.

Chapter 9

Ethan and I froze at the sound.

"Now, ya'll turn around slowly and don't do anythin' stupid, you hear?" a very Southern male voice rang out.

Ethan and I shared a look of dread before we put down our haul and turned around slowly. I could hear the blood pumping frantically in my ears and had no doubt that the color had drained from my face. *Oh god, what about the others?* I hadn't heard any gunshots, so I could only hope that they were unharmed.

A well-worn cowboy hat was the first thing to come into my peripheral. Our captor wore blue jeans, a tight plaid button down, and a pair of old cowboy boots to finish off the Southern look. Judging by his face, I placed him in his fifties. His lips were set in a grim line and his muscles moved under his sleeves as he kept his gun trained on us.

"Now, I don't want no trouble, okay?" his voice was calm and collected.

If I had to venture a guess, I would say he used to be police or military. There was something about the air around him, the way he carried himself. He was confident holding the handgun and had no qualms about pointing it at us.

"We don't want any trouble either," Ethan replied in an equally calm voice. "What did you do to the others?"

Confusion washed over the man's face before he answered.

"I didn't do anythin' to 'em; only saw you two so far."

Ethan visibly relaxed at the man's words.

"What're your names?" he asked.

I swallowed the lump in my throat before replying,

"I'm Bailey, and this is Ethan. We don't mean any harm. Just needed something to protect ourselves."

"Well Bailey, my name's John. I'm the owner of this here establishment." After a second, John lowered his pistol and placed it the holster on his belt.

The relief I felt when he lowered his weapon was unparalleled. It was like I had been taken off of death row right before I was due to face the executioner.

"Look, we didn't know anyone was in here. We would have never come in otherwise," Ethan reasoned.

"A bit late for that, isn't it, boy?" John said, raising an eyebrow at Ethan.

"Um, we don't have the money to pay for the guns, but maybe we could work something out?" I said, trying to defuse the situation. "We could make a trade, or put them on... layaway?"

I silently cursed myself for making the stupid comment, but John cracked a smile.

"Don't think credit works anymore," he grinned at me. "I'll tell you what, ya'll can keep the guns and ammo you have if you take us with you."

Ethan narrowed his eyes, "How did you know we were goin' somewhere or that we even had a plan?"

"Ya'll got that truck loaded up in the back and a map on the dashboard with an area circled," John replied. "Plus, last I heard most people were headin' into the cities for the refugee areas."

"They're all gone," I said. "Well at least the school we were at is. The city was overrun, infected people running rampant and shots going off everywhere."

"Wait you said *us*, who else is there?" Ethan eyed John.

"Just me and my son Taylor," John said.

A high-pitched scream echoed through the small store. John looked at us then bolted toward the sound and we followed right behind him. In the middle of the sales floor, Zoe had her arms wrapped around Chloe with Darren beside them. A few feet away was a guy who looked freshly eighteen, holding them at gunpoint.

"Pop, I found three," the guy said to John.

John raised his arm and made a motion to put down the gun, "It's all right Taylor, they ain't gonna hurt us."

"But they stole a bunch of our guns," he said, with his eyes quickly darting to Ethan and I behind his father.

He was the spitting image of his father, except the younger version that was barely out of high school. Cowboy to the max, complete with boots and a hat.

"Not like we can use 'em all," John said, staring Taylor down until he lowered his own pistol.

Chloe unlatched herself from Zoe and ran to Ethan, who grabbed her immediately. I glared at the asshole that had the nerve to hold a kid at gunpoint.

"What's your problem? *You* broke into *our* store," he sneered at me.

"Just wondering what kind of asshole would point a gun at a child," I sneered right back at him.

He had the good graces to look ashamed, and I hoped he felt it.

"Now nothin' happened, Taylor was just doin' what he thought was right," John reasoned. "We had no idea who broke in."

"Well, what now?" Darren asked, still giving Taylor an accusing stare.

"We were going to make a deal," I said.

"What kind of deal?" Zoe looked at me, questioningly.

"John said we could keep the guns and ammo if we let them come with us," Ethan restated the terms.

"Hell no, this guy just pointed a gun at us!" Darren yelled, stabbing his finger toward Taylor.

"How was I to know you weren't gonna hurt us?" Taylor yelled back.

"What did you think we were going to do, send the nine-year-old after you?" Darren retorted.

"I'm nine and a half!" Chloe piped in, and Taylor looked stunned that she even spoke.

John chuckled at that and got in the middle of the two.

"That'll be enough. We're all keyed up from what's been happenin'. Let's calm down," John looked at both of them.

Darren reluctantly nodded at him, whilst Taylor placed his gun in his own holster.

"All right then how to you suggest we do this?" Darren asked.

"Do what?" John asked.

"We don't have enough room in the truck or even enough supplies for ourselves," Darren answered.

"We got a car and there's a small grocery store down the road some," John suggested. "It's like our own small community this far out. There's even a gas station in the same parkin' lot."

"All right, grab your things and we'll meet outside," Ethan said, tugging Chloe toward the door.

"We'll only be 'bout five minutes," John said motioning for Taylor to follow him.

Once we were back to the truck, we all tossed our duffels into the back.

"This is a bad idea, Ethan," Darren said running his hand through his hair. "We should just take off before they get out."

"We can't do that. They let us keep the guns," Ethan said back.

"They just held us at gunpoint; you really think we can trust them?" Darren kept trying to make his case.

"Plus, we'll need them to show us where the grocery store and gas station are," I added.

Darren looked away, defeated.

"Look, I agree that we can't just blindly trust 'em, but we owe 'em for the guns and extra bodies could come in handy," Ethan sighed, leaning his arm against the truck.

"And that guy seems military or at the very least, has training," I added.

"That would be useful," Zoe added.

We saw them emerge from the door, both packing giant bags on their backs. They opened the Mazda's trunk and stashed their stuff before starting toward us. I was expecting a big, obnoxious redneck truck, but instead they had a small sedan.

"So what's the plan?" John asked as soon as they approached our huddle.

"We need supplies so we can at least stay put for a week or so," Ethan said. "My family has a cabin west of here, but we only have so much canned goods and supplies there."

"Well if it's out in the woods, we could do some huntin'," John added.

"Yeah, the game is pretty good out there, and we just fixed up the property 'bout a year ago. New fencin', solar panels, and even a meat smoker."

I perked up at the sound of that. I hated the taste of wild meat, it was to gamey for me, but a smoker meant jerky which tasted better and lasted longer.

"Sounds good," John said, impressed. "How's the water situation?"

"We have a well that the cabin draws from, but since we will be needin' lots from it, we'll need more water softeners to keep that rust taste out."

"Good thing we're goin' to a grocery store," Chloe added.

"Good thing we have an extra vehicle, hey?" John smiled down at her and she nodded.

"You should lead the way since we have no idea where we're goin'," Ethan said opening the truck's driver door.

"It's just down that road," John pointed to the road heading to our left. "'Bout a three-minute drive due south."

"We'll be right behind you," Ethan said.

John and Taylor headed to their car and started the engine. Once they pulled out of the parking lot, we followed closely behind. I could hear the gravel crunch under the tires, then the sound stopped once we hit pavement. The road was cracked and worn, definitely in need of a new layer of asphalt.

People must have really all fled into the main part of the city. There was not a soul anywhere, not even an infected person. The buildings were all locked up and dark inside with no vehicles sitting out front. I was half expecting a tumble weed to go rolling by.

"Wow, it's like a ghost town," Zoe muttered.

I could see the big sign that read Brookshire Grocery Company and John's car veered off in that direction. The parking lot was empty except for a few cars and shopping carts. The small Shell station that shared the parking lot was not lit up either. John pulled up right in front of the doors and Ethan followed right behind.

"How are we going to get in?" Darren asked. "Your shop may not have had an alarm, but I'm guessing this place does."

John looked at the door for a second then walked up to it, the doors parting open for him.

"Well that's kind of ominous," I muttered.

"Ya'll should grab some of those guns you *borrowed*," Taylor motioned to the truck.

We rummaged through our bags and picked our weapons. I grabbed one of the Beretta's and fiddled with it until the magazine fell out. I looked to see what Ethan was doing and started to copy him. Grabbing a box of bullets, I popped a bunch into the magazine until it was full. I had counted fifteen bullets which I hoped was more than enough. I slid the magazine back into the handgun, impressed with myself but when I grabbed the silencer I realized I had no clue how to put one on.

Taylor held out his hand, "Pass that here."

I gave him a narrowed look. In response he rolled his eyes and kept his hand out for the gun. I grudgingly handed him the pieces which he put together with practiced ease.

"You make that look easy," I sighed.

"Well I've been 'round a gun or two before," he said with a smirk, handing the assembled gun back to me.

The silencer added some weight to the gun and made it feel even more awkward thanks to the increased length. I examined the gun and found the switch, which I assumed was the safety; after all, I had seen a movie or two. The small light beside it was green and when I moved the switch to the other side, the light went red. I had no idea which color meant what. Green usually meant go, but did that mean go as in ready to shoot? Or green as in the gun is okay to move without accidently shooting it? There was no way in hell I would ask that out loud, though; I had *some* dignity.

"You guys ready?" John prompted.

Everyone nodded except for Ethan. He was going to stay in the truck with Chloe to make sure nothing happened to her while we were all inside the store.

"Maybe John and I should go in first," Darren said peering into the store.

"All that will do is put you two into danger and waste time," I said. "Safety in numbers, remember?"

Darren looked back at me and nodded.

"Well if we're worried about safety, maybe you shouldn't wield that gun," Zoe pointed to me.

"I've got to learn somehow," I retorted. "But to be on the safe side I'll stand off to the side, *not* behind you."

"Wait, haven't you ever shot a gun before?" John eyed me warily.

"Well, not a real one," I admitted and I could see the concern flash across his face.

"I swear to God, I better not end up with a bullet in my ass," Taylor said pointedly.

I flicked the safety to green, secretly praying that was the way to arm the safety and tucked it into the front waist band of my jeans. I held up my empty hands.

"Happy now?"

"Well happy wouldn't be the right word, but I feel a hell of a lot safer," Taylor admitted.

I could just tell he was going to be a drama queen.

Chapter 10

With John in the lead, we entered the quiet store. The emergency lights were on, and muted sunlight leaked through the front windows, but the store was still a bit too dark to see properly. The shelves and displays gave off elongated shadows, making the space appear sinister, like a cheap haunted house. I couldn't hear any movement except for the sounds of our group's footsteps as they hit the linoleum. We all split up, going into different areas of the store in the interest of time. I had claimed the pharmacy; after all, I'm sure the guys wouldn't think to grab tampons.

I picked up a handbasket along the way and started to peruse the aisles. I grabbed all the first aid items I could, focusing on bandages and anti-septic. I peeked around the corner to see Zoe adding items to her shopping basket with all the hygiene items we needed. After filling my own basket, I sat it down on the pharmacy counter and hopped over the counter, careful not to pull on my scratches again. Somehow this felt more wrong than breaking into a gun shop.

The shelves were still stocked with all the different kinds of medicines, and I had no idea where to start. I started to skim-read the labels and grabbed anything that sounded like it would be an antibiotic or pain killer. I tossed all of the bottles I could into a new basket and jumped back over to the customer side. With both shopping baskets in hand, I went in search of Zoe.

As I rounded one of the corners, I ran straight into another body; the force and shock knocking both of us down. The baskets contents spilled all over the floor, surrounding us, like insects scurrying away from light. I looked up into the discolored face of an infected. I quickly scrambled back as the thing snapped at me, my hands slipping on the linoleum with each stride. My back hit the pharmacy counter and I used it as leverage to get myself onto shaky feet.

Once up, the infected reached for me as it stumbled forward. Its eyes were clouded over so bad that I couldn't even see the iris' color. There was a big chunk missing from its neck, and the wound leaked discolored blood onto his grocery store uniform with every step. In my panic, I had completely forgotten about the gun holstered in my waistband. I pulled it out and flicked the safety until I saw the small red light. I pointed it at the infected, but my hands were shaking so badly that I couldn't hold it steady. I took a deep breath and squeezed the trigger. I missed and the bullet whizzed by the thing's head, embedding itself in one of the shelves.

It was still coming at me, and I only had time to make one more shot before it was on me. Never taking my eyes off of it, I shot again. This time the bullet hit its mark, well, sort of anyways. It caught the infected in its left shoulder causing him to spin around from the impact. It landed on the ground with a hiss and pushed itself back up again, not bothered by the bullet hole now adorning his body. I raised the gun to try again when the infected's head whipped to the side, brain and blood spraying in the air along with it. I looked to my right to see Taylor lowering his gun.

"You okay?" he asked as he ran up to me.

All I could do was nod dumbly, too shocked from what just happened to speak at the moment.

"Oh my god Bailey, are you all right?" Zoe dropped her basket and ran over to me.

"She's in shock, I think. I don't see any blood," Taylor said giving me the once over.

Everyone else ran over to the scene at the sound of Taylor's pistol. After deciding I was fit to go, John spoke up.

"We need to hurry. That shot was loud, who knows what else heard it."

The others flew off into their areas to finish, while Zoe stayed behind with me.

"Are you sure you're okay?" Zoe asked, placing her hand on my shoulder.

"Yes," I said weakly then cleared my throat. "I've just never had to shoot a gun before and the fact that I actually hit that thing freaks me out."

"They don't seem to feel it or even notice it," Zoe tried to reason with me.

"Yeah," I said and looked up at her, not realizing I had been staring at my feet. "It just got up and kept coming for me."

"But you're fine," she stated again.

My hand flew up to rest on my side where my scratch wound was still healing.

"I could have been one of those things," I said quietly.

I'm sure the others wouldn't be too keen on finding out I had been attacked before.

"You're not though. We saw how fast it turned Mike and all those other people. If you had been infected you would have turned by now," Zoe pointed out.

I wasn't sure how convinced I was of Zoe's words, but I nodded and bent down to gather up the supplies I had dropped. Maybe I was immune or maybe a scratch didn't work the same as a bite. If that was the case, then at least we wouldn't have to worry about being scratched in the future. The fact that my wound was healing like a normal cut would made me feel relieved, but how would other people react? The last thing we needed was for people to go around killing each other because they thought others were going to turn when they might not.

Once Zoe and I had finished stuffing all the supplies back into the overflowing baskets, we headed back to the front doors. As we walked out I gave one last look to the fallen infected on the floor, content with the fact that he was no longer moving. At the entrance Darren was handing out plastic grocery bags and we started to stuff our looted supplies into them. Taylor propped a mesh bag against the wall.

"What's that?" I asked.

"A tent. I'm assumin' we all can't fit into a huntin' cabin," Taylor grunted as he added the other camping gear and sleeping bags to the pile that he had found in the small supermarket.

"We're goin' to need more supplies like gas stoves, but time isn't somethin' we have right now," John added.

"Once we get settled, we can make a run back into town," Darren said, hauling all his bags out the doors.

We divvied up the bags between the Mazda's trunk and the back of the truck.

"We need some bungee cables or something to hold all this down," Zoe said, wiping the sweat from her forehead.

The sun was right above us, glaring down on the parking lot pavement. The temperature was perfect this time of year, but the closer it got to the summer months, the closer we got to experiencing that Southern heat. Zoe and I were too Canadian to deal with that much heat. Hopefully, this would all be resolved before that time came.

"All right, I saw some in the back of the store with the campin' gear," Taylor said. "I'll head back in and get some."

He took off back into the store before anyone could answer and John followed in after him.

"Where are they goin'?" Chloe asked, as she stepped out of the truck behind Ethan.

"Just ran to grab some ties for the back of the truck," Ethan answered, as he gave the area another once-over.

"Did ya get anythin' good?" Chloe asked.

Darren smirked, "Define *good*."

I snaked my arm over the truck side and rummaged through my bags looking for the items I had grabbed on impulse. Once my fingers found what I was looking for, I pulled them out and handed the pieces to Chloe, not realizing everyone was staring at me. Her eyes lit up when I handed her the Scooby-Doo mystery books I had spotted in the pharmacy waiting area.

"Thank you!" she squealed and launched herself at me.

"Yeah, yeah, you're welcome," I muttered, slightly embarrassed.

She took the books and skipped over to the passenger seat to flip through them.

"Awww," Zoe smirked at me and I flipped her the bird.

"Thanks for that," Ethan said, flashing me an appreciative smile.

"Yeah well, it wasn't completely unselfish. I just didn't want to listen to 'are we there yet?' the whole way," I waved it off.

"Fair enough."

We had just finished tossing in the last bag when Taylor and John re-emerged from the grocery store with the bungee cables in hand. John had empty red gas canisters in both hands and tossed them into the back of their car.

"So, are the gas pumps even working?" Zoe asked as we climbed back into the truck.

"Only one-way to find out," Ethan said.

The truck pulled up to pump number one while the Mazda took pump number three. We all jumped back out of the truck, except for Chloe who was engrossed in her books. Ethan lifted up the nozzle and the machine sprung to life. He grinned triumphantly as he placed the nozzle in the gas cap opening of the truck. Three canisters later, we had a good amount of gas that would hopefully last a while.

"Good thing we don't have to pay for this. It would have been more than the guns," Darren remarked.

"So now do we just head out to your cabin and wait?" I asked, propping myself up against the side of the truck.

"Wait for what exactly?" Ethan asked.

"I don't know. Order to be restored. The infected to be cured," I listed off. "What I meant is: what's the plan?"

Ethan raked his fingers through his hair and glanced briefly at Chloe before answering,

"There is no plan. Gettin' to the cabin was the plan."

"Maybe the military will start taking over," Zoe said hopefully.

"That's not necessarily a good thing," Darren muttered.

"It's better than chaos," Ethan said.

Darren didn't answer, but I could tell he was not one to be easily convinced.

"Why isn't the military here yet anyways?" I asked.

"Too much ground to cover," John answered me as they approached the truck.

"There's got to be safe zones set up or something," Zoe said.

"Probably somewhere, just not here," Ethan sighed.

"Although, it would probably end up just like the school did," I said.

"Not necessarily. The military have trainin' and fire power, plus they would be more organized than a bunch of volunteers trying to run an emergency shelter," Ethan said back.

"I have an old radio I grabbed on the way out," John said. "When we get to your cabin, we can fire it up and see if we hear anythin'."

"Sounds like a plan," Ethan nodded relaxing at bit at John's words.

"How far is your cabin from here?" Taylor asked.

Ethan reached into the truck cab and pulled out the map. We followed him to the hood of the truck and he spread it out.

"The cabin is here," Ethan said pointing to the circled spot on the map. "And we're here."

"Hmm, looks about three or four hours, dependin' if we run into anythin' or not," John said eyeing the trail Ethan made with his finger.

How he could tell that from looking at a map is beyond me. I needed Google Maps for that.

Chapter 11

If I had to listen to one more word about My Little Pony, I was going to shoot someone. Literally. I had a gun now. I brought Chloe those Scooby-Doo books so I wouldn't have to put up with something like this for the whole ride, but alas being a nine-year-old took over and the books no longer held her attention. So here we were listening to the epic tale of the Cutie Mark Crusaders trying to hook up their teacher and some dude with a magic potion. All I could think while I listened to the story was, *We have something like that in real life, and we call it alcohol.*

I grinned out the window at my internal conversation and tried to drown out her rather demanding little voice. We had finally got out of the city using the back roads and horribly designed one-ways. Luckily we didn't run into any infected, just a couple of other vehicles heading in the opposite direction. They all had junk piled on their roofs, as they sped into the city, no doubt trying to get to the emergency shelters. I knew most of those shelters would fall just like the school had, but the travelers wouldn't listen. We even flagged down a minivan and tried to tell them about the city being overrun, but they refused to believe us. I guess if you hadn't seen it yourself, you would have a hard time swallowing the truth.

"Hey look it's a van!" Chloe exclaimed suddenly.

We all peered out the windshield to see a newer model of a Dodge Caravan barreling down the one-way. Unfortunately, we were going the wrong direction on it, so Ethan slowed and moved over as far as he could with the truck. The van would be able to squeeze through, if they slowed down that was. Just before they reached us, they finally reduced their speed and stopped. The driver got out of the van and started to approach the truck.

"Stay here," Ethan said firmly to Chloe and she just nodded her head.

We stared at the dark skinned, middle aged man walking calmly toward the truck. Ethan rolled down the window before getting out, no doubt to allow us to hear the conversation.

"Uh, you're kind of in the way," the man said to Ethan.

"Sorry 'bout that, had to use these roads to get out of the city," Ethan said back.

"Why not the interstate or main arteries?" he asked confused.

Ethan sighed, obviously not liking to be the bearer of bad news. "We just came from one city shelter they had set up, and it was overrun. We figured the safest thing would be to lay low for a bit in the country while we waited for the government and military to organize everythin'."

"We're heading to the stadium one, was that the place you guys were coming from?" the man asked.

"No, the high school near downtown."

"Well, maybe the stadium is fine."

"I wouldn't take that chance," Ethan looked over at the van. "Especially with your family in tow."

"We don't know what else to do." The guy shrugged, helplessly.

Ethan better not ask them to come with us. The last thing we needed were more liabilities, although in all fairness, that's all we were to Ethan when he offered.

"You should turn back around and stay outside city limits."

"Thanks for the advice, but I think we will stick with our plan."

Ethan looked really torn as he almost pleaded with the man.

"Look, I have a huntin' cabin 'bout another three or four hours from here. You and your family are welcome to come with us."

"That's really kind, but we think an official shelter would be best. I got to look out for my family, you know?" the man gave us a crinkled smile. "Name's Roy by the way."

"Ethan."

"Well, thanks again for the offer, Ethan," Roy said, as he started back toward his van.

Slowly the van inched past us and Roy waved. I could see the curious faces of his young daughters pressed up against the van windows, watching us as they slid past us. I watched the van go by us and then the Mazda. Soon the van disappeared behind us and I found myself hoping they would find what they were looking for.

The buildings had given way to a two-lane highway surrounded by trees in every direction. It seemed so surreal considering we were just in the city, pretty much blocked in by buildings on all ends. The road was clear. This was kind of creepy in my books; it reminded me of when I would have the unholy 6 AM Saturday shift at my part-time job, and the roads would be empty the entire way. We drove on, speeding with the Mazda still in tow.

There was a car pulled over to the side of the road. We gave it a wide berth as we passed; the driver side window was smeared with blood and the passenger side door was left wide open. The window was so covered in blood that I couldn't see in, but Ethan didn't give us much of a chance to gawk as he sped away from the abandoned car. Suddenly no one felt like talking, even Chloe had stopped her tirade.

"So, anyone want to play I-Spy?" Darren quipped.

Zoe smacked him on the arm and he feigned being hurt. Honestly, the joke was in bad taste, but at least it helped to relieve some of the tension. I felt the truck slowing down and

Ethan flicked on his right signal light for John and Taylor behind us. The pavement ended with the highway and the sound of gravel crunching under our tires filled the cab. I could barely make out the Mazda behind us through the dust and gravel the truck was throwing up.

"I hope they can see," Zoe said as she peered out the back window.

"I hope he's not too attached to that paint job," I said back.

"So I hate to be *that* guy, but are we close yet?" Zoe asked.

"The gravel road turn-off means about another forty-five minutes or so," Ethan answered her question, glancing in the rear view mirror.

"Look!" our trusty guide pointed out from the passenger seat.

There was a deer bounding along the tree line.

"Hmm, you weren't kidding about the game up here," Darren said.

"Yeah, it's pretty good 'round this time of year, even though it's technically not huntin' season anymore," Ethan pointed out.

"So what does that mean?" I asked.

"It means were only allowed to hunt for a few months out of the year and generally it's around October until January, so we're a little out of the limits," Ethan answered.

"What happens if you hunt outside of the season?"

"Jail or a fine," Ethan said. "But I think that's the least of our worries."

He wasn't kidding.

"Once our dad took down a white-tailed buck that was almost four hundred pounds!" Chloe exclaimed proudly.

Ethan chuckled.

"Yeah, I remember that day all right. Took me, dad and Uncle Paul just to lift it onto the back of the truck. Damn near dropped the thing on me as we moved it."

"We had deer for months," Chloe giggled. "Mom made dad give the rest away 'cause she said she'd go crazy if she had to eat any more deer meat."

"Sounds pretty good right about now," Darren said. "I could go for some food."

Great, now I was hungry and we still had forty minutes to go. By the time we pulled up to the heavy iron gate, I was officially starving. Ethan got out of the truck to unlock the gate and swing it open. Darren jumped out and drove the truck through and the Mazda followed. When Ethan relocked the gate, he kicked Darren into the back again.

The immediate property was lined with barbed wire, the only break being the gate. I assumed their land went much further than I could see. Trees lined the area creating the feeling like we were in the middle of a forest, the only trail being the dirt road that led up to the cabin. The cabin itself was actually bigger than I expected. I was imaging a log cabin, but instead it was modernly designed, with dark brown siding. I could see the solar panels lining the roof and a few propped around the cabin on the ground. At the peak was a little window and I assumed that was a loft area.

"Nice," Darren said, clearly impressed.

Finally, we were able to get out and stretch. I grabbed one of the bags from the back and took out a pack of beef jerky. Everyone grabbed some of the dehydrated meat, and soon we were all busy gnawing on the chewy junk food.

"So do we get the grand tour?" I asked, after taking a drink from my water bottle.

"Sure is a nice place you got here, son," John said, eyeing the solar panels.

"My dad loves to hunt," Ethan said proudly. "This place used to belong to my grandfather, but when he passed, my dad redid the cabin. He added the fencin', all the amenities and hook-ups."

We followed Ethan around back where there was a little garden with a few plants starting to sprout and a well a few feet from that. There was a small shed with a pile of wood beside it, no doubt for the camp fire which was located a few meters from the side of the cabin. Then he took us inside.

The air was musty from being locked up for so long without even a window cracked. The inside was furnished with very utilitarian type furniture that would last forever. Then I saw something that had me actually excited.

"A bathroom. Thank god!" I exclaimed.

No bathing in a pond somewhere.

"There's also an outhouse a bit further from the cabin."

I made a face at that, and Ethan laughed. The kitchen was small, and a mid-sized, black contraption stood about half my height. The fridge was only an apartment-sized one when the spot could have held a full one, so I assumed this thing wasn't a second fridge.

"Meat smoker," Ethan said when he saw me eyeing the thing.

"Bailey and I dibs this room," Zoe said as she flung her bag into the room.

I walked over to the room, which was barely big enough to host the two single beds. I dropped my backpack onto the floor and peeked at the other room, which was just a mirror of ours.

"I dibs the loft," Chloe said excitedly as she climbed the wooden ladder that lead to a small ledge area.

I guess that window was really for a loft after all.

"Wait, does that mean we're bunking together?" Darren asked Ethan with a perplexed look on his face.

"Well, it's that or the couch," Ethan said as he dropped himself onto the couch in question.

Dust flew up and Ethan started to cough as he waved away the motes surrounding him.

"Not much of a choice," Darren muttered.

"Guys," Zoe rolled her eyes. "So touchy about things like that."

I grinned at the look they shot her. At least they wouldn't have to share a bed, but to be fair calling those cots a bed seemed like an insult.

"At least you don't have to put up with Zoe's snoring," I joked and she punched me in the arm.

"It's not that bad," Zoe said as I rubbed my arm.

"I honestly don't know how you don't wake yourself up," I said. "It's like a chainsaw."

Chloe laughed from her perch in the loft and Zoe just rolled her eyes.

"You guys brought sleeping bags right?" Ethan asked John and Taylor.

"Yeah and a couple extras, if you need any," John nodded.

"Maybe you guys should camp out in the livin' room until we make sure it's safe," Ethan suggested.

"Won't hear me complainin'," John said.

"You might when you hear Zoe snore," I grinned and Zoe lobbed a pillow at my head.

"It isn't that bad, dammit!" she yelled back.

Chapter 12

I slept like the dead that night. Pardon the pun, but it was true. We all did. The lack of sleep from the previous nights and the constant stress really did a number on a person; I even slept through Zoe's snoring. The others were already up by the time I rolled out of bed, following the very welcome smell of coffee. It was only instant coffee, but I gratefully accepted it from Ethan as he passed me a steaming cup. Chloe was up in the loft keeping an eye out the small window. If anyone saw something, it would be her. John was tinkering with the dented radio he brought, trying to get it to play anything but static.

"How long have you been at that?" I asked after downing about half the cup of coffee.

"Not too long, 'bout five minutes or so," John answered.

"And still nothing?"

"A few words here and there, but unless I know the frequency I'm lookin' for, it's just a shot in the dark," John shrugged.

"You got a workin' radio in here or anythin'?" Taylor asked scanning the room.

"Here," Chloe announced as she climbed down from her perch.

She placed the plastic, bright pink radio on the counter.

"Better than nothin'," Taylor shrugged and flipped the on switch.

Immediately the room was filled with more static, but as he scanned down the channels a voice soon caught our attention, but was gone too soon.

"Go back," Ethan said jumping right next to Taylor.

Carefully, as if he was doing surgery, Taylor turned the knob back and the needle barely moved.

"...indoors as much as possible. Gather all the supplies you can and wait for further instruction. Again, we repeat, under no circumstances are you to engage the infected. The virus is passed through contact and is not airborne. All those with firearm licences are strongly encouraged to obtain a weapon, only to be used in the case of extreme emergencies. We ask that you hold tight until the military is able to make it to your region. We are doing what we can to stabilize the remaining population and restore order. Keep strong and God bless...This is an emergency broadcast. The date and time is February 13th, 8:15 AM, and martial law has been declared. The President has fallen and Vice President, Mr. Biden, has taken the position in this grave time to lead our great country. The virus has gone international and now has been classified as an epidemic. You must avoid infected at all costs and try to stay indoors as much as possible..."

Taylor flicked off the radio when it started to repeat. It was clear the message was on a continual loop.

"That was yesterday," Zoe said quietly.

"Holy shit, the President's gone," Darren said in disbelief, sinking further into the couch.

I was no expert, but I was pretty sure the situation must be dire for them to announce something like that. I noticed how they didn't tell us to go anywhere like the newscast had a couple of days ago. Either they thought we really were safest in smaller numbers or there was no safe place left standing to go. I looked down into my coffee cup wishing I had something stronger, maybe some tequila.

"I can't believe they're encouragin' folks to get guns," Ethan said astounded.

"A situation like this is unprecedented... basically they're sayin' we're on our own," John said placing his cowboy hat on his head. "Well, if we are goin' to go around armed, we best get some practice."

"Why do I have the feeling that was aimed at me?" I grinned a little, despite the grim newscast.

"Because it was," Darren smirked back, pushing himself off the couch.

"We can't do it here though, we need to move away so that the sound isn't linked back to the cabin," John said. "You know of any fields within ten miles or so?" John seemed like a very practical man, never one to not have a plan or not think things through.

Ethan thought about it. "Don't know, there're some crop fields back a ways."

"Guess that'll have to do," John said.

"What'll we use for targets?" Zoe asked.

"Empty water bottles and whatever else we can find along the way," John suggested.

"Wouldn't this be a waste of bullets?" Darren asked.

John stared down Darren, "It's not a waste if you're learnin' an important skill that could mean the difference between life and death, son." That shut Darren up.

Everyone sprang into action while I finished my coffee. I was no good to the world without my coffee. I pulled out my cellphone again, noticing I only had thirty percent of my battery left. I would have to conserve what I could and hope that I would be allowed to recharge using the solar panels. Once again, I dialed my house number except I was met with a no signal tone this time. I peered down at the screen, the red circle with a line through it laughing at my efforts. *Am I ever going to talk to my family again?* I didn't want to think about it, so I put it out of my mind for now.

I grabbed my Beretta with the silencer still attached and shoved the piece into the holster, making sure I checked that the safety was on, only around seven times. It wouldn't really help my case that I could manage a gun if I shot myself. And I didn't think to bring a belt, so Ethan let me borrow one of his. The holster I grabbed was the one with a hole in the bottom, so even though the handgun had a silencer on it, it still fit. Then I looped on my holstered hunting knife on the other side of the belt. Needless to say, I felt pretty badass walking out of my room with all my weapons.

Although the gun and knife kind of looked out of place with my outfit, it felt like it was hot outside so I opted for my shorts and a T-shirt.

John was the only one by the truck when I finally exited the cabin. He nodded at me as I approached the truck. "You ready to go?" he asked.

"Yep," I said, looking at his outfit. "How are you wearing jeans and a long sleeve shirt when it's this warm out?"

He cracked a grin, "I grew up here, kind of used to the heat by now. Plus this ain't even that hot. Just wait until it's summer, that's when you'll really be fryin'."

"Great, something to look forward to." I squinted up at the intense sun. Again, I fervently hoped that by summer everything would be sorted out and I wouldn't have to worry about boiling to death in the South, but instead be back home.

"Glad you decided on the shorts because I won't be dragging you back," Zoe joked as she approached us.

"Glad to know I have such great friends," I retorted.

Zoe plunked the bag she had into the back of the truck and then turned to us.

"So, decided which way we should go yet?" Zoe asked John.

He pointed to a section on the map, "According to Ethan, this is an empty field, and it's fenced almost all the way around. This should be our best bet."

As the others joined in our little pow-wow, I could hear the tinkling of cans as they shifted around in the plastic bags they were carrying. With the location in mind, we headed off.

Instead of going back the direction we came, we went even further into the rural area. All the roads were gravel this far out and again the Mazda was stuck following in our dust trail. The tall trees helped to shade us from the unrelenting sun, which made the trip slightly more bearable. There wasn't even a cloud in the sky to filter out some of the rays. From the passenger's seat, Chloe informed us that it was unusually warm for February, which was just my luck.

We came up to a rotted gate with a *NO TRESPASSING* sign hung at an odd angle. Ethan jumped out of the cab to kick the gate open enough for the truck to pass through. The dirt path eventually ended and all I could see for miles was row after row of grass and crops. As we walked away from the vehicles, we stayed close to the fence line so that we could easily find our way back.

"This looks pretty good," Ethan said as he scanned the immediate area.

"'Bout as good as any," John agreed and we started to set up the cans and bottles.

Using some of the well water, we poured a little bit of liquid into the containers so that they would stay put, and upright on the fence. I voluntarily took the targets at the very end.

Chloe had brought a blanket to lounge on while she did some reading, setting up in the tree shade. She said that she didn't want to shoot, since she already knew what she was doing and that it would just be a waste of bullets. Smart-ass kid.

"All right, so as you may have guessed, I served in the military. The first thing they teach you is gun safety," John said, standing slightly in front of us, pointing to various spots on his gun. "This is your safety, this is your magazine release, and this is the trigger."

Darren rolled his eyes at that last one.

"You must keep your trigger finger on the side until you are ready to shoot; otherwise, we will have some trigger happy accidents," John continued on. "These notches are for aimin'. The one in the front must align in the middle of the two on the back."

He went on for a while before finally using his own gun to demonstrate taking a shot. He lifted the pistol to eye level and took aim. He looked calm as he slowly squeezed the trigger. One of the bottles flew back off of the fence as the shot rang out. That was one thing movies never got right, just how loud an actual gun shot was. Admittedly, it was less loud than the shots in the grocery store, but that was because we were out in the open.

We all spread out a little bit more to try it ourselves. I flinched at the sound of the others shooting, but once I started myself, the other sounds faded into the background. My first few shots missed by miles, but as I got more comfortable I started to at least hit the fence and even one bottle. I hit the release button and the empty magazine slid out. I fished the other loaded magazine from my bag and reloaded the gun. Everyone else was doing pretty well, but some bottles and cans remained untouched on the fence. It was almost as if they were mocking us.

"You need to slowly squeeze the trigger. You're jerkin' it which jolts the gun and ruins your aim," John offered as he came up beside me.

I took my time in lining up the next shot and slid my finger to the trigger. This time I took a deep breath and released it at the same moment that I slowly squeezed the trigger. The shot landed on the very bottom of one of the bottles, but it still went flying into the grass behind the fence.

"See, there you go," John grinned, patting me on the shoulder. "Also make sure your gun goes up when you fire, not down or else the shot goes off target."

"Thanks," I said before I turned back to my targets.

With renewed vigor I took my time, and managed to hit the remaining bottles and cans. Had they been moving, that would have been a different story. I'm sure the infected wouldn't stand still for me, even if I asked politely. I wondered how John planned to train us with moving targets. Dangle a bottle with a string from a tree branch?

"Wow. You hit them," Darren's eyebrows shot up when he saw the empty fence in front of me.

"Damn straight," I grinned proudly back at him.

"Ya'll did good," John said, making me feel less special. "But chances are, those *things* ain't gonna stand nice and still for you."

Looks like he had been thinking the same thing.

"Well, what would you suggest?" Ethan asked, as he slid his empty magazine out of the gun.

"That's the question, ain't it?" John said contemplating what to do.

"We could do real target practice," Darren suggested.

"Maybe you should elaborate slightly on that," I said, concerned.

Darren grinned like he had made a joke, "I meant, go find a bunch of the infected in an area and they can be our target practice."

The idea creeped me out, but Darren had a valid idea. The whole reason we were in this field right now was to practice shooting so we could defend ourselves against those things. But was I or anyone else ready to unload on a bunch of infected?

"Okay, say we did that. Where would we go?" Taylor asked.

"It would start with us having to head back toward the city because there would be more infected than out here," Darren suggested.

No one said anything; no one seemed too keen on heading back to the place we had just fled from.

"Well, we can't all just pack up and go. What if somethin' happened here while we were gone?" Ethan pointed out.

"Like?" Darren prompted.

"Infected wandered in or what if some other people come by and took the cabin?" Ethan listed off.

"We could split into groups I guess, and take turns going," Darren compromised.

"And we could also pick up some more supplies when we went in," Zoe pointed out.

"All right, let's head back to the cabin and plan this out properly," John said.

Seeing that we were done for the day, Chloe ran to us, her blanket flowing behind her like a cape. No one said anything as we walked back to the vehicles, our minds too preoccupied with thoughts of heading back into that mess. As much as I hated the idea, it was the only way to familiarize ourselves with the infected and learn how to defend ourselves against them. If we just hid out at the cabin for who knows how long and infected showed up, we would be sorely out of practice in dealing with them.

"How about we just give it a couple of days?" I suggested. "Let us get more experience with the bottles and stuff first."

John nodded. "Probably a good idea."

My side was now stinging a bit, but it was getting better everyday. I moved my arm around a bit to stretch the sore muscles. That's another thing they don't show you in the movies – the pain that accompanies the recoil of the gun.

Chapter 13

"Okay, how about two Reese's Pieces for some deer jerky?" Zoe pleaded again.

"No way, the jerky's mine!" I stood strong in the face of the chocolaty temptation.

We were running extremely low on supplies so we resorted to bartering amongst ourselves. We never made that trip a couple of months ago; *was it just a couple?* Man, it felt like a lifetime ago. All radio stations had quit broadcasting, even the emergency ones. We could no longer see the lights from the city, so the nights were beyond dark with the stars providing our only light.

In addition to all that, cell signals had also stopped, rendering everyone's cellphones useless. I wasn't addicted to my phone like some people, but I still found myself trying to check for new texts or calls from my family every once and a while. So I stowed it away in my backpack to keep it from getting damaged, hoping that one day it'd be usable again.

We had opted for the safer route, which was to wait here and see if help came instead of running head long into the city we just tried to escape. Well, obviously, since we were stuck here arguing over junk food, it was a wise choice. So now we really did have a decision to make: starve, or chance a run into a nearby town to grab some much needed supplies. On the plus side, with nothing but time on our hands, we had gotten lots of target practice and I had even been on a few hunting trips.

Not that I was much use on them. Basically it was to show me how to use my rifle. Damn Taylor showed me up every time. But at least he got his comeuppance a few weeks earlier.

"This is unholy early," I yawned, as I pulled the rifle strap back up my shoulder.

The stupid thing slid off repeatedly as I trekked behind Taylor in the rough-terrain of the forest. Well, it was rough to me anyways.

"Six in the mornin' is the best time to catch game," Taylor, once again, pointed out. "Hey, it was you who wanted to learn anyways."

"Yeah, but I didn't know it entailed getting up at five o'clock in the morning!"

Whatever the opposite of a morning person was, that was me. I saw Taylor clench his jaw before he picked up his pace and left me to scramble behind him just to keep up in the face of all the protruding tree roots. They were like the grabbing hands of the dead crawling their way out of the grave. This trek kept up for another hour, and I really regretted my decision to attend this Taylor hosted event. I heard the crunch of leaves off to our right and Taylor held up his closed fist which I assumed meant, "Sit still and shut up," so I did. Slowly Taylor slid his rifle off of his shoulder, and moved quietly toward the noise.

I decided to stay still since I would most likely trip and fall, and thus have ruined any chances of us actually catching something. Or worse, I might alert something to our presence. I turned my head and squinted, in an attempt to see what had made the noise. I couldn't see much, but I spotted a mass of brown fur with a white tail. I may have been a city girl, as Taylor called me, but I knew that was deer. The grin on Taylor's face reinforced my guess and he crept silently closer while he brought the rifle up to eye level. What happened next was quite strange.

One minute Taylor was approaching the deer and the next, he was gone. It was almost like the ground had swallowed him up. I heard him let out a yelp of surprise which made the deer bolt off in the opposite direction. I ran to where Taylor had disappeared and heard him yell, "Stop!" I came to a halt just in front of what looked like a pitfall where Taylor stood at the bottom. This was not a natural formation, which lead me to believe this was a manmade hunting trap. I peered down into the trap at Taylor and I couldn't help myself.

"It puts the lotion on its skin or else it gets the hose again." I burst out laughing.

Needless to say, Taylor didn't look amused.

"That's real hilarious," he drawled and I clutched my sides from laughing so hard.

Roots were stuck out in every direction and dirt was constantly sliding down the sides only to land on Taylor's cowboy hat and shoulders. The hole must have been seven or eight feet deep, but wasn't very wide; maybe enough for two people who knew each other pretty well to fit.

"Gimme your hand," he demanded, as he held out his own.

Still chuckling, I leaned down to offer mine as I said, "Give me the ring," before I burst into side splitting laughter again.

He rolled his eyes, but I could see a semblance of a smirk on his face. Finally, with much effort on my part, I stopped laughing long enough to help him out of the hole. I strained to lift as he dug his boots into the loose soil while grasping at the gangly roots. It took a couple of tries because he would lose his footing and I had to let his hand go or risk being pulled down with him.

"We never speak of this again," he huffed.

Both of us sat side by side, on the forest floor trying to catch our breath. I started to chuckle again at the bizarre situation, and Taylor shook his head.

"Come on, when would I ever get a chance to say that again?" I laughed.

Taylor grinned, "Fair enough. But not one word."

"Fine," I muttered. "Bad karma's a bitch, huh?"

"Whatever, let's just see if we can track that deer down," he said, dusting off his pants which were covered in loose soil.

A few hours later, the sun had gotten relentless and even bore down through the thick roof of foliage. I could feel the start of a sun burn on my nose and shoulders.

"Hurry up."

"You better be a bit nicer country boy or else I'll tell the whole camp," I grinned. Wasn't leverage great?

He turned his attention back to the fresh deer tracks and studiously ignored me. To be fair, he had taught me a great deal about tracking. The older the tracks, the more leaves and twigs that covered them, but usually the leaves and twigs were crushed and broken. The fresher tracks usually weren't covered but stood out in the dirt floor. The tracks we followed fell under category number two, so we were close to something. I could hear the faint sound of rushing water, and Taylor had mentioned that brooks and ponds were the best place to find game.

I mirrored what Taylor was doing and followed closely behind him as we approached the brook. Luck was finally on our side. The deer had stopped to take a drink and I could have jumped for joy, except that would have put us back to square one. Taylor didn't dare get any closer as he lifted the scope to his right eye and took aim. I plugged my ears, now fully aware of how loud a rifle really was thanks to the copious amounts of target practice. The shot rang out, but before the deer could react, the bullet hit it sending it to the forest floor. We ran up to the fallen mass and saw that the animal was still alive. Taylor pulled out his hunting knife and stabbed it in the head to end its misery.

I couldn't understand why, but I felt bad. I was by no means a vegetarian or a member of PETA, but having witnessed this first hand, I wasn't sure I wanted to do it again. Well at least this was a legal way to get out your serial killer tendencies. Taylor turned to me with a grin plastered on his face.

"Finally! That took forever," he exclaimed.

"So what now?" I asked, not sure I could stomach him gutting it.

"We should gut it here so it's lighter to take back," Taylor said. "But it will rot faster if we cut into it."

"Plus, it will leave a nasty trail leading back to the cabin," I pointed out.

Taylor seemed to think about it as he pulled out a compass and map to give us a rough idea of where we were.

"Looks like the deer took us back around. We're actually only 'bout an hour's walk with draggin' the deer back, from the cabin," Taylor noted as he scanned the map.

So we got to work and found a strong, lengthy tree branch to truss up the deer on. I felt like a caveman dragging a kill back to it's cave. We both had an end of the branch with the deer between us, hanging from its tied legs. Taylor had brought the extra strength rope with him in his small backpack, which I never would have thought of. He said we were lucky because the deer was a small one, but to me it seemed like it weighed a ton. I got the end with the head which made me cringe every time I looked at it; supposedly it was the lighter end.

I was about to demand we stop for a break so I could give my shoulder a rest, when the trees started to thin out and more light started to shine through. I sighed in relief knowing this meant we were finally getting out of the forest and back to the cabin. John and Darren met us at the property fence, where I gladly handed the thing over to them.

"Look at that," John smiled as he inspected the deer. "We better get this thing cut up, right fast."

"I'll take a pass on that," I said as I massaged my shoulder.

"You should learn how, just in case," Taylor grinned, flexing his own sore shoulder.

"Unless you want to see someone throw up, it's better that I don't," I insisted.

"Why are you covered in dirt?" Darren eyed Taylor and I burst out laughing again. See, this is what happens when I don't get my sleep; I get delirious.

I don't know how they gutted and disposed of the parts, but I didn't ask. That night we had fresh cooked deer, and it was delicious. I still felt bad about having to kill it, but my hunger washed away my hesitation. They decided it wasn't worth the risk to keep it for fresh meat any longer than a few days, so they smoked the rest of it, and I guessed we would be dining on deer jerky for quite a while.

John's voice cut into my reminiscing.

"All right, so we're down to the nitty-gritty of our food supplies and essentials," John said as we all situated ourselves around the camp fire.

"I thought we had a bit more left," Darren said as he rubbed his chin in thought.

"Nope, so this means we really have to make that trip into town," John said. "But we have to plan this right."

I toyed with the ring hanging from my gold necklace. I completely forgot that I had packed the ring and matching necklace, but it was a nice surprise to find it at the bottom of my backpack. My parents had gotten me the jewelry as a graduation present, and at the time I thought I would have to end up pawning off the pieces just to help pay off my student loans, but I'm glad I didn't. It was a nice reminder of my family, and I felt a little less despondent when I wore them. The necklace reminded me of home, even though home was so far away. The crackle of the walkie-talkie grabbed my attention.

"Guys, we got a situation over here," Taylor's voice sounded out. "I just found our first infected."

John picked up the walkie-talkie before anyone was even able to get up.

"What marker are you by?" he asked.

"The fourth one," Taylor's voice answered.

"We'll be right there," John said as he made sure his guns were on his belt and bolted off toward the direction of the marker. A month into our stay, John had the brilliant idea to lay out markers around the perimeter with whatever we could spare. It made it easier to organize watches and get to certain locations faster.

I jumped up and followed John, briefly registering that Darren was right behind me. The good thing about all this exercise was that I lost those ten pounds that had been haunting me since my first year of university.

The sun was setting but it was still light enough that we could see without flashlights. In the distance I could see Taylor's silhouette against the rays from the setting sun. I could also see a second figure, which seemed to be stuck on the barbed fence. Taylor was standing far enough from the thing that its grabbing hands were uselessly flinging up and down in an attempt to reach him.

The odd thing, aside from the being presumably dead part, was that the infected was wearing torn and dirtied hunting gear from being out in the forest. This guy must have been camping out in the woods and gotten infected, but the question was, *How?* I thought it took actual contact with a sick individual to turn someone. Maybe the infected had started to fan out from the cities and towns, which was an unsettling thought. His face had become so decayed that it was barely there. His lips were chewed off, and a chunk of his cheek was missing. The other side was so sunken in that his cheek bone stood out painfully against his emaciated and discolored face.

"What should we do with him?" Taylor asked.

"Shoot it," John said with finality.

"Then what?" I asked.

"Burn it," John said back, and I made a face at that.

There was no way that would smell good.

"How about we bury him?" Darren suggested and I nodded in agreement.

"Fine."

Taylor raised his gun to shoot the now snarling infected, but John grabbed his arm.

"We're on the cabin property and that shot will be loud," John reprimanded Taylor.

"Well, then what do you suggest?" Taylor huffed.

John turned to me, "Bailey has a suppressor on her Beretta."

I didn't like were this was going. And I really didn't like the smirk that had encroached on Taylor's face either.

"By all means," Taylor smiled, far too nicely.

"If you hand me your gun, I can shoot him," John offered, but I knew I would never live this down if I chickened out.

"No, I'll have to do it one day, why not start now?" I said, proud that my voice hadn't given way to my unease.

They backed up a few feet, and I removed the silenced Beretta from my hip holster. The brushed metal coating reflected the dimming light, as I lifted the pistol to eye level and flicked the safety off. I took a deep and slightly shaky breath as I aimed, and slowly squeezed the trigger.

Chapter 14

I stared up toward the ceiling, as the scene from earlier kept plaguing my mind. The problem wasn't that I missed, it was that I didn't. In fact, my shot was dead on, which wiped the smirk off of Taylor's face. I remembered how the infected's head whipped back as a mass of discolored brain matter and blood sprayed out behind him. It was like someone had spit out a mouthful of Campbell's Chunky Soup. I was mixed up in what I should be feeling; I mean that guy was alive once, maybe he had a family who was still waiting for him to come home.

Was I technically a murderer? Were the infected even alive? I mean no living creature could survive with the amount of damage and decay that guy had.

"Stop rolling around so much," Zoe hissed from the other cot.

"Oh, I'm keeping you up? That's rich."

She mumbled something as she flipped away from me, and I assumed it wasn't her telling me how awesome I was. Finally, I gave up trying to sleep and decided to get some fresh air. I closed the front door quietly behind me and was surprised to find Ethan sitting on the open truck gate. He glanced up at the sound of my approach and visibly relaxed when he saw it was me, not an infected.

"Can't sleep either?" he asked as I hopped up onto the gate.

"No, I keep thinking about that infected guy," I admitted.

"Me too."

"You weren't there," I pointed out.

"No, I mean if one got here then how long before more show up?"

"Oh joy, now there's that to worry about," I sighed and I could see the corners of his mouth lift up.

"You upset 'bout shootin' the thing?"

"Wouldn't you be?"

He seemed to think about it, "Probably."

"Very helpful," I muttered.

He shrugged. "It was bound to happen sooner or later. And it will happen to the rest of us, too."

"It's depressing."

"Yeah it is, but it's 'bout survival now so we gotta do what we gotta do," he said with conviction.

"But we live in a society that punishes those who kill; even those who kill in self defense are persecuted in a way."

"Society changes. It never used to be that way, look at Western times compared to now,"

Ethan brought up a good point. "Touché, country boy. Touché," I smirked.

"I did learn a few things down here in the South," he said exaggerating his Southern accent with a grin. "'Sides learnin' to suck the heads off crawfish."

"That sounds...dirty," I scrunched up my face and Ethan laughed.

"So you gonna be okay on our supply run tomorrow?" Ethan eyed me as I yawned.

"I'll be fine thanks."

"You can stay here with Zoe if you want."

Zoe had opted to stay here with Chloe and even though he put up a fuss about it, Darren reluctantly agreed to stay behind in case something happened. So our scavenging group consisted of Ethan, Taylor, John and I.

"You trying to get rid of me?" I eyed him back.

"Naw, just with what happened earlier I thought maybe you would want to."

"The last thing I want to do it sit here and think about it," I sighed. "Plus, the more hands the better."

Ethan nodded, disbelief marring his features. Hell, I don't think I believed myself, but I knew that sitting around here wasn't going to help. And we really did need supplies since it looked like a rescue wasn't about to come for us after all. We hadn't seen or heard so much as a helicopter since the beginning of all this two months ago. It was hard to believe we were that screwed; there had to be some sort of military operation somewhere. Maybe we just had to go to them instead of waiting to be rescued. *Lazy government.*

We made small talk for another hour, staring at the blackened sky. The only illumination came from the moon and the stars which I could see clearly, as if I were looking through a telescope. I said my goodnight as the yawning began and trudged back to my uncomfortable cot to try for sleep. That night I didn't dream of zombies, but for the first time of my family back home.

We took our turns showering that next morning. The lukewarm water was still better than no water. Chloe was quietly bristling in her loft. She was mad that Ethan was going without her and refused to talk to anyone. Zoe was trying to get her to say something, but all it earned her was a glare, so she gave up. I dumped out my backpack contents and filled it with water, some measly amounts of food and extra ammo. My second pistol was thrown in there, with the safety on, and the other one was secured to my belt. John had the map spread out on the picnic table to try to plan the route out.

"Okay, so our best bet isn't to go back into New Orleans, but to hit up a town or city around it," John said, his fingers swiping across the arteries on the map. "I was thinkin' Duson since it's not too far off from our location."

"What's the population like?" Darren questioned.

Even though he wasn't coming on the trip, he still wanted to be part of the planning.

"Decent size. We'll find lots of stores and houses to gather supplies from. There's even a police station we could check out," John answered. "But it's not so big that we would have a sea of infected to go through."

"Zombies," Chloe finally spoke.

"What?" Ethan asked, his face scrunched.

"You keep callin' them infected, but they're zombies," Chloe said exasperated.

Well she wasn't wrong; I guess we still felt stupid actually saying it out loud.

"All right, we won't have as many *zombies* to worry about like we would in New Orleans," John reiterated.

"How far is it from here?" I asked.

"Two hours give or take, dependin' on what we come across," John said.

"How do you always know these things?" I asked, genuinely curious.

John chuckled, "I grew up here darlin'. I know the area pretty well and have been readin' maps since before I was five."

I couldn't even tell you what direction I was facing at the moment.

"I think we should take my truck," Ethan said. "Even though it's not as quiet as your car, it will carry more."

"Probably a good idea, just in case we run into a group of infected somewhere. Your truck will have a better chance of not gettin' caught in it," Taylor added and John nodded.

"You three packed?" John looked around at all of us with our backpacks and gear on.

"Looks like it."

We tossed our bags into the back of the truck along with some cable ties, which we would need for when we brought all the supplies back. Chloe grabbed onto Ethan and refused to let go, he had to basically pry her off. Zoe came up to me and gave me a giant hug.

"Can't breathe," I wheezed out through her squeezing.

"Don't die, okay?"

"Well since you asked so nicely," I grinned. "And same goes to you. Use your secret hillbilly skills if need be."

"I knew I shouldn't have told you about the gopher hunting," she shook her head.

Next Darren gave me an awkward, one armed hug.

"Please don't accidently shoot anyone."

"Hey, I've improved!" I said indignantly.

"Just saying," he shrugged, and I resisted the urge to kick him in the shin.

Ethan got into the driver's side and John went into the passenger seat since he was the navigator. Which left Taylor and I to share the back. I walked past Chloe and ruffled her hair.

"Don't be too big of a pain, kid."

She grabbed my arm to stop me.

"Please take care of my brother."

Her eyes were glassy as she pleaded with me.

"Don't worry, I'll make sure he doesn't do anything stupid," I said. "I know how brothers get."

She smiled a little at that and nodded.

"And make sure you bring me back somethin' good," she added for good measure.

"Barbies it is," I grinned at the horrified face she made and jumped into the back before she could yell at me.

Ethan gave me a questioning look, as I jumped in, but I just shrugged in response. With one last wave goodbye, we were off. The sight of the three standing at the top of the dirt driveway slowly faded as we sped away. The bright morning sun shone through the windshield, reflecting off the rock chips as we headed toward the main drag. We had decided to try out the interstate first because it would be the fastest route, but if it was too clogged, we would opt for a detour. John already had a few back up plans up his sleeve.

The overpass we used to get onto the interstate was unobstructed. The road was also clear up until we hit the more populated areas; that's when the exit ramps became clogged with abandoned vehicles. Some cars had been left on the side of the road, some even in the middle. Since the interstate was multi-lane, we were able to get around the parked cars with no problem. As we slowly passed by the abandoned vehicles we got a better look.

Some were just left with their doors hanging wide open, while others had long dried blood smeared up the windows. An infected- *sorry, a zombie*- launched itself from the inside of a Kia against the driver's rear passenger window. This surprised us all and I jumped back from the window instinctively, right into Taylor.

"You know he's stuck in there right?" Taylor said as he rubbed his side where I accidently elbowed him when I made my hasty retreat.

"Still, it jumped out of nowhere!" I shot back, easing myself into my own seat once again.

The rest of the drive was virtually quiet except for any directions John gave. We passed a few straggling infected, which stumbled after us as we passed. They weren't very fast, it seemed like they couldn't even run and most were in a state of major decay. Their clothes hung off them in tattered rags and all had discolored scaly skin. One that used to be a woman, at least I thought it was a woman because of the long stringy hair dangling from its scalp, was even missing a major portion of its arm. No blood poured from the wound as she wagged her stump back and forth in an attempt to gain speed to chase us.

I knew we were still a ways from Duson, but I saw a sign calling in the distance. It was no longer lit up, but I could see it in the perfect late morning light. Walmart.

"Guys, I think we might not even have to go to Duson," I said as I pointed out the giant, warehouse looking building.

Ethan stopped the truck as he spotted the far away blue writing. We all looked at each other.

"Best place as any," John stated.

"Which exit should I take?" Ethan asked.

"The one labelled Crowley," John said as his eyes scanned one of his maps. "That's the town it's in."

We slowly drove up to the one signed Crowley only to see that an old Dodge was blocking the entrance.

"Come on Taylor, let's push it outta the way," John said as he unbuckled himself from the front seat.

We peered out all the windows to see if they would make it unnoticed, but a few of our groupies were still hanging on and closing in on the parked truck.

"You got your huntin' knife?" Ethan turned to me and I gulped.

"Yeah."

"All right, Bailey and I will take those three out while you two push the truck outta the way," Ethan rattled off and before I could voice my unease, everyone vacated the vehicle.

As soon as my feet hit the pavement, I unsheathed the hunting knife strapped to my belt and followed Ethan who had a machete now gripped in his hand. I kind of wished I had brought a bat or something else with length so I didn't have to get so close. I saw Ethan hesitate as the first one approached him with its arms outstretched and it let out a loud groan. Ethan's Adam's apple bobbed as he swallowed before he launched himself at the infected.

The machete came down hard on the zombie's head and embedded itself deep inside its skull. The thing dropped like a stone and took Ethan's weapon with it. He placed his boot on the infected's head and heaved the blade free with a sick, sucking sound. After waving the blade around to clear it of the muddy blood, he looked at the other two closing in. I wasn't being much help as I stood there terrified, so I approached the remaining two. Ethan took the one on the left, which meant the one on the right was mine.

I saw the infected's teeth clang together in anticipation, as it neared me. It was once a teen girl. Too bad she wasn't wearing a Justin Bieber shirt; maybe I would feel better about this. My blood pumped faster and faster the closer she got. I wrinkled my nose at the smell, which was worse than road kill left in the summer heat.

I swiped my leg underneath both of hers and she hit the cement hard. Unfortunately, it didn't faze her, but it bought me time to kneel and bring my knife down into her left temple. The decaying skull gave way to the sharpened blade extremely easily, her movements ceased and her flailing arms dropped beside her.

I sat there for a few seconds, just staring at the aluminium handle sticking out of her skull. I had just taken out one of the infected, but I felt no better for it, in fact I had the distinct urge to vomit. I breathed through my mouth to avoid the smell which would only further my need to throw up. Once I centered myself, I wrapped my hands around the hilt and pulled. The blade slipped out of her head, slowly at first, then completely dislodged with nasty wet sound. I took a bunch of steps backwards with the bloody knife still in my hands. I saw Ethan motion for me to head back to the truck, the body of the other infected down by his feet.

"You okay?" he asked, his own voice a little shaky.

I nodded in response not wanting to say anything. I heard the Dodge hit the meridian and the sound of metal scrapping against concrete rang out in the eerie silence. John and Taylor ran back to the waiting truck panting.

"We should probably get movin' before more come 'cause of the noise."

Chapter 15

Everyone was tense as we fled down the exit ramp, going faster than we probably should have. Ethan handed me a leftover fast-food napkin from his glove compartment to clean off my hunting knife before I put it back in its sheath. I rolled down the back window and tossed out the blood-matted napkin, happy to be rid of it. I wish I had brought some hand sanitizer with me. It was like I could feel the infected germs on me. I noticed Taylor looking at me out of the corner of my eye, but he didn't say anything even though I could tell that he wanted to. Instead of confronting him, I opted to stare out the window.

Grime and dirt coated the front of buildings and any vehicles parked on the road. It was amazing how dirty everything could get once it remained stagnant for just a couple of months. Old flyers and trash had gathered in street corners adding to the abandoned look of the city. The straggling infected were roused by the sound of us passing through, so naturally they came after us. We were going slowly enough that they were able to bang and grope on the side of the truck as we passed. Ethan picked up speed, causing the ones trying to latch on to be propelled backwards, and I could see a couple rolling in our dust.

I spotted the Walmart logo in the distance, but my visual was cut off as Ethan rounded a corner suddenly.

"What the hell are you doin'?" Taylor yelled from the back seat.

"You want those things followin' us all the way there?" Ethan asked a bit too loudly.

Taylor's jaw popped out as he clenched his teeth. Ethan continued to zig-zag down random streets and avenues. I was starting to get sore from being jerked against the seat belt, so I held the abrasive belt in my hands. I hadn't seen any of the old followers after we rounded that first corner, but we kept running into more infected with every turn we took.

"We're just picking up more as we lose the old ones," I pointed out, and I heard Ethan let out a breath of frustration.

"Maybe get off these main streets and use the back alleys," John suggested and pointed to the alley opening a few meters ahead.

Ethan turned down the alley only to slam on the brakes. I went flying forward and the safety feature in the belt kicked in, stopping me from hitting the front seat. The belt slicing my hands hurt more than slamming into the back of the seat would have. I looked up to see what had caused him to stop so suddenly. There was a blockade of infected on the narrow tarmac, all of which had their attention focused solely on us. They started to stumble toward the truck, so Ethan hit reverse and we flew back out the alleyway entrance, dust and rocks encasing the crowd.

One of the infected that had come up to the alley entrance hit the back tailgate and was sent flying to the ground. Judging from the sound of bones crunching under the tires, I knew it wouldn't be getting back up again. Ethan fled back down another road, avoiding the main artery to the supermarket. Somehow we had end up in a residential area, passing by house after house. Strangely there were not as many infected in the neighbourhoods as I thought there would be. I guess most people chose to go to the shelters rather than take a chance on their own. Either way, I was glad for it. We had enough on our tail already.

"All right, I think we've gotten away," John said as he peered in the rear view mirror.

"'Bout damn time," Taylor muttered.

I had to agree, I was getting pretty tired of being yanked around in the back seat.

Ethan nodded and started back toward the Walmart. The houses gave way to businesses as we got out of the residential area and back on the main roads. Taylor pointed out the Chevron station to our right, so I guess this would be our first stop on the tour. We hopped out once Ethan pulled up beside the last pump so we could make an easy get away of need be. He lifted up the nozzle only to have the machine remain dead from lack of power. He slammed it down in anger and ran his hand through his hair.

"Maybe we should see if we can boot the pump up from inside?" Taylor suggested, pointing to the matching convenience store with a garage attached.

The rusted sign boasted "Best oil change prices in town!"

"But there isn't any power, how will we get it to work?" Ethan questioned.

Taylor shrugged. "Dunno, but we might as well go see what's in there. Who knows what we'll find."

He and John raised their pistols while Ethan picked his machete. I unbuckled my holster and removed my silenced Beretta, secretly wishing I wouldn't have to use it. John motioned for us to stay put as he approached the front door. He stopped right before it and looked around, grabbing a full jug of windshield washer fluid. The bell above the door jingled when John opened it. Then he placed the jug down to prop the door open and took a few steps back.

When nothing emerged right off the bat, John whistled rather loudly to attract anything that may be in there. I really hoped we were out of here before anything else around heard that. John went rigid and I spotted the figure emerging from the darkened store. I assumed he used to be the mechanic for the attached garage, judging from his grease stained coveralls.

He growled lightly as he stumbled out into the daylight, he looked like he hadn't seen the light for months. He was in decent shape as far as decay went, maybe he was recently infected.

John raised his pistol, which had its own matching silencer, and shot the thing right in the forehead. It fell backwards from the momentum of the bullet and laid still. Taylor kicked its leg a couple of times to see if it was actually dead.

"What kind of name is 'Macky'?" Taylor asked after he stopped kicking it.

I was confused on how Taylor knew the thing's name, but then I saw the name tag sewn onto the coveralls. We waited for another minute to see if anything else followed him out, but we were met with only silence. John motioned with his head for us to follow him. With his gun at the ready he checked all the corners of the store and shut the *Employee's Only* door that was left wide open. The convenience store looked like any other gas station one. We all could see over the shelves, which was to our advantage. Taylor went around the counter to see if he could activate the pump somehow, but all the electronics remained unresponsive.

"Well, let's at least grab what we can," I suggested, opening one of the cooler doors.

I pulled out all the unopened water bottles that were left and started to stuff them into the Chevron plastic bags. The others started to do the same with anything that was non-perishable. I wandered over to the small automotive section to find a few car wipes and air fresheners, but that's not what caught my attention. I found a couple of crowbars and the idea suddenly hit me.

"Guys, how strong would you say you are?" I grinned at the confused looks on their face.

"Why?" Taylor asked suspiciously.

"We could use these to try to open that manhole thing that the gas trucks pump the gas into," I said holding up my find.

John looked like he was considering it, "Well, we could try."

We walked back outside carrying our spoils and tossed them into the bed of the truck. I handed one crowbar to Ethan and the other to Taylor. Kneeling down, they positioned the crowbars into the narrow slots in the circular rim. They strained and grunted with all the force they were putting behind it. Just as I was about to curse myself for thinking of this stupid idea, the lid shifted up and they were able to shuffle it to the side.

"Damn, that was on there good," Ethan huffed.

We all looked down, not knowing what to expect. From my limited view through the hole, I could only see a part of the silver tank; the part with the sealed top.

"Great," John muttered.

Taylor reached down and grabbed the red colored handle and heaved, but it refused to budge. John rummaged through our bags and produced a wrench to twist of the seal that the handle was attached to. When Taylor was finally able to loosen the seal, he tried the handle again which actually turned this time. The tank groaned as the pressure was alleviated and we took a few steps back not sure of what would happen. Taylor popped off the top and we retreated even further as the overwhelming smell of gas made our eyes water.

Through watery eyes I said, "See, what did I tell you?"

"Hey, I'm the one bustin' my ass over here," Taylor panted from all his exertion.

"How do we get it out of there?" I asked.

"I bet that garage has some plastic tubes we could use to siphon the gas out," Ethan pointed his thumb toward the gas station add-on.

"Let's go check it out," John motioned to Ethan. "You two stay here and keep an eye out. Holler if you see a bunch comin'."

Taylor and I nodded as they ran back into the gas station. I went to the back of the truck and pulled out two water bottles. I tossed one to Taylor and took a big drink of my own. The water was warm, but it tasted so much better than the well water back at the cabin, that I didn't care.

"Thanks," he said before he downed his own drink.

I spotted them before Taylor. His back was turned to them so he could face me. There were about five or so stumbling infected heading toward our location.

"Taylor," I whispered, not wanting to make any more noise.

He looked at me, then to where I was staring. He stilled at the sight of them and put down his water bottle gently on the pavement.

"What should we do?" I asked quietly.

"We need to take 'em out to buy more time," Taylor said as he pulled out his pistol and silencer.

With ease he attached the accessory. I pulled my own weapon back out, only this time I knew I would have to use it.

"Should we try to warn the other two?" I asked glancing back to the store.

There was no sign that Ethan or John would be emerging soon.

"No, we have to take care of 'em now," Taylor said. "Stay close to me."

He took off in a light jog toward the group and I followed right beside him. The group was five in number, a mix of tall, short, young and old. One at a time was manageable, but a group would be harder to deal with. I chewed on my bottom lip as we approached them like a couple of gunslingers in an old Western movie. I had to take a couple of deep breaths to calm myself and Taylor seemed to be doing the same thing.

"We need to take out the sides of the group instead of shootin' in the middle. We have more of a chance hittin' 'em that way," Taylor said in a low voice beside me.

He raised his pistol and with a muffled pop, the shot flew into the fray. The east-most infected went down causing another one beside it to stumble over the body and hit the pavement. This left three up. I took my time to aim and fired off a shot only to have it sail through the group without hitting anything. I swore under my breath, knowing the closer I let them get, the more nervous I would become. The next shot I made hit the body cavity of one, but it just kept walking.

Taylor let off another shot which took down the one I had previously hit in the torso. I sent him a glare for taking the one I was trying to hit. He just smirked at me, which made my blood boil. Two of them were close enough that the smell of decay under the high noon sun reached us and I scrunched my nose at the odor.

The one that had tripped earlier managed to get itself upright and was now trailing behind, its face a mess of road rash. He would have made a good poster for why you should wear a seatbelt.

I gritted my teeth and aimed slightly to the left because I noticed my shots were going to the right of where I wanted them to land. My third shot rang true and the remnant of a soccer mom dropped to the cement like a puppet that had their strings cut. I resisted the urge to jump in triumph and rub it in Taylor's face. I looked over at him and he grinned at me. Bastard had somehow turned this into a competition and I fell for it; my competitive side taking over. I shouldn't be rejoicing that I had just killed something or at the very least, re-killed it. Taylor looked at the closest one, then at the one further away and opted to take the furthest one. It took two shots, but he did it.

"This one's all yours," Taylor said, cockiness coating his voice.

The last one was maybe two cars lengths away.

"You're a dick, you know that?" I hissed at him, but he just shrugged off my insult.

I had found its head with only one shot this time, my anger and pride not allowing me to mess up. I put my gun back into its holster and calmly turned to Taylor so that I didn't give away my intention. His grin was replaced with a grimace when I kicked him as hard as I could in the shin.

"What the hell?" he yelled angrily, as he massaged his shin.

"That's for being a dick!" I yelled back. "Now was not the time for it."

John and Ethan choose that moment to reappear. They trotted over to us, not sure of what had happened.

"What's going on?" John asked as his eyes darted from us to the corpses lying all over the road.

"Your son's an ass, you know that?" I said to John, storming back to the truck.

Ethan shot Taylor a look of venom and followed me back to the truck. "What did he do?"

I told him what happened.

"So you kicked him in the shin?"

"Yes I did, and I hope I did some damage."

Ethan chuckled. "Well if you really want to injure someone, go for a throat punch next time."

"Will do. You find what you were looking for?"

He held up the rubber tubing, and it wriggled like a trapped snake. "Not quite, but hopefully it'll do."

Chapter 16

Ethan moved the truck closer to the manhole so that it was easier to pack the full gas cans. John had found a couple of empty jerry cans when they were inside, and we had brought a few as well. I didn't want to be the one who had to suction the gas out but Taylor said he'd do it; you wouldn't find me objecting. He sucked profusely and sputtered when the gas started to flow, quickly shoving the tube into the empty jerry can. He spat a few times on the ground and swished his water around in his mouth.

"Wow you're an expert at that," I taunted, and the look he gave me made me grin even wider.

Ethan burst out laughing and even John coughed to cover up his snort of laughter. I felt like I had gotten my revenge, albeit petty revenge, but whatever. After a few seconds, the gas stopped flowing and we all peered down at it, as if by miracle our staring would make it run again.

"I didn't think this would work," John sighed as he took off his hat and ran his hand over his head. For someone his age, he had a pretty good set of hair.

"The tank needs to be higher for this to work properly," Taylor pointed out.

"I'll do another look around for somethin' with a hand pump." At that, John jogged back to the garage for something more useful.

The three of us just stood around, not saying a word. Taylor and I traded some more squinty eyed looks, while Ethan tried not to notice the tense atmosphere. I was about to say something about his rusty sucking skills when John emerged from the garage, this time with a device that looked like the bicycle tire pump we had back home; just with two hoses instead of one.

"This should work much better. Must've missed it the first time around," John announced as he placed one of the hose ends in the jerry can and the other hose running from the pump into the underground tank.

The handle of the red pump was on the top and reminded me of the detonators in the Looney Tunes cartoons. After thirty seconds of using the pump, the gas started to flow again much to our relief.

In the end we had half a dozen canisters full of gas which had better last us a while. Taylor reclosed the tank just in case we needed to come back for more gas in the future. There was still a good amount left; we just had to hope that no one else found our treasure trove of gas. John mentioned that gas does go stale, but desperate times meant we had no choice but to try it. We made sure the hand pump was placed securely inside the truck so we didn't lose it.

After putting the cans into the back, we reconvened in the truck. Taylor and I refused to acknowledge one another as we shared the back seat. We were walking distance from the Walmart and the area between only had a few infected roaming. The rest seemed to have disappeared for the moment which was a relief and worrying at the same time.

The massive parking lot was abandoned except for a few cars neatly parked in a spot, a handful of tipped over carts and a manageable amount of infected. I'd say the place looked to be in pretty good shape, but I suppose looks can be deceiving. Ethan pulled up to the front door and killed the engine. We scoped out the place before we got out of the truck. There were three infected using the parking lot like their own personal walking track, but as soon as we had pulled up they started toward the noise.

I unloaded my magazine to see how many bullets I had left; I counted seven. We clambered out of the truck to confront the three, but John shot them in a quick succession before we had the chance to lift our weapons up. Luckily he was still using his silencer; he wouldn't risk shooting out here without one.

"How long were you in the military?" Ethan asked, as he placed his put his pistol away.

"Fifteen years," John answered. "I've been stationed all over the world with my platoon."

"Got any 'Nam stories?" Ethan asked.

John chuckled, "I ain't that old, son. That war ended the same year I turned old enough to enlist. But I got many other stories."

Oh joy, back-in-my-day stories.

I walked up to the front doors and peeked inside. Since the power had been out for quite some time, it was no surprise that the doors didn't part for me as I approached. The light from outside barely broke into the cart lobby, and I had to wipe away some of the dirt caked onto the glass doors just to see inside better. From what I could gather, there were no infected nearby, and the second set of automatic doors were wide open unlike the set I was currently peering through.

"Come on and help me pry these apart," I said, wishing they weren't dead bolted.

I stuck my fingers into the little slot where the doors met, and with Ethan grabbing the other side, we heaved. Slowly the doors parted for us as, squealing at the sudden use after being neglected for so long. If the doors weren't locked, that meant anything could be in here. We gave the parking lot one last look to make sure it was devoid of infected and with our bags in hand, we reclosed the glass sliding doors behind us.

Once inside, we flipped the dead bolts, which only required a key to get in, not to lock up from the inside. Then we did the same for the second set of doors.

"Should we be locking ourselves in without checking the place out first?" I asked.

"Even if somethin' is in here, it would be even worse if anythin' outside got in, too," John pointed out. "At least we know the front is secured."

"For all we know, the back door could be wide open," Ethan mentioned.

"Good point," John said as he took his gun from its holster. "Let's check the perimeter first. Bailey and Ethan, you check the emergency exits and doors around the floor. Taylor and I'll check the back."

"Splitting us up? That's horror movie talk," I said nervously.

"We need to get this place locked down as soon as possible," John insisted. "Which means we need to cover as much ground as possible, fast."

We all rummaged around in our bags for our flashlights and clicked them on. The sunlight coming through the front doors only shone so far. I pointed my beam all around to see if I could spot anything, but the immediate area seemed to be clear of infected. The smell of rotting food hung in the stale air, but if you breathed through your mouth, it wasn't so bad. The grocery section took up the left side of the store while the non-food items took up the rest of the supermarket.

The store didn't seem to be in as bad of shape as I thought it would. There were carts here and there and some of the shelves were picked over, but that wasn't out of the ordinary for this store. John and Taylor took off down the middle aisle toward the back, while Ethan and I decided to start along the left wall and make our way around.

I made sure I was breathing through my mouth as the stench of rotten food got stronger. The produce section had created its own compost heap so we pretty much ran past that part. The first door we spotted was the one that lead to the back room. John and Taylor had that section, which apparently ran around the whole building in a U-shape. I pointed my flashlight along the wall while Ethan pointed his ahead.

"Ethan," I whispered as I spotted the first emergency exit door.

It was closed; I could only see the light from outside trying to peek through the bottom. Ethan wiggled the bar handle to make sure it wouldn't swing open easily. Once we were satisfied that it wouldn't open from the outside, we continued on. At the careful pace we were going, it took us just under an hour to check the perimeter. We had made it all the way back to the entrance part, which only left the washrooms and the janitor's closet.

We rounded the corner of the women's washroom. Ethan stepped in first to make sure nothing was hiding in the darken space. The sound of the creaking hinges rang out in the small space as Ethan pushed open all the doors one by one. I heard footsteps behind me and whirled around to see the half eaten face of a former employee. His blue vest was ripped and stained dark red. His decayed skin had taken on the same colors as his dirty vest. With a growl he launched himself at me, knocking both of us to the floor.

I focused all my energy on keeping his discolored teeth away from me. The thing was relentless with his snarling and snapping. I turned my head to avoid the dribbling blood and saliva that the thing was spraying with every attempt to bite into me. I was about to yell for help when the body was ripped from me and flung across the floor, its arms flailing. Before the infected could get back up, Ethan stomped down hard on its head. The decayed skull gave way fairly easily to the pressure of his foot and soon a pulpy mess covered the white floor and walls.

"You okay?" Ethan ran back over to me and heaved me up.

I gave myself a once over and nodded, "Yeah, I managed to keep him from biting me."

I was shaking slightly from the adrenaline and fear. For a second I thought I might throw up. The nasty, rotting smell didn't help with that either.

"You gonna be okay to keep goin'?" Ethan asked, seeing that I was slightly shaken.

"I'll be fine," I said curtly and he let it go.

I pulled out a handful of paper towels and wiped myself down, trying to dislodge the mess the infected had sprayed me with. When I was done, we stepped over the mess and checked the rest of the front area. So far, the peeping Tom infected was the only thing we had run into.

"Should we go look for them?" I asked. "They're taking a long time."

"Let's head down the middle aisles on the way then."

As we passed by more empty lanes on our way to the back of the store, growling became the first sign that we were not alone in the center. I shone my flashlight in the direction of the sound and once it landed on the infected, I realized that had not been a good idea. The infected's attention was now honed in on us and we took a few steps back. Ethan whipped out his machete as the thing started toward us.

"Down here," I said, pointing my light to one of the home accent aisles.

Ethan nodded and we bolted toward the land of bathroom mats. The infected chased after us but I suppose it couldn't see too well; it ran straight into the massive display of frying pans that was plunked down in the main throughway. The display was knocked over and the crashing noise was so loud that I cringed. That would surely attract anything that was lurking in here.

"Shit!" I heard Ethan hiss behind me.

The flashlight bounced all around in front of me as we ran, making it hard to keep a steady eye on anything.

"Turn back!" I yelled at Ethan, stopping dead in my tracks.

A handful of infected had managed to cut us off. Their mangled bodies created a blockade at the end of the aisle. Ethan yanked me back toward the way we had come with the six on our trail forcing us to keep moving. The first infected that had caused the noise was still trying to get itself untangled from the display, making more noise in the process. As we ran past its reaching hands, Ethan brought down his machete on the things head. One swing was all it took and it stopped moving. Ripping the weapon from the things skull, Ethan and I ran even faster away from the approaching crowd.

It seemed like we had garnered the attention of every infected that was in here. Somehow we had not run into them during our perimeter check; they must have been hiding in the center aisles.

"Maybe we can try to lose 'em." Ethan grabbed my hand and pulled me toward another aisle.

We weaved through all the aisles, trying to shake the ones following us. I hoped this worked as well as it did in the truck. Finally, we had made it to the back of the store, but I could still hear the mass of infected approaching somewhere in the aisles near us. They hadn't wandered off like I hoped they had. Having been trapped in here, they probably haven't come across fresh meat in a while and the thought made me grimace. The shuffling and groaning was getting louder by the second.

I looked over at Ethan, who had the exact same look of desperation plastered on his face as I did. Our eyes darted back and forth until we simultaneously spotted the set of scuffed plastic swinging doors that lead to the back room. Neither of us had to say anything as we bolted straight for them.

Chapter 17

We crashed through the doors like a couple of battering rams. I felt Ethan's hand grab my arm, and then he yanked me to the left, just as I started to contemplate which direction we should go. The narrow back room was lined with jam-packed shelves as high as the warehouse ceiling with pallets of product sticking out dangerously, making the aisle difficult to run in. I heard the sound of the plastic doors swinging open again as the mini-horde pursued us.

"Get behind me!" a familiar Southern accent rang out.

We spotted John and his worn cowboy hat just around the west corner. Once we were clear of his line of fire, he raised his gun to eye level, as the infected approached in a crowded mass; some fell to the others insistent shoving and some to the littered alleyway. Muffled shots came from John's raised weapon, and soon a blockade of dead infected clogged the passage.

"Did you alert every one of those things in the store?" John asked us as he reloaded his gun.

"They were hidin' in the aisles," Ethan said indignantly.

"Where's Taylor?" I asked, noticing it was just John.

"Unloadin' some of the pallets we found. Come on, I'll show you."

We followed him around to the other side of the backroom. Taylor was slicing up one of the shrink-wrapped skids of product with a box cutter.

"Found a whole bunch of protein bars," Taylor beamed at his find. "Should last us a good while too."

"Now that we made sure the back is clear, we should move the truck 'round back to load this stuff in," John suggested.

"Well, I'm sure as hell not lugging it all out the front door," I said as I eyed our year supply of protein bars.

Ethan and I headed back into the main part of the store, a lot more alert this time. We stuck close to the outer walls just in case there were more lurking inside the aisles. Luckily, we made it all the way back out and to the truck with no more infected, but I'm sure there were some left inside. We would just have to stay on our toes.

The massive steel loading door squealed as John and Taylor tried to open it up. There was a manual pulley system as a backup that required two people to tug on the rusted silver chains just to lift it a little. Ethan backed the truck right up against the loading dock, which was about three feet higher than the bed of the pickup. Together we tossed the protein bar cases in the back in a matter of minutes.

"We also found a flat of water and some dried goods we can use," Taylor huffed as he lifted the wooden pallet outside and out of the way.

We kept a wary eye on the back lot just in case some roaming infected decided to stop by. There was only one out there that we could see, so Ethan jumped from the dock and took the thing out with his machete, leaving a nasty stain on the tarmac. He grimaced at the mess that now coated his weapon and he flung it to the side to dislodge the decaying matter.

"Now, should we just load up what we can find back here or look around?" John asked.

"We're here, we might as well grab all that we can," I shrugged.

I desperately needed new clothes and hygiene products. You would be surprised how rough living out in the sticks and washing on a scrub board, like a housewife from the 1800s, can be on your clothes. Plus, we needed deodorant, and trust me that was a necessity, not a luxury. John glanced down at his watch.

"We don't have many daylight hours left. Maybe we should make camp here?"

A supermarket and now a hotel chain? Walmart really did have everything. Ethan looked around nervously. "This was supposed to only be a day trip. I don't want the others to be worried."

"I'd rather spend the night sheltered than chance drivin' 'round in the dark. There aren't streetlights anymore," John reasoned.

He had a point. If anything happened while we tried to get back in the dark, we would be even more screwed than normal.

"Looks like I'm outnumbered," Ethan sighed and I looked away guiltily.

Normally I would take his side, but not this time.

"All right then, let's finish loadin' what we can back here."

Between the four of us we managed to completely fill the truck bed with food products. Looks like any extra supplies would be crammed with us in the seats. John released the roll-up door while Taylor and Ethan stood underneath to gently place it on the ground. The last thing we needed was a big crash to alert more infected to our whereabouts.

"Everyone got an idea of what they want?" John asked just before we pushed open the swinging doors.

We all nodded.

"There can't be that many more of them in here," Ethan said, pointing to the mass of bodies that piled up where John shot them. "So do you each want to take a section?"

I tried not to let my concern show on my face, but I was not happy with being sent on my own. We walked out onto the main floor, no infected or even a sound greeted us.

"All right, Ethan and I will split up the grocery section. Taylor, you take campin' supplies, and Bailey you take the pharmacy area. Grab what you can and bring it back here so we can load it all up at once."

As we were about to take off, Ethan stopped me and whispered quietly. "If you get into trouble, just holler, and I'll be right there."

I was going to point out that the food and pharmacy sections were on opposite sides of the store but instead just nodded. Then I took a deep breath through my nose and clicked on my flashlight again, starting towards my designated section. All I could hear was the blood pumping in my ears and the sound of my feet quietly hitting the cold floor. I stuck with the main aisles to get to the other side. This way, I had a larger view path so it would be harder for anything to sneak up on me. I calmed my breathing, making it easier to listen for the sounds of infected. Looking to my right and left rapidly was starting to make me dizzy, so I opted for just looking straight ahead. I shone my light onto the wall and saw the giant red pharmacy sign like a lighthouse beacon.

I realized I had not brought anything to carry all the supplies in other than the backpack currently resting on my back. *Shit.* I walked up and down the aisles and spotted an abandoned cart. I placed my flashlight down and holstered my gun so I could take the items out. Looks like someone had grabbed all the toys they could but never made it to the register with them. I shoved the boxes onto the empty spots on the shelf closest to me. I had a bad habit of doing that even before the outbreak.

My head whipped around at the sound of something hitting the floor a few aisles over. I held my breath and started toward the noise, one of the toys still in my hand. As I gingerly rounded the corner, I spotted the light purple liquid that now coated the floor. The smell of chemicals and lilac perfume hung in the air. A bottle of shampoo must have fallen over but what could have done that? I squinted further into the dimly lit aisle, but no one was there. The skylights didn't provide much light down here.

I went rigid at the gurgling sound one aisle over. I swallowed and tiptoed to the front of the aisle. There was an infected about halfway down the aisle. It was once a teenage boy, his body now ravaged by the disease. His clothes were in shreds, and he was missing a few fingers; it almost looked like they had been gnawed off. His head was whipping around stiffly, and if I wasn't mistaken, it looked like he was sniffing the air. All I could smell was the cheap perfume of the spilled shampoo. Maybe that obscured my smell, and that's why he wasn't charging at me.

Well if I was going to do something about him, it would be better if it was on my own terms. I brought my arm back and threw the toy with as much power as I could muster while hurling the awkward shaped box. It hit the infected square in the back, and he turned around at the impact. The infected looked down at the toy as it hit the floor, confusion showing in its jerky body movements. I couldn't believe what I was about to do.

I ran as fast as I could toward the infected, slipping my hunting knife from its holster on my belt. Before it could even register that something was moving in front of it, I sunk my blade into the part where the head met the neck at a slight upward angle.

I had to grab the thing's shoulder to gain leverage, and when the blade hit home, the infected tumbled backwards taking me with it. I rolled to the side instinctively to avoid landing on it, then turned right back toward it. The infected was laying still, the blade protruding from its neck. I counted to ten before investigating. I got up and kicked it with my foot and when it didn't react, I grabbed the knife back. It slipped out of the creature's neck easily, leaving an open wound behind. The rotten smell now coated my knife, so I used the infected's destroyed shirt to clean off the blade. Not that he'd mind.

I stared at the unmoving infected. I hadn't realized my heart was pounding and I had to hunch over to catch my breath. The adrenaline was starting to dissipate, leaving me a bit shaky. I hadn't even taken the time to think my plan through. All the images of what could have gone wrong played through my head, mocking my impulsive choice. I was lucky it has worked out this time, but would it again? Slowly I walked back to my flashlight and cart, the smell of decay and lilacs mingling in the air.

A feeling akin to triumph, like when I used to play soccer as a kid and scored, bloomed within me. I found this confusing. On one hand I should be upset, but on the other it was either me or the infected and like any other human, I choose myself. I looked down at the blade in my hand and scowled, as I put the knife away.

I grabbed what I felt we needed, dropping a few items in the process thanks to my shaky hands, but soon my cart was almost over flowing. We really should have brought another vehicle. Not that John's little car would hold much more. The cart wheels squeaked for a few meters until I got a steady pace going as I pushed it to the back. The rush of taking out the infected had finally worn off, and my hands were steady once again. For a second I pretended I was back home doing some shopping, mentally trying to tally up the bill in my head and failing.

"Geez, you got enough stuff?" Taylor asked as I approached him.

He had some small propane cylinders and other various camping supplies lying by his feet. He must have made quite a few trips. There was a camo painted hunting rifle leaning against a bunched up sleeping bag.

"Walmart sells guns?" I asked, incredulous.

Taylor raised a brow, "They don't have guns in the stores where you live?"

"Nope," I shook my head. "Canadian, remember?"

"Well, it was pretty much picked clean anyways. Only got this one and a few random sized bullets."

"Do you know if the others are done?" I asked.

"Pop is. He's stackin' stuff by the back door. Dunno about Ethan though."

"All right, let John know I'm done and I'll go grab Ethan."

I left my cart in the care of Taylor and went off in search of Ethan. I found him in the granola bar aisle tossing boxes into his cart.

"What do you think of those bars with fruit jam in the middle?" he asked, hearing me approach.

"That they were invented by people who knew nothing about children."

He placed the box back on the shelf. I almost squealed like a fangirl when I spotted the blue box and shoved all three into his cart. Ethan raised an eyebrow at me in question.

"Frosted strawberry Pop Tarts," I grinned at the find. "I love those."

"Well, we do have a toaster back at the cabin."

"Hell, toaster or not, I'm eating them."

"Everythin' go okay in the pharmacy?"

I hesitated and Ethan stared me down.

"What happened?"

"There was an infected, but I took him out." I shrugged, playing it off like it wasn't a big deal.

Ethan's mouth formed a mulish line. "I told you to call out of you ran into anythin'."

"What was I supposed to do? Run around the aisle like a hysterical woman until the big strong man came to save me?" I glared in response.

We stayed like that for a few seconds before Ethan cracked a grin and laughed.

"It's not that funny," I muttered.

"Sorry, I just got this image of you runnin' around in old fashion dress yelling 'Lord save me!,'" Ethan said through his laughter.

"That would mean I've officially lost it," I grinned at the image he painted.

"You two done tellin' jokes?" John asked as he rounded the corner.

With John prodding us along, we managed to grab what we wanted and brought it to the back. I looked at our haul; it was like a giant mound at the garbage dump minus the smell of course. I felt like I was in an episode of Hoarders.

"Look, I'm no engineer, but how is all that supposed to fit into the truck?" I asked skeptically.

John took off his hat and ran his fingers through his hair, "Dunno, but it's gonna be mighty squished in there. Maybe we can grab another vehicle nearby."

"There were a few in the parkin' lot," Ethan suggested.

"Do you know how to hotwire one?" I asked John and he smirked at that.

"I may have had the need to a few times in my life, but chances are the cars out there are alarmed so we can't afford to have 'em go off, even for a moment."

"Maybe the keys are still in here?" I offered, and the three looked at me strange. "I mean the cars probably belong to the employees we found in here. We could search the employee lounge and their pockets."

"Quick thinkin'," John nodded in approval.

I knew all that education would come in handy one day.

Chapter 18

We dug through the pockets of the dead infected in the back, managing to find four sets of keys. Whether or not they had the keys for the vehicles outside, who knows. I jogged back to the one I had downed in the pharmacy. It was still lying where it dropped and I rummaged through its disgusting pant pockets. I almost threw up, managing to only gag at the nasty substance that covered my hand, but at least I got a set of keys for my trouble. I copied what I did earlier and wiped my hand on the infected's shirt.

Then I remembered what area I was in and headed off to find the baby wipes and antibacterial gel. A handful of wipes later, I finally got my hands clean, but I still itched to wash them with soap and water. If I was lucky, maybe the sinks in the washrooms would still work. But that was just wishful thinking on my end. All the power had stopped and therefore, so did the pumps that made the water run to the various locations in this giant building.

I met the others at the door that said Employees Only so we could check for more keys. John pushed it open to reveal a set of metal stairs leading to the top office area. With our flashlights in hand, we ascended the stairs. At the top was a long hallway with windows to the outside on the left and cork boards, lockers and doors to the right. We followed John as he slowly made his way down the walkway. The few offices that were up here had the doors open and were empty of people or infected.

The last door on the right was closed and had a frosted window on the upper half reading *Loss Prevention*. John's hand went to open the door when a figure on the other side slammed itself against it. We all jumped back in shock, as the thing snarled and crashed against the door trying to get at us. Blood and spittle coated the inside of the glass as the door continued to rattle from the impact. I could see the outline of the nasty figure through the frosted glass and had an inkling as to what John was going to do next.

"Cover your eyes," he barked, lifting his handgun.

I placed my arm over my face as he shot through the glass. The only sound I heard was the tinkling of the glass hitting the floor along with the thump of the body. John peeked in.

"It's clear, I think."

John motioned for Taylor to open the door while he stood at the ready with his gun in case anything tried to charge out. The door opened and the fading sunlight coming through the windows showed us the infected sprawled out on the ground not moving. Behind it was, well, a mess. A chewed up corpse was spread all over the back part of the office. I grimaced at the sight of half eaten intestines and the hollowed out chest cavity. The smell was beyond anything I had smelt before, and I fought the urge to vomit on the spot. The head was still intact and to my dismay, it started to stir. Its teeth clanged together as it snapped, defying all laws of nature.

Ethan paled at the sight. "That's disgustin'."

John approached the disembowelled corpse, lifting his knife from his belt and brought it down into one of the eye sockets. The head stopped moving, and we all looked at each other searching for answers we knew none of us had.

We checked the open lockers for keys and the pockets of the coats hanging on the hooks beside the lockers. Coming up here was a bust. We didn't end up finding anything useful so we headed back downstairs.

"Should we try out the keys now or wait until morning?" I asked.

"I think we should try to get as much done tonight as possible," Ethan answered.

John nodded, "We've got maybe an hour of sunlight left, so we should get to it."

The setting sun shone through the murky doors as we approached the front. We opened the double set of doors and peered out into the parking lot. Nothing had changed. The cars were still parked in their spots, and the fallen infected from earlier were where we left them.

"Psst," Taylor hissed and we all looked to where he was pointing.

A couple of infected were starting to walk over from the parking lot of the stores next to us. John handed me the keys he was holding.

"You and Ethan go try these while Taylor and I take those lurkers out."

I nodded and started off toward the beaten up Chevy Cavalier with way too many bumper stickers on it. Two of the sets of keys had the Chevy symbol on them, so I tried those first. But neither one opened the door. We jogged through the parking lot, zig-zagging to all the other vehicles. I looked up to see John and Taylor use their melee weapons on the first two infected they encountered.

When it looked like we were shit out of luck, we finally got a key to work. It was for the old minivan with the cliché family member decals on the back window. I jammed the key into the ignition and the engine sputtered a few times due to it sitting here for so long, but after a few moments it roared to life. The fan belt squealed like an unoiled door hinge, and I held my breath.

"Figures," Ethan muttered. "Pop the hood."

I pulled the lever and the hood unlatched. Ethan looked but couldn't really do anything without tools. The sound stopped, and I looked at him.

"Did you do that?"

"No, must've just needed to work the kinks out."

He slammed down the hood as gently as he could and climbed into the passenger seat.

"I feel ridiculous driving this thing," I muttered.

"Hey, at least it has lots of space."

"Spoken like a true soccer mom."

We pulled up to Taylor and John who were making their way to us.

"A van? Really?" Taylor tsked as he opened the sliding door.

"Good find," John said as he joined Taylor in the back.

I dropped them off at the front doors and headed around back to meet them at the roll-up door. The truck was still blocking the loading bay, so Ethan jumped out to move the overstuffed truck. Once I backed into the bay, I killed the engine not wanting to waste any gas. The red needle was currently sitting at slightly over half a tank. Ethan parked the truck right beside the van and got out, so I did the same. The sun was setting on the front of the building, leaving a large shadow to eclipse us in darkness.

"Maybe we should wait in the van?" I suggested, not liking being out here in the open.

"I'm sure we're fine. John will be quick about it."

As if on cue, the metal door started to rattle. I opened the back door to the van and shoved down the folding seats for more room. I would never say it out loud, but it was kind of handy. We threw in all the stuff as fast as we could and there was even a bit of room to spare, hopefully for clothes. After closing all the doors, we moved back out into the store.

"Well, how should we set up camp here?" Taylor asked.

"We could start with the furniture aisle. I think I saw a futon display," I mentioned.

The aisle in question mainly had office furniture, but there was a set up futon that we could steal the mattress from and the boxed up sets underneath. We found three in total which meant someone doubled up, which was a pretty decent trade off in my books. Taylor came back with four sleeping bags and camping pillows in a cart and we started to move out the other furniture boxes to create a wall around us just in case. After a bit, we had quite the fort going on. Now all we needed were sheets as a makeshift roof to finish off the look.

"We need some food," John said as he headed off to find us some snacks.

"While he's doing that, I'm going to try to find some clothes," I said, starting off toward the middle.

"Yeah, I could use some too," Ethan said, pushing off our fort wall.

We kept a stern eye on our surroundings as we made our way to the clothes section in the middle. The department was out in the open with no walls to block it off, so the infected could come from anywhere. I headed straight to the T-shirt section and started to stuff my backpack, then moved onto the shorts. I didn't think I would ever have use for pants here due to the Southern heat. I wandered to the underwear section while Ethan was picking out some clothes for himself.

Hand washing everything on a scrub board actually seemed like it was harder on your clothes than the regular spin cycle on a washing machine. So basically, I needed to replace everything I had with me. We had left our suitcases behind at the school emergency shelter when it was overrun; leaving me with just the clothes I was wearing and the emergency ones in my backpack.

"You done yet?" Ethan asked.

"What do you think? The blue or the purple pair?" I held up the lacy underwear I was looking at.

Ethan sputtered and turned a tad bit red, "I'll be over there." He made a quick retreat back to the guys' section.

I grinned at my joke as I stuffed the items in my bag. I grabbed a pack of generic, unflattering underwear for Zoe. *What were friends for, if not that?* After, I found Ethan in the little girls' section, which normally would have been a red flag, but he had a sister to get things for.

"You should get her only pink things," I smirked.

"She would kill me."

"Need some help?"

Ethan eyed me, still wary from the underwear incident, "Sure."

We picked out some clothes that looked about her size and I found some T-shirts with snarky kids quote on them that she would undoubtedly love.

"I've never had to buy little kids clothes before," he admitted.

"Me neither," I shrugged. "You have to get her this coat."

I passed him the little leather jacket.

"If you say so."

"I promised her I would bring her back something good, any ideas?" I asked.

Ethan smiled, "She told me the same thing."

"Sneaky kid. Probably got to John, too."

"Well I was thinkin'," Ethan sighed. "Hell, I have no ideas."

"Let's go check out the kid's toy aisle."

With our backpacks full, we moved onto the kids' section. Our weapons were at the ready as we passed all the aisles, not sure if anything was lurking in them. I was beginning to prefer my knife because you didn't have to be a good shot to use it. My aim was drastically improving, but it wasn't perfect; there's nothing like the apocalypse and end of civilization, to force you to learn. I had never really thought of it in those terms before.

Was this the apocalypse? The end of civilization as we knew it? There was no way of telling until we saw more of the world other than the southern U.S.A. I thought about my family more and more as the last two months passed by. I wondered if they were still alive; if it was as bad back home in Canada as it was here. They also had the cold to compete with.

"Don't you find it odd that we haven't seen another person all this time?" I asked Ethan.

He was caught off guard by my sudden question and took a few seconds to think about it.

"Well, we've been holed up at my cabin for most of it."

"True, but how about today? How come we didn't cross another human?"

"Maybe there aren't any left?"

I gave him a look, "There has to be. Hell, if I've survived this long then others more qualified should have."

"You do happen to be with a group of highly functional people," Ethan grinned.

"Be that as it may, I still feel like there should be others out there."

"They're probably holed up somewhere like we used to be."

"Do you think we could find a radio for communicating?" I wondered out loud.

"Possibly, we just won't find it here."

"What about that police station in Duson that John was talking about?"

Ethan ran his hand through his hair. I noticed he did that a lot when he was struggling with what to say.

"Maybe, but we should definitely head back first."

"I know you're worried about leaving Chloe for this long, but we're only about a half an hour away," I reasoned.

"You wouldn't understand. She's my responsibility now," Ethan said rather angrily.

I was kind of taken aback because he rarely got like that. I knew if I said anything back, a fight would just ensue so I held my tongue. Turning my attention to the aisles, I started to look for something to bring back to Chloe.

"You know, she's also got all of us looking after her, too," I admitted after a while. The kid sort of grew on you, like an unwanted cat that followed you home but you took it in anyways. She wasn't the whiny brat that you expected a nine-year-old to be, but acted like a little teenager. This made it all the funnier.

After a beat, Ethan replied, "Sorry 'bout that, didn't mean to get all upset. It's just that I feel like she's my responsibility and truthfully, I don't know what I would do if I lost her, too."

I nodded in response, acknowledging his apology. Looks like I had finally found what to bring Chloe back. It was a make your own bookmark set, filled with everything she would need. I stuffed it into my already over flowing backpack.

"Good choice," Ethan nodded his approval.

"What did you find?"

"High school Barbie."

"Not even close."

Chapter 19

We headed back to our fort, which would make any kid proud, only to be grilled by Taylor.

"Why we're you lookin' at toys?" he asked.

"None of your business, that's why," I retorted and I saw his left eye twitch.

"The little one asked you, didn't she?" John grinned around the pepperoni stick he was eating.

"We figured she'd asked you to," Ethan laughed.

"She asked for some Oreos so I packed a few boxes for her," John grinned. "Hope that's okay."

Ethan shrugged, "Why not."

"So y'all find what you need?" John asked.

"Think so."

I plopped down on one of the futon mattresses. It was comfier than the cot bed back at the cabin, which was rather sad.

"We were just discussin' the plan for tomorrow."

Taylor sat down on the mattress opposite from me.

"We were talking about that too," I replied. "I think we should still go to Duson for their police station. Maybe we can get a transistor radio there."

"I was thinkin' the same thing. Maybe start lookin' for other survivors," John nodded in agreement.

"I think we should go back," Ethan added. "Look how much stuff we got. And the police station isn't goin' anywhere."

"But we're only like half an hour from Duson," Taylor pointed out.

Ethan clenched his jaw, frustrated that again he was going to lose out.

"You could take one of the vehicles back," I suggested.

Without hesitation, John retorted, "No, we should stick together."

"I don't like leavin' Chloe," Ethan ground out through gritted teeth.

"I understand that son, but we're so close that we can't pass this up," John said calmly. "And we could sure use the ammo, unless you want to make another long trip back to my store."

Ethan glared off into the distance, then got up and walked off. I guess he needed some time to cool off.

"I'm sure he will come around," John said as we watched him walk away.

"I've been wondering this since we met you at your gun shop. How come your store is called Bobby Joe's Gun Shop when your name is John?" I finally got around to asking.

John chuckled, "Bobby Joe was my father. He started the gun store and when he passed, I took it over after I was in the military."

I nodded, accepting his answer, "So we would be back at the cabin by tomorrow night right?"

"Easily. Duson is only a half an hour away, give or take," Taylor answered.

"Might be longer dependin' on if we run into trouble or not," John added. "But if we leave bright and early tomorrow, I don't see why not."

"Do you think there are other survivors out there?" I asked both of them.

John grinned at the thought, "There has to be. We don't have a military for nothin'."

"Then how come we haven't seen any military presence? Not even an armoured vehicle on the interstate?"

"Maybe we just haven't gone far enough. This country is filled with people who were in the military; chances are they're hunkered down waitin' out the storm, too."

"Plus, we don't even know if this is global or not," Taylor piped up.

"True, but I haven't seen any planes in over two months. So even if they are untouched by this plague elsewhere, they sure as hell haven't come to lend a hand," I pointed out.

"Let's leave the 'are we alone' debate until another time, kids," John butted in. "We have more immediate concerns."

We decided that we would leave at first light for the Duson police station. If the journey became too much, then we would turn right around and head back to the cabin. When John and Taylor began discussing firearms, I started to zone out. I've taken all the gun talk I can over these last few months. I'd like to think I've become rather proficient in my knowledge of them, which I suppose is a necessity now. Ethan still hadn't shown up by the time they started talking about high caliber rounds, so I slipped away with a nod to find him.

Ethan had headed off toward the left side of the store, so I started that way. With my knife in hand, I looked around for signs of him. I caught the faint sound of rustling, like metal on a rack, and quietly followed the noise. The aisle marker showed *Sporting Goods* when I shone my flashlight over the sign. I found Ethan comparing two different fishing rods.

"You fish, too?" I said.

"Yeah, so which one do you think?" He held them up for me to inspect, knowing full well I knew nothing of fishing. The name of the one caught my eye.

"The black one labelled The Ugly Stick; at least you can hit someone with it and get a few jokes out of it."

Ethan looked me in the eye. "I'm taking the van back tomorrow."

"But John–"

"Who made John leader? We sure as hell didn't take a vote."

"He's not our leader." I frowned at the term because in a way, John kind of had taken charge.

"Really, so that's why he's the one callin' the shots?" Ethan was starting to get louder.

"Look, I know you're upset that we're not heading right back to the cabin, but we have come this far already," I used the calmest tone I could manage, hoping that Ethan would stop his fit.

"Why are you takin' their side?"

"It's not a matter of sides, you idiot. We're all in this together. By getting a transistor radio and maybe even a police scanner, we might be able to locate other people; don't you want that too?"

Anger was starting to slip into my voice. I just didn't understand how Ethan, who had always managed to see reason before, was so opposed to adding on an extra couple of hours to our trip for such a worthy cause. My hand clenched around the handle of my knife in frustration.

"Of course I do, but I have family back there that I hate to leave."

"So you're the only one who gets to worry about your family? What about my family, huh? They're practically a whole country away. I don't know if any of them are alive or dead!"

He turned to me in an angry rush, "I don't know if my family is alive either! For all I know, all I got left is Chloe!"

I opened my mouth to yell my retort, but John cut me off as he appeared around the corner. "What in God's name are ya'll hollerin' about?"

"Ethan is taking the van back tomorrow while we go to the police station."

John looked over at Ethan's angry face and sighed.

"Son, this is a free country so I ain't gonna stop you, but think of how much we need you out here."

"Chloe needs me."

"Yes, but she's safe at the cabin with two adults watchin' over her. We're out here in the middle of nowhere, full of infected and no idea of what else is out there; we could use you more."

Ethan yanked his hand through his hair, "Fine, but we get in and out. No more side trips. No more stallin'."

"That's more than fair. Now come on, we need our sleep."

We trudged back to our home base in silence. I was mad that Ethan kept freaking out and somehow, I managed to be the recipient of it. I refused to acknowledge him the whole way back and even as we settled down on our futon mattresses for the night.

John had managed to get Ethan to see reason, where I had failed. This kind of pissed me off since Ethan was only moments ago complaining about John. It was clear that John had military training and maybe that extended to dealing with difficult soldiers. To answer Ethan's earlier question, I guess that's why John sort of had become our unofficial leader. He managed to organize us all, while in the middle of this mess and keep a level head. I still had a lot to learn on that front.

The next morning came too fast. I felt like I had been run over by a bus, having been up most of the night tossing and turning, as my thoughts drifted toward my family once again. My throat constricted at the thought of never seeing them again. As much as I complained about them, I still loved my family. Up until now, I had never lost anyone I was close to, besides my grandma. Wondering if they were dead created a panic in me that had my heart racing all night long.

I poured out a water bottle into the ladies' washroom sink that I had plugged and washed my face, waking me up a little bit. I stared into the messy mirror. My appearance hadn't really changed; my blonde hair was slightly longer and the paleness of my skin was replaced with a minor tan. Well, it was a tan to me. Those pesky last few pounds had disappeared thanks to our new lifestyle, which was probably the only benefit. *The apocalypse diet.* I giggled at the thought, which turned into full-fledged laughter. I had to bend over the sink I was laughing so hard.

My family always complained about my ability to laugh at the worse times, but I suppose it was my version of crying. I wiped at my moist eyes, feeling even hollower on the inside. There was nothing funny about this situation; it was the polar opposite of funny. I missed my family, my home; hell, I even missed my crappy part-time job. What I missed was regular life, the way you could go to the grocery store without a weapon. Well, at least in Canada that wasn't an issue.

I finished washing my face, feeling a bit back to my normal self. When I left the women's washroom, I passed near the front doors to get back to our fort. The sound of banging caught my attention. I fumbled with my bathroom stuff as I whirled around at the sound. The morning light was blocked off by a barricade off bodies pounding at the glass doors. *Shit!* I held my stuff to my chest and ran like the devil was on my heels. I rounded the furniture display aisle and ran face first into Taylor, who went flying back.

"What the hell, Bailey?" Taylor demanded, as he rubbed his face.

"There's a whole bunch of infected crowded at the front door," I said in a rush, my eyes darting between the guys.

John hopped up instantly, and we ran back to the entrance with our weapons in hand. The crowd was still banging on the glass doors insistently.

"They must have heard us drive here and all that noise we made yesterday," John gritted. "We need to get a bird's eye view of how many are out there."

"I saw a ladder and roof hatch in the back," Taylor mentioned.

John nodded, "All right, Ethan and Bailey, you stay here and keep an eye on this bunch. Taylor and I will go to the roof to see just how many are out there and see if our escape route in the back loadin' area is blocked off."

Before we had a chance to answer, they took off toward the back, leaving Ethan and my terrified self to keep watch on the front doors. We stood there powerless, unable to do anything about what was going to happen. The sound of glass starting to crack reached my ears, and that's when I noticed the snake like fissures slithering over the first set of doors.

"All that pressure is going to shatter the doors." I took a step back.

"We still have the second set to hold 'em off," Ethan offered.

As soon as the words left his mouth, two panes of glass exploded in a mess of glass. The horde poured into the cart lobby, only to be met by the second set of doors. Their grabbing hands banged and their teeth scratched uselessly along the glass, as smears of blood and other substances started to coat the inside of the doors. It was hard to see at this point, but it looked like the lobby was full to the brim of infected, like a mosh pit of rabid teen girls at a One Direction concert. The pushing of the crowd was starting to make the doors groan with the increased force.

"I really don't think us standing here is doing much good," I pointed out. I was starting to sweat from the mixture of the heat and fear.

"There's nothin' we can do, unless we want to go down with the first wave. Screw John, we're not waitin' here. Let's go."

Ethan grabbed my arm and we ran back to our camp. We hoisted our backpacks on and grabbed John and Taylor's bags. Even though we were in the middle of the store, I still heard the sound of the second set of doors give way to the horde in a spectacular crash. I looked at Ethan, my eyes wide. I had never seen so many infected all at once, not even when we were still in the city. There must have been at least fifty of them. Ethan used his head to nod toward the back, and we sprinted to the swinging doors.

"Did you see that ladder Taylor was talking about?" I asked, panic saturating my voice.

There was no sign of either John or Taylor or even the roof hatch he was talking about. For a brief second, the uncharitable thought that they had left us for bait while they escaped crossed my mind. Our heads whipped up toward the ceiling as the distinct sound of gun fire erupted. They must have been trying to shoot the infected from the roof.

"Those idiots! The sound will just draw more in!" Ethan yelled angrily.

He looked like he could punch someone at the moment while I started to seize up, unsure of what to do. We had maybe a couple of minutes before the infected spread out in the store, and there was no telling how long it would take until they got back to where we were. I looked around wildly, searching for any kind of answer. The ray of sunlight that was shining down caught my frazzled attention. There stood the brightly painted yellow ladder Taylor must have been talking about, illuminated from the sun leaking in through the roof hatch. My fingers dug into Ethan's arm, and he jerked at the pain. I pointed toward the ladder and a small smile flashed across his face.

We threw down their bags and our own. I don't think we would make it through that hole wearing a giant backpack. I wasn't a fan of heights, but I didn't see much of a choice in the matter. The metal rungs were cold on my palm as I ascended the ladder with Ethan right behind me. I grabbed onto the top and hoisted myself onto the roof. I noticed the rusty, metallic smell clinging to my hands so I wiped them on my shorts. John and Taylor were on the south side of the building shooting.

"Hey!"

They turned to me, confused that I was up there. I ran to the side and peered over. Our vehicles were unharmed, but there were quite a few roaming infected. The main horde must have been the ones at the front since I only counted about ten or so still standing back here. There were fallen bodies littered around the vehicles, all shot with their guns.

"They broke through both sets of doors, we only have a bit before they will reach back here," I filled them in on what happened.

"Shit!" Taylor yelled.

"Calm down!" John yelled back, more stressed out than I had ever seen him before.

I could clearly see the worry lines etched into his face that I had managed to overlook until now.

"We gotta go before this gets worse," Ethan declared, as soon as he poked his head out of the roof hatch.

All of us scrambled back down the ladder, planning to roll up the receiving door just enough so that we could escape through. It groaned and squeaked as John and Taylor yanked on chain. Light spilled in as it slowly opened and soon there was enough room for us to crawl out. They tied the chain around the handle on the wall, testing to make sure the door wouldn't roll back down and squish us on our way out.

I threw our bags first, then followed suit and rolled out. The rising sun and fresh morning air greeted me. I pulled out my Beretta and shot the infected closest to me. The bullet landed in the thing's torso, the impact knocking it to the tarmac. In three steps I hovered over the infected and shot it in the head. The body jerked at the force and laid still. I looked up, only to see the rest coming straight for me.

Chapter 20

A bullet whizzed by my head, and I turned to glare at the idiot who thought it was all right to shoot so close to me. John had his gun raised and was picking off the closest threats. I trusted John with a gun more than anyone, but I still didn't approve of him shooting so close to me. The slide of my gun popped back, signaling that the magazine was empty. All those bullets used and I had only taken down three infected. I really needed to work on my aim when under pressure.

"Bailey!" Ethan yelled over the fray.

I spotted him opening the truck door, stabbing the keys into the ignition. Taylor jumped into the passenger side since he was closest. I dug into my pocket and produced the van keys.

"John, let's go!" I screamed, as I ran for the van.

He held up his hand for the keys, and I tossed them to his opened palm, missing my target by a foot. I was too worked up to fight over who was driving and with my shaky hands I wouldn't be very good at it anyways. The engine sputtered, but started quickly when John turned the keys. He put it in drive and floored it, smashing into the infected that was right in front of the grill. Blood and goo splattered all over the windshield and the body crunched under the wheels as we ran it over. John flipped on the wipers and the mess smeared all over the windshield.

I let out a nervous laugh at the sight, and John gave me a questioning glace out of the corner of his eye. I waved it off. After a few more wipes, the windshield was clear of the mess. John avoided hitting anymore of the infected, steering the vehicle away from the bodies coming toward us. We peeled out onto the road that passed behind the Walmart, the wheels squealing in protest. The smell of burnt rubber wafted into the van.

I turned to look out the back window only to realize I couldn't see over the mound of supplies crammed into the back.

"They're right behind us." John pointed to the side mirror.

I spotted Ethan's truck a few car lengths behind us and breathed a sigh of relief. John led us out of the town and back onto the interstate.

"So I take it we are still going to Duson?" I asked, noticing we were not heading back in the direction of the cabin.

"We need to see if they have a police scanner or transistor radio. Maybe we can start broadcastin' and see if anyone hears."

I glanced back at the side mirror to see that Ethan's truck was not right behind us anymore.

"Ah, John." I pointed to his side mirror.

"Shit!" He put on the brakes and slammed his hand against the steering wheel.

We were sitting in the middle of the three-lane highway, a few wrecked and abandoned vehicles sitting nearby. There was an unmoving body lying face down by a rusty Mustang.

"Are you going to turn around?"

"We will give 'em a few more minutes. I'm guessin' Ethan tried to go back to the cabin."

There was no way Taylor would allow that, so I fervently hoped they didn't start fighting. Taylor would easily throw a punch, and Ethan was worked up enough that he would return it. We waited in silence for a few more minutes, our breathing and the engine the only sounds in the van. I opened my mouth only to shut it again when I spotted the black Chevy coming up behind us like a shadow.

"See." John put the van back into drive and we continued along the interstate.

"Do you think that horde will follow us? Or at least start moving our direction?" I mused out loud.

"Dunno, I hope not. But let's just pray they head this way instead of the other direction."

We approached the Duson turnoff in just under forty-five minutes. I only counted a handful of infected during our jaunt down the interstate. John easily avoided them, making use of all three lanes. The turnoff wasn't blocked with cars like the last one, so our entry to Duson was already smoother than the last.

"Any idea where the police station is?" I asked.

"I got a rough idea, I've only ever set foot in Duson once before. Had no reason to go to the police station."

The town was a decent-sized one, not too large or small. We passed by the main drag of stores then ended up in a relatively new development of houses. They stuck out amongst the rest of the aging infrastructure.

"Are you also noticing the lack of any infected? Or bodies?"

"Just thinkin' that myself. A town this size should have some out and ab–"

"Stop!"

John hit the brakes without question, and I stepped out of the car. The last portion of the new subdivision was all just empty lots. But that wasn't what had caught my attention.

"Ho-ly shit," John said in a low voice as we approached the last lot.

It looks like they had managed to dig the basement but instead of being filled with cement, the hole was filled with charred and burnt bodies. The stench of scorched charcoal and gasoline mixed with a foul smell I couldn't place drifted off of the massive pile. There must have been at least a hundred bodies in there. Whether they were the corpses of infected or not, I had no way of telling.

"You can still smell the burned flesh, whoever did this must have added to the pile recently," John observed, making me even more nervous.

Taylor and Ethan had joined us, both just as disturbed by the sight as we were.

"What the hell?" Ethan asked to no one in particular.

"You think whoever did this is nearby?" I asked.

"I'd bet on it, and to do somethin' on this scale, it would need more than one person." John rubbed his hand along his jaw line.

"Well, this is probably the most efficient way to deal with the infected," Taylor said.

"If they were all infected." I'm sure the others were thinking it, too.

"Come on, let's keep movin'," John prompted.

We drove in silence, following the blue signs that showed us the way to the police station. John made sure to drive slower, trying not to draw attention to ourselves. Since we were the only moving vehicles on the road, driving slower was futile. We stood out like a speck of dirt on a white floor. The police station appeared on our right; a chain link fence surrounded the perimeter.

John spotted them before I did. "I'm willin' to bet these are the folks who did the burnin' back there."

There were two men stationed at the makeshift front gate. The chain link had run all the way along except for the break in the front, which was now covered with a brand new moveable chain link gate; you could tell due to the shininess of the gate compared to the rest.

Now aware of our presence, the two men approached our van with their weapons drawn. Both had automatic weapons pointed right for us. They weren't wearing any police or military type clothes, just green cargo jackets and jeans. One man veered off toward Ethan's truck while the other came up to the driver's side. I gulped as the man opened John's door.

"Get out," he said forcefully.

"All right, we don't want any trouble," John said calmly.

"You too," the man said when he noticed me in the passenger's seat.

I reached for the door, fear making it hard to grip the handle. *Were we being taken hostage?*

John looked me in the eye and nodded. "It's gonna be fine."

"Now!" the armed man demanded.

After a few attempts, I managed to open the door. My legs were shaking, as I clambered out of the van. It'd been two months since we'd seen other people and these were the first one's we'd run into. This wasn't a good sign. Ethan and Taylor were ushered out of the truck by the other guard.

"Turn off the van."

John did as he was told. The guard grabbed the key chain from John's hand while keeping the gun trained on him. The other guard followed suit and took Ethan's keys from him. They were both average height and not particularly muscled, but they had automatic guns aimed right at us.

"Get over there," he pointed at John with his weapon.

My legs were like a hundred pound weights, fear making my limbs seize up. It made my journey to John's side more difficult than necessary.

"Open up," the other guard yelled and the chain link gate started to move.

It took two men from the inside to lift and swing open the wide gate. They were dressed in similar attire; they almost looked like a hunting group. All with their own weapons.

"Move."

I looked at John, the terror clear as day on my face.

He whispered to me, "Just follow my lead, and we'll get out of here."

With the guns pointed at our back, we were ushered into the compound. There was not much room between the fence and the building, especially along the sides. Our vehicles would not have fit inside. The gate was closed behind us and the two men who had opened it, joined the guards in pointing their guns at us.

The front doors to the police station opened, and one man strolled through as if he owned the place. He was wearing a faded green wife-beater top and army cargo pants. His belt boasted two gun holsters, which were not empty, and a rather large knife. Tattoos covered one of his arms, and he wore a pair of motorcycle gloves. As he got closer, the taller and bigger he became. He must have stood well over six feet and had the body of someone who devoted at least two hours a day to weight training. His face didn't show any emotion, as he approached us.

"Conner, did you check them for weapons?" he barked at the guard who had forced us out.

Conner panicked and motioned for the others. "Will do."

They descended on us, and I instinctively backed up. John shook his head at me, silently telling me to remain still. The guard patted me down, opting to remove my entire belt containing my holstered Beretta and knife, while the other guards did the same to the rest of our group. They gathered up our weapons and accessories, placing them in a large garbage bag. Now we really were screwed. There was one man stationed on the roof with a hunting rifle. He didn't seem too concerned with us, as his weapon remained impassive at his side.

"Now what brings ya'll to Duson this fine day?" the muscled man asked, trying to sound conversational.

"We just wanted to see if we could find a police radio or scanner, that's all," John spoke up on our behalf.

Not that any of us were considering speaking up. I'm pretty sure that if I was forced to speak, that my voice would come out in a squeak. I have never been so terrified in my whole life; even the infected didn't scare me as much as this group did. I flexed my fingers, trying to get the involuntary stiffness out of them. Apparently extreme fear made my joints buckle and stiffen. This was something I would have been happy to go my whole life without knowing.

The man smiled at us while the rest of their crew remained silent. It was clear he fancied himself the leader of this paramilitary type group. They looked like a rag-tag bunch of macho men, not proper military like John. John's demeanour was a lot more professional than theirs.

"Why don't you come inside and maybe we can discuss a trade? My men tell me you have two vehicles full of supplies."

It wasn't until then that I noticed the walkie-talkies they all sported on their belts.

"I think out here would be best," John eyed the man warily.

"Now you've hurt my feelings," their leader tsked. "I would have liked for you to take the offer voluntarily. Now, I must insist you come inside."

He nodded his head toward us and the guards sprang into action. The one closest to me grabbed my forearm in a vice like grip. He started to drag me toward the police building. I wanted to struggle, but none of my limbs were cooperating with what my brain was telling them to do. The others didn't bother putting up a fight either, now noticing that the sniper on the roof had hoisted his rifle to eye level.

John stared the leader down as we were ushered against our will into the building. The leader just smiled politely as we passed. He shot me a wink, as I walked by, and I just stared. *Have I mentioned how screwed we were?*

Chapter 21

We were brought through the main doors and into the police station. It looked like any small town station would – a couple of desks in the main space and some offices for the higher-ups lining the area. The guards led us to the back portion labelled *Holding Area*. The first thing that came into my view was the large, iron bars that kept the prisoners inside.

The guard holding John pulled out a ring of keys and unlocked the first of the two holding cells, both of which were facing one another. Pushing his self through the now crowded walkway, their leader whispered something into the guard's ear. He nodded at whatever the large man had said. He shoved John in first then Taylor and Ethan, locking the door back up behind him.

Now I was starting to sweat.

"What about her?" John ran up to the bars.

"We can't have male and female *guests* in the same cell. That would just be unprofessional," the leader shrugged. "Keys."

The guard handed the ring off and the muscled man unlocked the opposite cell.

"After you," he smiled at me, and I resisted the urge to shiver. He gave off major stranger danger vibes.

Not seeing any way to escape, I did as I was told and with the help of the guard still hooked onto my upper arm, I walked into the cell. The lock clicked behind me, and I rubbed at my arm where there was undoubtedly a bruise starting to form from that guy's grip.

"How rude of me, my name's Riley," the leader announced. "Now you."

John spoke for us again, "I'm John, and this is Taylor and Ethan." He pointed to them both, then to me. "And that's Bailey."

"Nice to meet you all. Lovely name." He looked at me for the last part, and how I wish I could have replied with my usual retort, but I just nodded stiffly.

All of the others filed out of the room at Riley's request, leaving just him and the guard named Conner.

"Now what exactly do you all have in those vehicles of yours?" Conner asked.

"Just food and general supplies," John answered.

I don't know why he was humouring these lunatics, but he was.

"Just you four?" Riley eyed us up.

"Yes, had a bigger group before, but we're all that's left," John lied.

"Where's your main base?"

"Well, you see we're in the market for one."

"Well you see, I know you're lying to me, and I don't take well to that." Riley stalked to the front if their cage.

To John's credit, he didn't back up or even bat an eye.

Riley grinned at him. "You're military aren't you?"

"Maybe, but I know enough to see that your crew isn't."

Riley turned to Conner. "Bring their supplies in."

Conner nodded and took off. If they got a hold of all of our stuff, then our trip will have been for nothing. My legs finally gave out and I plunked down on the nasty cot in the cell. *They wouldn't keep us prisoners here? Or worse, kill us would they?* I looked at Riley's face and something there said he's done worse.

His hawk-like eyes kept returning to me and not in a flattering way. I had been leered at by drunken college boys before – I was in the South for Mardi Gras, after all – but this look made the hairs on the back of my neck stand up. This guy was dangerous, possibly unhinged and he was rather too focused on me for my liking.

The others must have noticed this, too, and were shooting me concerned glances. Not that I wasn't already worked up as it was. I hadn't seen another woman here, just the male guards. All sorts of horrible thoughts started to run through my head, and my breathing neared panic attack proportions. I needed to calm down; I wouldn't be able to help myself if I got worked up. I tried to focus on my breathing while John answered more of Riley's probing questions. John refused to tell him about the others and the cabin, but Riley insisted that he was lying.

Conner interrupted the interrogation when he came back in and fetched Riley.

"Now, don't go anywhere." Riley laughed at his joke and left us to stew in the cells.

"Bailey, you okay?" John asked me through the bars.

"Y-" I had to clear my throat. "Yes."

"If they try anythin', just kick them in the balls and run," Ethan said, now grasping onto the cell bars.

"You're not helping," I muttered, more to myself since the volume in my voice was not working.

"How are we going to get out of this, John?" Ethan whirled around on him, clearly blaming him for our predicament.

"Give me a minute, son," John growled, his calm demeanor fading.

"I got an idea," Taylor said, and we all turned to him expectantly. Taylor dug into his pocket and produced a set of keys, "The spare to your truck and the only key fob. You left them 'em the glove compartment." I hadn't known he was a Klepto.

Ethan didn't even look mad as realization lit up his face, "The panic button."

"Exactly. We need a distraction, and this will bring in the infected for miles."

"What about when they come back looking for who set off the alarm?" I asked, my voice deciding to return.

"They will need to open the cell to get the key fob, so when they do, we rush 'em and steal their weapons."

"I dunno son, this could go bad real fast," John hesitated, unsure for the first time since I had known him.

Without further warning, Taylor hit the panic button for the truck and the shrill alarm echoed all the way into the building. We froze at the sound trying to listen for footsteps. I heard yelling outside and a gunshot. What they shot at, I had no idea. I got up from the cot, my legs popping at the sudden use. Standing on my toes, I tried to peer out the tiny window. All I could see was the side of the chain link fence.

"These guys aren't military, just a bunch of thugs. So they won't know how to handle us rushin' 'em," John quickly explained. "Waste no time when they open the cell door. Go for the head and try to knock 'em out as fast as you can. Don't give 'em time to reach for their weapons."

A few minutes later I heard the front doors crash in and angry footsteps carried to the back. Two guards, one of them Conner, burst into the holding area.

"All right, which one of you has the keys?" Conner barked, in no mood for joking.

The alarm was still sounding in the background, like a glorious beacon. Soon infected would be swarming this place, and maybe we would be able to escape. Or, maybe we had just made it a whole lot worse. When no one said anything, Conner ripped the cell keys from his pocket and opened the guys' barred door.

But they were waiting. When Conner yanked the cell door open, all three of them rushed him and John swerved around to grab the other guard. John punched him square in the face as the guard reached for the weapon on his belt. He crashed against my cell, the back of his head connecting with the thick iron bars.

John didn't leave him time to recover, as he punched him in the gut with a forceful uppercut. He keeled over, and John shoved him to the ground, grabbing a bunch of hair and smashing his head to the cold cement floor with astounding power. Some blood seeped out from underneath the guard's skull as he lay limp on the ground. John got off of him just as Conner fell unconscious to the floor. Taylor and Ethan had made quick work of knocking him out.

I gripped the bars tight. Conner had dropped the keys in all the confusion, so John swooped to pick them up. Bringing the key ring to my cell, John had to try five different keys before the one that matched my cell lock was found. I rushed out of the cell, glad to be free. I hadn't realized just how lucky we were to have found each other and the cabin. It could have gone a lot worse, in a lot of ways. I had the uncharacteristic urge to hug John, grateful that he got me out of here. "Thank you."

John didn't need to say anything, instead he gave me a one armed, brief hug, and I returned it with a squeeze.

"We don't have much more time before the others come, too," John said as he pulled the handgun from the guard he knocked out.

Ethan grabbed the one from Conner and passed the knife to Taylor. John also handed me the guard's knife, although I had no idea what for. No matter how creepy they were, I don't think I was up for stabbing a human.

"I've got a plan," Taylor announced.

Apparently he thought very well under pressure, but didn't feel the need to share as he took off toward the back of the holding cell. There was an old, metal rung ladder that led to the roof. I had never noticed before, but did most places have a fire escape to the roof? They were proving very useful for us thus far. As he climbed the ladder, he voiced his plan.

"I'm gonna jump from the roof, over the fence. There couldn't have been more than two feet of clearance on the sides. You keep 'em occupied."

He pushed up the roof latch as John ran over to him, "And do what, son? Go for help? There ain't no help."

"I'll think of somethin'." Taylor disappeared into the afternoon light streaming through the square opening at the exact moment more guards entered. This time, Riley was in the lead, and he looked pissed.

"Now which one of you has the keys?" His eyes flashed to the downed guards, ripping the gun from his belt holster.

John instantly responded by lifting his stolen gun, and Ethan followed while I stood here uselessly with my little pig-sticker. Behind Riley the other two guards looked at each other, and then raised their own weapons. I had never been in a standoff before, and I can't say I enjoyed it. Riley stood there menacingly, with a fake smile plastered on his face.

"We can do this the easy way or the way that ends with you dead," he said matter-of-factly.

"I'll take neither," was all John replied with.

None of the guards had their guns trained on me; obviously they didn't consider me a threat. In a flash, my arm rose of its own accord and I whipped the knife at Riley. He spun, my movement catching him off guard, and the blade sunk into his upper chest. He howled in pain, shooting off one bullet before dropping his gun in the process. I ducked instinctively, praying for the first time that I would be safe from bullets. Luckily, the bullet was way off course and landed somewhere in the cell.

The guards behind him fumbled in confusion, readying to shoot. John reacted quickly and shot them both dead. Two shots and two lives later, the guards landed on the ground behind the kneeling, cursing Riley. John went to pull the knife out of him, but Ethan burst out from beside us and delivered a swift kick to Riley's head, rendering him unconscious. We all stood still for a few seconds, needing to process what the hell just happened.

John had just killed two men – two men who were ready to end us. I had just stabbed Riley, something I still couldn't believe I did. It felt so surreal, like I was watching a really high-definition version of an action movie.

John was the first to come to his senses. "We need to move, now!"

I nodded, keeping an eye on Riley as we stepped over their bodies to get back to the main part of the station. Ethan yanked out my knife from Riley's torso as we passed by and handed it back to me. No one else was in the station; the rest of the minions must have been outside. The alarm was getting louder the closer we got to outside. I heard a gunshot go off on the roof and John ran to the front door like a man possessed. Taylor was up there. He flung open the door just in time for us to witness a body fall from the sky. The sound of bones crunching and an unnerving splat sound reached my ears. *Dear God, don't be Taylor.*

Upon closer inspection, we realized it was the sniper on the roof, not Taylor. It was hard to tell since the body made such a mess, but the clothes were the same Army surplus type as the rest of the individuals. We closed the door, not wanting the other guards to know we had escaped and ran to the large front window. The gate was wide open, since they had been in the process of relieving us of our supplies.

A couple of men were hurrying to shut the gate, locking out anyone who was on the other side. More gun shots went off from outside, and that's when I noticed the infected in the distance. A whole bunch of them were ambling toward the noise of the siren. Some of them were already at the chain link fence, rattling it while trying to get in. We were surrounded and I wondered yet again, if we hadn't just made things worse.

Chapter 22

"Taylor must've pushed that sniper off the roof," John stated, as he craned his head to look out the wide window. "That's one less gun to worry about."

"How many more do you think are out there?" I asked.

"Dunno, we got their leader and four guards lying in the back room. I only saw those, but judgin' from the noise of the gun shots, there are at least three more out there with weapons."

"So what are we goin' to do? Wait until Taylor does whatever he comes up with?" Ethan blurted.

I noticed he was not able to sit still, unlike my frozen reaction to everything. Ethan was moving restlessly from foot to foot and running his hand through his hair over and over again. John was wiggling his fingers, as his mind moved to come up with a plan. I remained still like a statue. Ironically, I looked like the calm one but inside I was beyond panic. My mind had started to block the freaking out part, probably due to some inherent survival instinct. The thoughts in my head finally melded into one. We needed to get out of here, and fast.

"I don't think we will have to wait too long." I pointed to the truck that was now reversing.

Shots were fired toward the retreating truck from the others that appeared out front. I watched an infected that had managed to get inside the gated area tackle one goon that was too focused on shooting at the truck to see it in time. They fell to the ground, the infected practically covering the henchman. The man screamed in agony as the infected tore at the side of his head with its bare teeth. Blood squirted from the wound like a punctured orange, as a mixture of skin and veins were torn brutally from the guys' skull. His screams turned to wheezing and then stopped abruptly, as he sank to the ground. The infected continued to tear into the corpse, chewing and ripping at his flesh.

"Move back! He's going to ram it!" a voice bellowed from the front, and the remaining men tried to run to the police station doors.

Seeing they were heading this way, we ran over to the doors to hold them closed. John flipped the deadbolt right as they crashed into the entrance with such a force that the doors shook from the impact, the hinges groaning.

"What the hell," someone shouted from the other side, "Is that mess Jensen?" They must have finally spotted the sniper lying dead on the ground.

"Who cares man, shoot the lock!"

In less time than it took to breathe, John grabbed my shoulder and dove to the side with me in tow. I hit the ground hard as bullets whizzed past us. The breath was ripped from my lungs, but I managed to crawl over further from the barrage of shots. Ethan was on the other side of the doors clutching his arm, blood leaking down his shirt.

"You okay?" I yelled once I had air in my lungs again.

"Just grazed me."

"It's not working!" the shooters from the other side yelled when they tried to kick in the door again.

I imagine the front doors to a police station were purposely made to withstand a certain amount of damage, but they wouldn't hold for much longer.

"The ladder out back!" a muffled voice responded, and I could hear the footsteps go around the building.

John braved a look out the window, "Ho-ly shit! He's really goin' to ram it. Get down!"

I heard the roar of the engine and then the loud *clang* of Taylor running into the chain link fence. Something hit the building with substantial impact and the window shattered. Glass rained down all around us, and I covered my head, diving underneath the nearest desk. I had once broken a vanity mirror years ago, but it was nothing compared to the size of this.

Once the shards lay still, I moved out from under the desk. The glass crunched under my shoes, as I walked over to John. He was crouched right under the window, shaking the glass off of himself. Ethan didn't appear to have been touched by the shards, as he flipped the deadbolt on the front doors with his left hand, his right arm still out of commission. The gate lay in a crumpled heap just outside the set of doors and the truck was half in and half out of the fence. Taylor was behind the wheel signaling for us to get in.

We climbed over the massive gate and ran to the truck. Infected were rattling the fence with renewed vigor, and it was beginning to collapse inwards, starting from the edges where Taylor had punctured a hole in it. John shot at the few that had managed to sneak in by the truck. Ethan passed me his gun, knowing he couldn't shoot while injured.

I gulped. Spending a bit more time on aiming than I should have, I started to shoot at the things that were invading the police station, like ants to a picnic. One down, two down, three down. I had taken out three in as many bullets but more were lining up to take their place. We had a small window before the make-shift opening would be overrun.

"We have to go now!" I yelled.

I started toward the truck, shooting at the ones coming up behind it. One tried to squeeze in the opening by the passenger side, so I switched to the knife Ethan had handed back to me in the police station and stuck it into the things left eye socket. It slumped forward, taking the knife with it. I pulled open the passenger door and jumped in, shuffling to the back seat. Ethan followed me in and maneuvered to the back while John came in last, slamming the door behind him.

"Go!"

Taylor hit reverse and floored it. We were catapulted against the front seats, and Ethan groaned in pain as his injured right arm was smashed against the seat. The map flew from the dashboard against the windshield impeding our view, but John quickly tore it down.

Shots were fired from the roof, and we ducked to avoid any bullets. The windshield cracked and fissured where the bullets had hit, but Taylor turned the wheel and hit drive, leaving the bullets behind us. We roared off to the side, running down mass amounts of infected. I didn't know how much more the truck could take; the grill was becoming a lumpy mess.

Bodies were flying everywhere, and one lifted over the grill and smashed into the windshield, shattering the glass. Taylor veered to the left and the body rolled off of the hood.

The back seat was still crammed with supplies. It looked like they hadn't got a chance to strip the truck clean. The bag of clothes I had tossed in last night were lying at my feet, reminding me that my backpack was sitting in the van. There went my other gun. I looked down at the piece we had swiped; it was a generic handgun, nowhere near as nice as my Berettas. But our lost supplies were the least of our concern. We had to get back to the cabin alive.

Once we were clear of the thickest part of the crowd, Taylor slowed down his reckless driving and become a little more defensive. We reached the main street, which previously was empty, now as busy as it would have been before the virus. Infected were stumbling across the street, drawn in by the truck alarm. At least, I assumed that's what brought them out. We passed by the cremated remains in the empty lot and then back out to the interstate.

As soon as we hit the main drag Taylor applied the brakes. The truck stood still in the middle of the three lanes, the engine still running.

"Why'd you stop?" John asked.

Instead of answering, Taylor opened the driver side door and got out. Ethan and I exchanged confused glances. John opened his own door to see what had gotten into Taylor. Not wanting to be left out, I vacated the truck with Ethan in tow. For some reason he followed me out my side instead of opening his own door.

"What is it, son?" John asked, concern lacing his voice.

We all stared in horror as Taylor rolled up his left sleeve to reveal a bloody set of teeth marks and some skin missing. John stood frozen in place, the shock too much for him. I heard Ethan swallow loudly beside me.

"I'm gonna turn aren't I?" Taylor asked in a low voice.

It was one thing to be dying; it was another thing all together to be a dead man walking. The irony was not lost on me. I had only witnessed a handful of people turn once infected, but I knew he didn't have long. The ones that turned fastest were the ones who had died while they were attacked, like in the school. The one's that didn't die during the attack turned a little while later, like Mike had.

A tear slipped down John's cheek, and I found my own eyes starting to cloud up with salty tears. None of us knew what to do. We had just left the supermarket this morning only to be taken hostage and here we were with more bad luck thrown our way. Only this time death was so much closer.

I turned back to the vehicle in a blur and started rummaging through the pharmacy supplies that were buried underneath the other items in the back of the truck bed. I ran back to Taylor with disinfectant and gauze; my own personal savior.

"That won't do any good," Taylor deadpanned.

"Give me your arm," I demanded, ignoring his words. "What happened?"

"Well first I shoved the sniper off the roof; he hadn't seen me comin' up behind him. Then I jumped off the roof, outside the fence and when I ran to the truck, there was already some of the infected around it. I pulled one off by the collar, but it twisted around and bit me before I could raise my knife."

He stopped his tale and held out his injured arm for me, so I got to work. Taylor hissed at the stinging disinfectant spray as it bubbled on the wound's surface. John was hovering, still eerily silent. The bite looked beyond painful. It was an angry shade of red and purple; it almost looked like it was pulsing. I wrapped the gauze firmly around his arm, but the blood was soaking through at an alarming rate. Maybe that's why people died so fast when attacked, the wound didn't clot.

"Leave me here."

"Never," John sounded angry.

"You might not turn, Taylor," I admitted.

He gave a humorless laugh, "And what are you basin' that off of?"

I handed my supplies to Ethan. They all looked at me warily as I began to lift my shirt. Taylor gave me an incredulous look, like he was worried I was about to strip. The nail marks on my skin had healed, but they left one hell of a scar, they looked like someone had dragged a hot poker across my skin. They were raised and red.

"That's from an infected?" Taylor asked, life coming into his voice once again.

"Back when everything first broke out. I was at the hotel, and an infected woman chased me down and scratched me. Zoe and I had gone to the hospital after, but it was too crazy there to get any treatment," I recounted what had happened, purposely leaving out the part about Mike.

"And you didn't turn," Taylor sounded hopeful.

"Obviously not."

John smiled at his son and put his hand on Taylor's shoulder.

"See, there's no need for us to leave you sittin' out here."

Ethan finally spoke up, "Maybe you're just immune."

Way for him to wreck the point of my little story time. I shot Ethan a sideways glance, silently telling him to shut up.

"There's no way of telling. So everybody get back in the truck and let's head back to the cabin," I used my rarely heard authoritative voice.

Taylor's lips quirked and he walked off to the passenger's side, John to the drivers. Ethan and I slipped back into the cab and I fixed up his arm once we were on the move again. It turns out the bullet had gone through his arm, which was lucky because I was pretty sure I didn't have the stomach to fish a bullet out. I sprayed some of the antiseptic on it then wrapped his upper arm in the remaining gauze. I was getting pretty good at that.

"I think you might need stitches?" It came out more as a question, since I wasn't actually trained to treat wounds.

"I can stitch you boys up once we get to the cabin," John announced from the front seat.

He kept looking over at Taylor, who was staring out the window silently. I threw the unused medical supplies back into the bag and sat back in the seat. None of us wanted to talk; we needed the time to sort through everything that happened today. My gaze kept returning to Taylor, looking for any signs that he was going to turn. Mike had lasted at least two hours before he turned, but that was only a guess on my part. He came to Zoe and me after he was bit, so there was no telling how long he was infected before we met him.

I turned in my seat, paranoid that we were being followed. The last thing we needed, on top of everything else, was to be followed back to the cabin by those psychos. Much to my relief, the road behind us was as empty as the road in front of us. Just a few abandoned cars, the only infected being the dead bodies that occasionally lay by the roadside.

Taylor let out a wet sounding cough, and I started to chew at my lips, my emotions fried. Mike had started to make those rattling coughs before he turned.

Chapter 23

The drive back to the cabin was fraught with tension, much more so than when we left. Taylor had resorted to shivers and sicklier coughs, like he was in the midst of fighting off the flu. His skin had paled even more than my own skin color, so John used his hand to feel for Taylor's temperature.

"You're burnin' up. Got any Tylenol back there?"

I rooted through the meager pharmacy supplies and produced the extra strength version. I passed two tablets and a bottle of water to Taylor, who regarded my outstretched hand with glassy eyes. He was starting to zone out. Weakly, he took my offerings, struggling with swallowing the pills.

"We're almost to the cabin, so just hold out a little longer." John pushed harder on the gas pedal, adding an extra twenty miles an hour to our speed.

The others must have heard us pull up the gravel road because they were lying in wait out front. It felt like we had been gone for weeks, when in reality it had only been two days. I felt both physically and mentally drained, struggling with processing all that had happened to us. And it looked like I had guessed wrong; Taylor was getting worse at an alarming rate.

Chloe ran up to the truck as we opened our doors. "Ethan!" She slammed into him, like a little midget linebacker. Ethan grunted with the force, but squeezed her back.

Zoe wrapped me in a giant bear hug. "You asshole, you were supposed to be back yesterday!"

"Something came up."

She let me go.

"Ah, what's wrong with him?" Darren asked, stepping away from Taylor.

Taylor had slunk out of the passenger's door and was now bent forward. John rushed from the driver's side to him. "Stay away," Taylor hissed, as he weakly tried to push his father away.

"Let me see," John pleaded.

Taylor collapsed to his knees, coughing up blood. The grass around him was sprayed in little red droplets. I heard Zoe gasp, as she grabbed my arm. Everyone backed away, except for John. Ethan clutched Chloe tightly and tried to steer her toward the cabin.

"Taylor." I shook off Zoe's grasp and tentatively walked over to him.

"All of you..." He gave a bloody cough. "...need to stay away." His eyes rolled back in his head and Taylor fell to the ground, his body going into convulsions.

Darren's hand moved to rest on the gun holster on his hip. "He's infected, isn't he?"

The look on my face answered his question, and he glared at Taylor. I held my hand up, telling Darren to stay back. John was hovering over Taylor's jerking form, his hands waving over his son uselessly. None of us knew what to do; there was nothing we could do. I knew Taylor would turn, and then we would have a big choice to make. After a few moments of spewing blood and spit, Taylor lay still on his side. He didn't appear to be breathing.

"Taylor?" John said weakly was he crouched over Taylor.

"John, don't get too close," I warned as I moved closer.

"Taylor!" John started to shake his motionless body.

"John!" I yelled, knowing full well how a turned person could react.

I ran over to try to pry John off of Taylor's corpse before he attacked. A hoarse growl escaped Taylor's lips, and he reached out to grab John's arm.

"Taylor?" John asked hopeful, but Taylor just let out a low, raspy moan.

I grabbed John's arm, yanking it free from his grasp on Taylor and tried to steer him backwards. Taylor rose in jerky movements, his eyelids opened to reveal a set of bloodshot eyes. All the blood vessels must have burst in his eyes, creating a sinister set of red orbs. He snarled and lunged for us from his half-sitting position. John was still lying on the ground, so I kicked out with my right foot, hitting Taylor's corpse under the jaw. He flew backwards but got up fast.

The brief question of why some infected moved faster than others crossed my mind in the confusion. Taylor spotted Zoe and decided to make a dash for her instead. His arms rose in her direction, snapping his teeth. She let out a scream and backed up, tripping over her own feet. Without fanfare, Darren whipped out his handgun and shot Taylor in the head. His body crashed to the side, discolored blood leaking from the wound. Then he laid still, for good this time.

We all just stood still, too afraid to even breathe. A distressed cry came from John, and I let go of the tight grasp I had on the collar of his shirt. He ran to Taylor's corpse, tears streaming down his face. I could barely make out him saying, "No, no, no," over and over again. I heard Chloe sobbing into Ethan's shirt, as he ushered her into the cabin, not wanting her to see anymore. Zoe stayed sitting on the ground, transfixed with Taylor. Darren put his weapon away and helped Zoe to her feet.

Darren hadn't hesitated to lay waste to Taylor; infected or not, we had lived with the guy for the past two months. When it came down to it, I wouldn't have been able to do it. That put me even more on edge.

I don't know what affected me more, the sight of Taylor dead on the ground or John weeping over his body. The sensation of liquid running down my face took me off guard. I wiped at my cheek, realizing I was crying. This was just too much to take, and the tears wouldn't stop. Taylor and I butted heads constantly, but I didn't want him dead. And I certainly didn't wish this on John.

I stood there awkwardly, not knowing what to do. When it came down to it, I was just an ill-equipped twenty-two-year-old with no comparable life experience. Not wanting to deal with this, I took off to the back of the cabin. Zoe looked like she wanted to follow, but I shot her a look that made her stop in her tracks.

Tears were making it hard to see, so I plunked myself down on the tree stump out back and let them flow. My mom always made remarks on how I wasn't very girly, never crying much as I grew up. The only person I have ever known to die was my grandmother, but I was seven when it happened and wasn't old enough to understand. Now I realized why I never cried a whole lot growing up; I had nothing to cry about, until now.

We had become our own little dysfunctional family. Taylor was like that brother you fought with, but at the end of the day still cared for. The tears had stopped now, leaving my eyes feeling swollen and my nose had become stuffed up. I felt gross. This is why I didn't like crying, you felt worse afterwards than you did before.

"Hey," Zoe said, as she hesitantly approached me.

I wiped at my face, trying to clear the streaks left behind by the tears. "Hey," my voice nasally from the stuffed up nose.

"So that was rough."

"Just a little," I muttered.

"Darren thinks we should deal with the body soon."

"Fuck Darren."

Zoe seemed taken aback by my reaction. "You know, someone would have had to shoot Taylor," she said quietly.

"That's not the issue. We'll give John as much time as he needs."

Zoe was right. If Darren hadn't shot Taylor, someone else would have had to. It did however, bother me how little it seemed to affect him and that he didn't use a silencer. That shot was loud.

I got up and we walked back to the cabin. John was still beside Taylor's body, but Darren had disappeared. When I opened the door, Chloe was chattering away nervously and Ethan was trying to calm her down. He stood up off of the dusty couch when we entered.

"He still out there?" Ethan asked.

"Yeah."

"What do we do?"

"I don't have a clue."

Chapter 24

Darren turned up a few hours later covered in dirt. He propped the shovel he was carrying against the cabin.

"I dug him a grave," he looked over at John, still sitting beside Taylor's body. "For when John's ready."

That was oddly nice of Darren. Or creepy. I couldn't decide. We had waited in the cabin for John, but he just remained by Taylor's fallen body. We had gathered outside in the hopes that John would do something or at the very least get up. I walked over to him. The sun was starting to set behind the treeline, creating an orange glowing effect along the tips of the trees. Their shadows were extending closer and closer to us, like silent, grabbing hands.

"John," I placed a hand on his shoulder. "We have to do something for Taylor. Darren dug a grave for him."

John took a deep breath before he replied, "Are there any extra sheets?"

"Yes there are, I'll be right back." Ethan ran back into the cabin.

He re-emerged a minute later with an off-white sheet. Together, we placed the sheet flat on the ground and lifted Taylor's stiff body onto it, then wrapped him fully.

"Where did you dig the grave?" I asked Darren.

He pointed to the east treeline, "Just under those trees."

I grabbed the shovel as Ethan and John lifted Taylor. We walked to the trees in a makeshift funeral precession. Chloe ran to the cabin flower beds and ripped out some blooming buds. Gently, they lowered Taylor's body into the shallow, uneven grave. I couldn't chastise Darren for the crappy quality; digging was hard.

The sheet clad body looked out of place among the wildlife. I stabbed the shovel into the soft ground, not sure how to proceed. I had never been to a funeral before.

After an awkward period of silence, John cleared his throat.

"Suffer us not, at our last hour, for any bitter pains of death, to fall from Thee. And we beseech thee oh Lord to receive with mercy unto thine arms the soul of our dear departed brethren today, that we may rejoice in their life and honor their passing to thy eternal care." He looked down at the grave, pain etched into his features as he took a breath. "Even though I walk through the valley of the shadow of death, I will fear no evil, for you are with me; your rod and your staff, they comfort me."

When he finished, silence reigned once again. *I guess I should say something.* I cleared my throat and all heads turned to me.

"Taylor was like family. We all are. And when we lose a family member, they cannot be replaced. He was like a brother to me. We fought and got along like siblings. At the end of the day all that matters is that we were there for each other, just like Taylor was there for us. He tried to teach me to hunt, unsuccessfully might I add. But he did manage to teach me something else: what is means to be brave. We would have never made it out that police station if not for his sacrifice. That is what it means to be family."

John looked at me with appreciation in his eyes. "Amen."

He bent down and grabbed a handful of dirt, sprinkling it onto the body. I went next and then everyone else after me. I started shoveling the dirt pile back into the hole, but Darren stilled my efforts with a hand on my shoulder. He held his hand out for the tool, so I passed it to him, and he continued where I had left off. Since the hole wasn't that deep, it didn't take long to fill. Chloe placed her freshly picked flowers on top of the grave.

Zoe had taken off and reappeared with a makeshift cross to use as a grave marker. She stuck it near where Taylor's head would be and Darren hammered it in further with the shovel. Darkness was now upon us, so we started to head back to the cabin. John was the last to leave as he whispered something to the grave that was not meant for our ears.

That night was awful; I laid wide awake staring at nothing. Zoe was snoring away beside me and there was no chance in hell I would get any sleep. Quietly, I crept out into the kitchen. A while ago I had spotted a bottle of Jack Daniels shoved to the back of one of the cupboards. Ethan probably didn't even know about it and I could really use a drink.

I snatched it from its resting place, careful not to wake John who was sleeping on the pull-out couch thanks to some strong sleeping pills I had forced him to take. I pocketed the match book that was sitting on the counter on my way out. The door clicked into place soundlessly as I carefully closed it. The fire pit out back was my destination. I did have my knife with me should I need it.

The starlight vaguely illuminated my path to the back, but I still wished I had brought a flashlight. I knocked into one of the camping chairs, which meant I was where I wanted to be. The match sprang to life as I dragged the head along the package rough patch. I tossed it in the fire pit and the dry wood caught on fire instantly, but the flames were dull and weak so I packed on some thin pieces. It crackled with the new addition and I shrank into my chair.

A quarter of the whisky bottle later, I was feeling pretty good. I felt warm. Invincible. *I wonder if I put my hand into the fire, if would it hurt?* Okay, maybe I was a little drunk. I tried to get up, but I fell back on my ass.

"Stupid chair," I muttered.

"You drunk?" Ethan drawled, suddenly very much beside me. Normally I would have heard him approach, but he had caught me off guard. I waved the bottle at him.

"Not yet." I took another drink from the bottle and then offered it to him. He eyed it for a second then took a drink himself, as he pulled up a chair beside me.

"Didn't peg you for a drinker," he said passing the bottle back to me.

"Really? The girl who was in New Orleans for Mardi Gras?" I took another drink.

"Touché," he smirked at me.

"Well, I'm not normally a get drunk drinker. I find this whole apocalypse thingy goes down a lot smoother with a bottle of Jack," I grinned drunkenly.

Ethan rolled his eyes and held his hand out for the bottle again. "You know, Taylor's death affected us all. Are you..." He searched for the right word. "...okay?"

I sighed at his anticlimactic word choice. "Someone just died. No, I'm not okay."

"Well, I'm here for you if you need to talk or anythin'. I care about you, Bailey." I couldn't really tell in the dim light, but he looked serious when he said that. That wouldn't do.

"Why Ethan, that's the nicest thing you've ever said to me." I batted my eyelashes at him and he scowled down into the bottle. "Gimme." I wiggled my fingers at the whisky.

"I think you've had enough," Ethan grinned evilly, taking another drink of my Jack Daniels –

well it was mine now. I narrowed my eyes.

"So that's how you want to play this? I should warn you I've been told I'm a mean drunk." I reached for the bottle, the grin widening on his face as I missed completely.

"That the best you got?" he mocked.

I shocked both of us when I jumped at him from my chair and knocked us over. I took advantage of his surprise by grabbing the bottle out of his grasp, my drunken reflexes working overtime. "Ha!" I yelled proudly as I held the bottle up.

"Jesus, woman!" Ethan said as he sat back up right.

"Told you not to mess with my Jack," I said matter-of-factly, taking a drink.

We were sitting really close, our arms slightly touching, but neither of us moved away. We just sat in comfortable silence, sharing the bottle on the ground instead of our chairs.

"I'm gonna need to pick up some more of this wonderful stuff when we make our next trip," I slurred.

"You can't hold your liquor, can you city girl?" Ethan shook his head beside me.

"Sorry, we can't all be country folks, who are used to Uncle Willy's 'shine," I retorted but my slurring kind of ruined the impact, and Ethan chuckled.

"We should go back inside."

"I don't wanna go back in there," I pouted.

Ethan shook his head, then gave into the booze and took another long drink. An ember flew from the fire and landed on Ethan's pants. He hissed in pain as he patted the spot where it had burnt a hole through his jeans. I laughed at his exaggerated response. He acted like his leg was on fire.

"S'not funny," he slurred, his accent becoming more pronounced.

He sighed and grinned at my chuckling face. He moved in closer, and I stopped laughing. I knew what he was going to do and I wasn't as opposed to it as I should be. His warm lips covered my own and I kissed him back. I rested my hand on his thigh and he gripped the back of my head, pulling me in closer. This would be awkward in the morning, but in my drunken state of mind, I found I didn't care.

He smelt of guy body wash and tasted like whiskey. Using his body, he gently pushed my back to the ground so he was on top of me. His lips moved to my neck, and I ran my hands through his hair, which really needed a haircut. He winced when my roaming hand went over his bandaged arm.

"Sorry," I said, breathless.

Instead of responding, he just crushed his lips back to mine. I ran my hands down his toned torso and felt his abdomen contract at the touch. He grabbed my roaming hand, not hard though, just enough to stall it.

"We shouldn't continue this." He was panting as he said this.

Rejection washed over me in a fierce tidal wave, no doubt worse because of the alcohol. I tried to shove him off, but he removed himself from on top of me without any more effort on my part. I stumbled, as I attempted getting up. Ethan tried to lend a hand, but I swatted it off as I stomped away from the fire pit. *How dare he reject me when he was the one who started it!*

"Bailey!" Ethan hissed behind me as he caught up to me. "You misunderstand." He latched onto my arm and swung me around so I was facing him.

"What?" I demanded.

"You misunderstand. It's not that I don't want to... well you know." He looked really uncomfortable as he tried to explain himself. "It's just that I don't have any precautions."

"You mean condoms?"

The dark was obscuring my view, but I was willing to bet he was blushing a little.

"Yes. Maybe when we get some, we can continue this?" He sounded hopeful, and I laughed.

I had to put my hands on my knees I was laughing so hard. Tears were threatening to over flow with my giggling. Now it was his turn to be pissed.

"It ain't funny."

"No, it kind of is, but you're right. I'm willing to bet Zoe thought to grab a box or two back when we were all at the grocery store months ago."

I found it funny how I prided myself on being the responsible one, but here Ethan was proving me wrong. Pregnancy was scary on a regular day, let alone when the world had gone to shit and there was nowhere safe.

"Maybe you could ask to borrow some?" He scratched the back of his head awkwardly.

"I'm sure that would be a bad idea. But maybe I'll sneak a few when she's not looking." I winked and he pulled me in for a kiss again.

"I still don't want to go back in there."

"We could sleep in the hammock."

I thought about it. "Sure." It beat listening to Zoe's snoring for the rest of the night.

The hammock in question was a freestanding one that you could buy from any outdoor store, and it was close to the fire pit. He laid down first and then offered his hand for me.

"How gentlemanly."

I took his outstretched hand and settled in the crook of his arm.

"Night."

I don't remember what I replied with; the darkness took over as soon as I closed my eyes.

Chapter 25

A shadow moved across the inside of my eyelids. Something was blocking the morning light, and I was a little too hungover to deal with that. I stiffened and cracked an eye open, readying to attack. The smirking face of Zoe peered down at me. She uncrossed her arms and produced the now empty bottle of Jack Daniels.

"You couldn't have saved even a little bit for me?"

I had to swallow a few times before I was able to reply. It felt like I had just been standing in front of an air-conditioning unit with my mouth open for hours. "Kill me." My head was pounding, and I felt like death warmed over.

Zoe laughed, "Come on, we'll get you some Tylenol and water."

I started to sit up; trying not to jostle the hammock too much, but with it being a hammock and all, that attempt was futile.

Ethan's eyes flew open as he was rocked back and forth. "What the?"

I chuckled at his complete disorientation, "I think we're being told we have to get up."

He scrubbed his hand over his face and hauled himself to his feet.

"You need some Tylenol, too?" Zoe grinned.

"Well, I ain't gonna say no."

We walked back to the cabin, probably looking as bad as we felt. Zoe was grinning the whole time and I could tell she was waiting for us to be alone before she tried to drag all the details out of me.

Inside, Darren and Chloe were making breakfast with the powdered eggs we had found, but John was nowhere to be seen.

"Where you been?" Chloe narrowed her eyes at Ethan then at me.

Ethan shot me a panicked glance, and I just grinned, "I dibs the shower first." I ran off, leaving him to explain.

The shower was lukewarm and had almost zero water pressure, but it beat bathing in a pond out back. The water also had a slight metallic smell to it, which usually meant the well needed more water softening salts. *At least we were getting our iron.*

I took two pills from the bottle Zoe propped on the kitchen counter and downed them with some instant coffee. I tried to eat some of the scrambled eggs, but my stomach could only handle so much.

"Ethan said ya'll had a bonfire without me," Chloe pouted.

I scratched the back of my head, not sure of what else Ethan had told her, "It was past your bedtime."

Judging from the scrunched-up look on her face, Chloe didn't like my answer.

"I'll tell you what, next time we'll all have a bonfire. We even grabbed some marshmallows on our run."

Chloe beamed at that, "What else did you bring back?"

I was amazed at how well kids recovered. She seemed to be back to normal despite the scene we had witnessed yesterday. I wish I could bounce back like that. Realization hit me that the bookmark making set I had brought back for Chloe was stored in my backpack, which was currently located at the police station.

"Bailey and I brought you back this."

Ethan appeared from his shower holding the My Little Pony choose your own adventure series I had helped him pick out.

Chloe squealed and jumped off of her stool excitedly. "Thank you!" She grabbed the books from Ethan and gave him a huge hug. Then came back over to me and gave me a hug as well. "I know you picked this out, so thank you," she whispered to me.

I grinned at little miss smart-ass. She opened the first book on the counter and got right into it. Ethan grinned at me, his hand resting on his right shoulder. I forgot he still had that bullet wound.

"Where did John go?"

"Don't know, he was gone before I got up," Darren answered.

Shit. That couldn't be good. We still needed him to sew up Ethan.

"Do you want me to help you patch up your arm?" I asked.

"If you could, that would be great."

We had unloaded some of the supplies yesterday, and it looked like they had been back at it this morning. There was a massive pile of stuff in the corner and pretty much on every surface. I grabbed the first aid supplies and began rewrapping Ethan's arm. The wound looked sore and wasn't starting the healing process.

"Still think I need stitches?" he said.

"I'd say so."

"Think you can do it?" Ethan looked me in the eye

"I've only ever sewn my clothes and not very well either. I'd probably make it worse."

Darren put down his coffee mug. "I can do it."

"You've stitched a wound before?" I asked skeptically.

"No, but I've taken advanced first aid training and we had to learn about giving stitches."

Judging from the look on Ethan's face, I don't think he trusted Darren to do it.

"Why did you take advanced first aid?" I probed.

"I was going to enlist in the army."

"So that's why you can shoot so well," Zoe added.

I wasn't sure if shooting an infected friend in the head amounted to being able to shoot well, but I suppose I should stop resenting Darren for that. Someone had to do it.

"Since John's not here, I guess I don't have a choice."

Ethan sat down on the stool and Darren started to rummage through the supplies. He set out the fish hook looking needle and sterile black thread.

"Come on Chloe, let's go read those outside." Zoe ushered Chloe out the door with her books in hand.

Ethan glanced at me, "You gonna watch?"

"Well I should probably learn, although Darren hasn't done this before so I'm not sure if I'll learn wrong or not."

"I'll have you know I aced that class."

Darren had the white rubber gloves on and dipped the hook into the peroxide. The wound bubbled as he poured the disinfectant on the opening before he started in. Ethan hissed through his teeth as the needle pierced the angry wound. His knuckles went white as he gripped the counter. It only took four stitches before Darren tied the end off and cut the extra thread off.

He added more disinfectant to the now even redder lesion, before wrapping it in gauze.

"Not too bad," I said, although I had nothing to base that comment on.

"Speak for yourself," Ethan grunted from the pain.

I slid the Tylenol bottle to him, and he swallowed two pills dry. At this rate, we would need another bottle soon.

Darren rounded up and tossed out the used supplies. "See, it's literally like sewing a seam, except you use a different shaped needle and generally the pants you're sewing don't jerk away."

Ethan glared at Darren's attempt at humor. I tried to hide my grin by sipping my coffee.

"Hey, I could have used super glue on it,' Darren said. "Would you rather that?"

"I thought that was just a myth?" I asked.

"If you clean out the wound beforehand, there shouldn't be an issue. It's when there are still lots of germs in the open cut that you get the infection setting in."

"Good to know."

"So are you guys going to tell us exactly what happened?" Darren asked, clearly he had been waiting to do so.

Ethan and I shared a look, neither one of us wanting to have to relive the nightmare of the last two days. But Ethan always the gentleman, decided to recount everything to Darren before I had a chance to.

Darren took a minute to let it all sink in. "You think those paramilitary guys are going to come looking for you?"

"I don't see how," I said. "They didn't follow us, and we are a good distance away from Duson."

There was no way to be sure, but I had this sinking feeling that Riley wasn't the type to let things go. I didn't have a chance to even think about that until now. Fear ran down my spine, its icy grip making me panic inside. *Would he want revenge?* The whole situation was their fault anyways, forcing us to become prisoners, but I doubt he saw it that way. Psychos never did.

"We should make a run back to John's gun shop to grab more ammo and to replace your weapons in case they do show up. Maybe get some sort of perimeter warning system going," Darren suggested.

"We just got back, Darren and just lost a person yesterday. Ethan is shot and John is MIA, I really don't think right now is the best time," I pinched the bridge of my nose. "Plus I have no idea where we would get a perimeter system."

"I didn't mean right now. And if we're lucky John's store will have something, if not, we look for a hunting or outdoors type store."

"I agree that we need more ammo and weapons to replace the ones we lost, but after what happened to us, we should not be goin' out in groups less than three," Ethan said as he tested his injured arm.

"So we have to wait until your arm is better then?" Darren didn't seem happy with this revelation.

He was obviously pissed about having to stay behind.

"In case you've forgotten in the last few seconds, we're down a person and one is no mental state to go out," I added.

Darren's jaw clench at that. "Well we should make it soon. Who knows, that group could have someone skilled in tracking." He roughly pushed himself away from the counter and walked outside.

I let out a deep sigh. I was at a loss as to what we should do. Normally John was here to tell us what the best course of action was.

"Fuck him," Ethan said angrily.

I laughed. From the shocked look Ethan shot me, I'm guessing that wasn't the reaction he was expecting.

"I said the same thing yesterday."

Ethan grinned at my explanation, "What do you think we should do?"

"I know you're probably tired of hearing this, but I have no clue."

"I don't know either."

We decided to head outside. Chloe was at the picnic table reading furiously. Zoe and Darren were talking quietly off to the side, and I didn't like the looks of that. Zoe had the worst taste in guys and there was something about Darren that still irked me, although he hadn't really done anything too bad in the grand scheme of things. After all, I had just stabbed someone a day ago. So maybe I was the dangerous one. *I guess I should have gone into psychology instead.*

"Ethan!" Chloe yelled. "Come look!"

She excitedly showed Ethan the story, and he pretended to be impressed by it. Zoe broke off from Darren and swarmed over to me. I knew where this was going, and I really hated girl talk.

"I just had to hear the whole story from Darren!" She was pissed that he was filled in first. I was slightly relieved that it was about our trip, not Ethan.

"We literally just told him, the gossip queen." I sent a glare in his direction.

"Jesus."

"That about sums it up."

We sat in silence for a moment.

"So you and Ethan huh?"

I knew it was a trap!

"Not that I didn't see that coming a mile away," Zoe grinned knowingly at me.

"Actually, I didn't take a page from your book last night. We kissed and then fell asleep in the hammock."

Instead of being angry at my insult, Zoe just laughed. "You are wise, young Skywalker."

See, true friends can insult each other and not give each other the silent treatment for a week afterwards.

"I don't think that's an actual quote from the movie." I raised an eyebrow.

"Whatever, I prefer *Star Trek* anyways."

"Blasphemy!"

Zoe's eye darted to something behind me and I whipped around in time to see a figure emerge from the treeline. My hand instinctively went for the gun on my belt, which of course wasn't there.

"It's John," Darren announced.

We watched the figure grow larger; the outline of his cowboy hat came into view first. As he got closer, I noticed he had a gun with a silencer attached in his hand. This got Ethan's attention.

"Chloe go back inside," he commanded.

"But Ethan–"

"Now!"

She grabbed her books and grumbled until she was safely inside. I had no idea what was going to happen; John didn't look like John. He had the look of a man possessed. I glanced back at Darren who must have had the same thing going through his mind that I did. Retribution. His hand rested on his gun holster, just in case.

I spotted the russet-colored stains that were smeared on John's clothing as he approached us. *What the hell?* Grief made people do all kinds of things; made good people do bad things. Darren moved to pull the gun from his belt.

"Don't you dare," I hissed at him.

Darren regarded me with cold eyes. The stains on John's clothes resembled the one's I got from the infected's blood. It was not human blood, much to my relief.

"John?" I asked hesitantly.

John stopped and looked down at the gun in his hand, and then wiped his other hand on his shirt. Looking anywhere but at us, it seemed like John wanted to say something. I had a hard time swallowing past the lump in my throat.

His sudden movement caught me off guard, and I flinched. John had sheathed his gun back into its holster, and then took a deep breath. "I ran into a couple of infected out there. They were pretty close to the property line."

I nodded, fully aware I had started to sweat from the tense situation, "I could tell from your clothes."

He looked down at his shirt and surprise registered on his face.

"Come on, you should change into something else," I urged, getting closer to John.

I tentatively put my hand on his shoulder and he looked at me, "Yeah, I look a mess."

Chapter 26

Two weeks later, everything was back to the way it was before.

Except that was a lie.

John was still acting like a husk, not at all the John we were used to. I don't blame him, but it was getting too much to be around. So here I was on my own, with his car, a fair distance away from our home base. Cabin fever was starting to set in and that, combined with the gloomy atmosphere, was becoming too overwhelming for me.

So I volunteered to do a perimeter check and when Ethan said he would go with me, I declined his offer saying that I would be fine. He was stubborn about it, but I fought for my independence in this matter. I needed to be properly alone. The others weren't happy about it, but I think they understood.

I packed the backpack borrowed from John with extra ammo for my stolen 9mm gun, some food and water for my day trip, and an extra pair of clothes and my shiny new hunting knife, just in case. I was planning on just driving around the roads that surrounded the property to make sure that there were no signs of infected or anyone else, but I got sidetracked. There was a road that went in the exact opposite direction of the cabin that had called to me instead. After all, the perimeter thing was just a guise so that I could get away for a few hours.

The gravel road led me to an open field surrounded by trees. I had been driving for almost an hour, so I stopped at the opening and killed the car. The sun was shining bright above me, as I climbed out. Not a cloud in the sky. I closed my eyes and inhaled deeply. I was starting to really appreciate the

Southern weather. Usually by this time of year at home, it was raining and overcast all the time. The air smelled fresh; the flowery fragrance of the field grass was a welcome one.

As you can imagine, six people living in close quarters did not smell all that great. I looked around for any signs of, well, anything. I was completely alone for the first time since the infection had taken over like a conquering army. I scooted myself onto the hood of the car and leaned against the windshield, my new backpack right beside me. I propped my hands behind my head, intending to fully enjoy this brief reprieve. The warm sun was making me drowsy and I let myself start to drift, listening to the sound of the wildlife.

That was one thing that didn't seem to be affected – the ecosystem. Animals, plant life, bugs, they all seemed to be thriving, while the humans were decimated. I hoped that one day this world would not end up lost to the bugs. That was an even more disturbing thought. *Didn't they say that cockroaches could survive nuclear war?* I stopped thinking about it, trying to push out the image of people sized cockroaches roaming the empty streets.

A gust of wind rustled the trees even more, and I sat up, making sure it was just the wind. I was trying to relax, but fear always was waiting silently in the back of my mind. You could never lower your guard in this new world. I sank back down to the windshield, confident that it was just the breeze.

Darren had been pestering us all about going back to John's gun shop to grab more ammo and guns. Unfortunately, John said he didn't have any type of perimeter monitoring equipment. He also showed no desire to go back to his store. Or anything for that matter. We had come to the conclusion that we would go in the next few days. Ethan's bullet wound was getting better, but we still needed as many capable people as possible. So it was to be Darren, Ethan and I, while John and Zoe stayed with Chloe.

Zoe didn't seem to have an issue with staying behind; she wasn't the most aggressive person, not looking to run head long into danger. I remember back when we had first started university and were at the bar with other students. Some drunken bitch was pissed that Zoe was getting hit on by a member of the school hockey team and decided to go up and shove her, all while calling her a chink. Zoe was like third-generation Japanese and barely looked Asian, but if there was one thing I couldn't tolerate, it would be racism. And that someone was heckling my friend.

Zoe just kind of stood there, not willing to shove her back, so in my drunken wisdom I decided to stick up for my friend. I shoved the girl from behind, and she whirled around and sucker punched me. At this point I got pissed and grabbed the girl's hair, smashing her face into the bar counter, then proceed to punch her on the ground. I wasn't lying when I said I was a mean drunk. Zoe pulled me off of her, and we ended up getting banned from the bar.

I remember all the pats on the back I got the next day a school, all the while trying to hide my shiner under makeup. The girl had a few inches of height and definitely had some pounds on me, but I had managed to win anyways. That was the most violence I had ever committed, up until now that is. Maybe it was there all along, and this apocalypse was just starting to bring it out. That was an unsettling thought.

It was nice to have quiet for once. Usually someone was talking or yelling in the cabin. I had never spent so many of my days outside, as I had during the last two and a half months. We were starting to grow restless. Obviously help was not forth coming and unless we planned to live out our lives in that tiny cabin, we had to come up with some kind of plan.

Maybe I could find a car and try my luck heading north, back to B.C. That plan seemed less and less crazy as the days went on. That was also a worrying thought. Looking at my watch, I realized that I had been laying here for two hours. I hopped off of the hood and threw my backpack into the passenger seat. I reversed back onto the gravel road and decided that I should finally get around to what I had supposedly come out here for. Trees whizzed past me and gravel was tossed up behind the car, as I sped back the way I had come.

An hour later, I had been up and down the main artery that passed by the road to the cabin, and it seemed clear. I wasn't sure, but I could swear I saw movement in the bushes. The car came to a slow stop, as I pressed on the brake and got out. Using my hand as a shield, I blocked out the mid-afternoon sun shining down from above. *Maybe it was just my imagination.* Everything seemed still now. I shook my head and decided that maybe a drink of water was in order.

I rummaged through my bag for my water bottle, as I started down the road again. It kept sliding away from my grabbing fingers, staying just out of reach. I sighed and turned my head toward the stupid backpack. Finally, I managed to fish the bottle out of my backpack of no return, just in time to see a body in my way. Slamming on the brakes did no good since I was on gravel and the car continued to skid forward.

I managed to swerve to the side, only clipping the human-shaped form. It went flying into the ditch as the car eventually came to a stop. Hurriedly, I dug through my bag for the hand gun. Gripping it tightly, I got out of the car leaving the engine running, just in case I needed a quick getaway.

"Hello?" I prompted.

A moan was all I got for a response and I had no idea if that meant the person was infected or just injured. I risked getting closer, peering down into the ditch dip. A mangled hand reached toward me, two of its fingers missing and not from the crash. The man was wearing a shredded business suit, and his dingy skin was starting to bubble and blister from the unrelenting sun. He tried to crawl to me, his teeth grinding together excitedly.

I took a deep breath and stepped toward the crevasse. I had a better chance of hitting it if it was down there. The gun was lighter than my Berettas were, so I had to watch how I shot with this one.

One minute the ravenous face was looking at me, the next it was face first into the grass. In a single shot I had hit the top of its head, ending its climbing attempt. There was no silencer on this gun, and you could tell from the echoing sound of the gunshot.

The rest of the drive was not a pleasant one. Now I was sure I had seen things moving in the trees. My knuckles were pulled taut, as I gripped the steering wheel and floored it back to the cabin, hoping it didn't take me an hour to get back.

Nowhere near soon enough, I finally turned left onto the road that lead to the cabin from the main one, immediately having to swerve around another infected standing in the middle of the road. I heard the sound of its fingers dragging along the car as I passed, no doubt wrecking the paint job.

More infected were lining the road and coming out of the woodwork. I felt like I was playing a driving video game, having to swerve all over the road just to avoid unwanted pedestrians. There would be no points awarded this time, just death if I managed to crash the car and have to make it through this on foot.

I needed to get back to the cabin to warn the others, if they haven't already found out for themselves.

"Get off the road!" I yelled to no one in particular, after yet another infected ran toward the car instead of away from it.

One of the headlights cracked from the impact, and a fair amount of dents were more than likely adorning the front grill. I gritted my teeth, my breath coming out in short spurts.

Finally, I reached the gate, cursing when I remembered that I had closed it behind me.

Except it wasn't closed. It was wide open.

A group of infected had formed behind me, chasing after the car so I had no choice but to go forward. The closer I got to cabin, the more I realized I should be panicking. Ethan's truck was gone, and I didn't spot anyone outside. Infected were everywhere; the whole property was overrun.

I got up to the cabin door and jumped out of the car, taking out the two that were banging on the front panels. The door banged against the wall, as I burst through and I slammed it shut. I looked into the two bedrooms, only to find them empty of people. The room was spinning, and I realized that it was me, so I stopped my feet from going in circles. It looked like things had been hastily packed, bags and supplies were everywhere. On the floor, counter, furniture.

It looked like I had been left behind. I braced my hands on my knees; breathing was starting to become difficult. There was no way they would leave me behind, they just couldn't have. All right, I would have to keep that thought out of my mind for right now. I ran to the ammo stash and threw as many of the remaining cases as I could find into a plastic bag, then grabbed some of the food bags and tossed them all by the door.

Peeking out the front window revealed that a couple more infected had made it this far up the driveway. I took a breath and flung open the front door, not wasting too much time with my aim, and managed to take the two that had just approached the car. I reached back into the cabin and grabbed the bulging plastic bags, then threw them into the back seat of the car.

My head whipped around as I tried to scan for signs of anyone, eyes landing on a bobbing head just beyond the fence line, and my heart sunk.

It was Chloe.

Chapter 27

Chloe was running wildly. All the infected in the area seemed to have honed in on her presence. The more I listened, the more I heard her screaming for help, ironically making the situation worse. She was over half the property away from me with over a dozen infected between me and her.

Leave her.

I turned toward the car, my hand on the driver's side door.

But I couldn't do that. I reached in and turned the engine off, but left the keys in the ignition. The last thing I need would be for them to slip out of my pocket. I had roughly ten bullets left in my gun and one extra magazine that we had found. I fished it out of my backpack and stuffed it into my pocket.

The door slammed louder than I hoped it would have when I shut it, drawing some attention. I started my jog toward Chloe's location, using the less populated path. Luckily, most of the infected had their backs to me, all intent on getting to the screaming girl.

I wanted to yell at her to stop screaming, but then the attention would be focused on me and make this rescue attempt harder. Dodging the grabbing arms and confused infected, I managed to gain some ground. I really wanted to avoid using my gun until I absolutely had to, because the noise would draw them to me like moths to a flame. I was so focused on what was happening in front of me, that I didn't see the one bounding toward me from the side.

We were knocked down from the collision, and I rolled away as soon as I felt the grass on my skin. A badly decayed hand wrapped around my ankle, using me as leverage to pull its emaciated form closer. I tried to dislodge it by wiggling my foot, but it was wrapped on my leg good.

Seeing no other option, I pulled out my gun and shot it between the eyes. Well, it was more like in the upper left corner of the forehead, but it worked all the same. Dark, viscous blood sprayed onto my leg and I grimaced. The body went lax, and I was able to pull my ankle free and get up.

All red and milky eyes were on me. I had just rung the dinner bell with that shot. It appeared I had also gotten Chloe's attention, because she was now sprinting toward me. Into the horde. *Shit.* I gained some speed and started to shove over all of the nearest infected, knowing I would have more success with that than with my gun at the moment. I felt like a quarterback running the football in for a touchdown. I hated sports.

"Bailey!" Chloe screamed my name.

I reached her in the middle of the chaos. She latched onto me and I had to pry her off.

"Come on."

With her hand in mine, I led us around the infected. As I steered her away from the relentless bodies, I was forced to pull out my gun. The gunfire had formed into a continuous popping succession. Bodies were dropping, but it looked like I had used all the bullets. Then more gunfire sounded off into the distance.

Chloe looked at me, us both knowing that came from one of our group. I elbowed a pre-teen infected out of the way and they flopped against the trunk of the car, bouncing right back up.

"Get in the driver's door!" I yelled out of breath.

Chloe didn't have to be told twice as she opened the door behind her and scrambled into the next seat. The infected that I had elbowed was by no means done. I swiped out my left leg, hitting it behind the knee. It fell back against the car again sliding all the way down this time, its arms flailing in the air. It reminded me of when a cartoon character would dramatically slip on a banana peel.

I hurried in after her and slammed the door behind me. Hands were groping on the sides, looking to get in. The rest were heading right for us.

"Go!" Chloe's high-pitched scream made my temples throb.

I turned the key and the engine roared to life.

"Seatbelt!"

Chloe quickly strapped in right before I hit reverse. The tires spun up dirt for a second before we actually started to move. The infected that had started to lean on the sides, suddenly found themselves sprawled out on the dirt path as we backed up. I had my head craned to look out the back window, and once I found a patch clear of infected, I turned the car around.

Now we were facing the open gate and numerous infected. I punched the accelerator and played yet another round of dodge-the-things-in-the-way. The seat belt was twisted in Chloe's grip as she held the scratchy fabric between her small hands. Once we cleared the gate, I chanced another look back. None of our friends could be spotted, if they were still there that is. There was no way Ethan would have left without Chloe, so he must still be somewhere out in the woods looking for her.

Now I was torn. I hadn't seen him in the flesh, but Ethan was more than likely out there somewhere. We had heard that gun shot in the distance, but in all the confusion I had no idea even what direction it had come from. I had a choice to make. Did we go back and look for him? Or did I keep going with Chloe?

I wanted to scream at the unfairness of it all.

"Chloe, what were you doing out there by yourself?" I asked, once I urge to scream passed.

"I wanted to see where John kept goin'," she said in a small voice.

"So you followed him out there?"

She nodded.

"Did you see anyone else?"

She shook her head and started to sob. "Ethan's got to be back there. We have to go back!" Tears ran down her face, and she was getting those heaving breaths that accompanied crying.

"We can't go back Chloe. If we go any further out, we'll just get bogged down with the infected."

I knew her next move before she even had time to think it through clearly. Her hand reached for the door handle, and I quickly hit the childproof lock button. She rattled the door all while crying profusely. "Let me out! I have to go back for him!" she wailed and then turned on me full force.

Her little fists wouldn't do much damage, but I was swerving the car all over trying to subdue her.

"Chloe! Settle down!" I yelled, in the most adult voice I could muster.

She wasn't stopping, so I shoved her back into her seat – not hard mind you. Chloe blinked at me, surprised that I had done that, and then started bawling again. I felt like an asshole, but she needed to calm down. I was having a hard enough time driving in this as it was. The right turn was up ahead, and the herd had thinned out, the majority of them surrounding the cabin.

"Chloe, I know you're mad, but I need you to answer me. Did you see who took the truck?"

She sniffed and took in some short breaths, "I dunno. I never saw the truck leave."

Damn. My best guess was that Zoe and Darren were driving to who knows where, while John and Ethan were out in the woods. Ethan must have realized Chloe had snuck away and went after her, probably getting trapped in the horde. And for all I knew, John had walked right into them, depressed about Taylor.

I had to stop this train of thought; it was making things even harder. It was like when you heard a noise in the middle of the night and your mind immediately began picturing all the horrible things that could be waiting for you outside of your blankets.

Speculating wasn't helping. I needed to get us to safety, and I now had someone other than myself to look out for. I was responsible for another human being. That knowledge was daunting and hit me like a ton of bricks. *Goddamn them for not watching her closer!* I smacked the steering wheel yet again, and Chloe flinched at my outburst. Again, I felt like an ass.

"I'm getting us out of here," I announced, more for my sake than for Chloe's. I felt like I needed to convince myself.

The main road that lead back to the highway was peppered with infected, but nowhere near as saturated as the cabin lot had been. I had apparently done an appalling job on my perimeter run. Maybe if hadn't left, things would have turned out differently. Maybe we would have all escaped together. *Was this my fault?* Guilt was gnawing away inside me, like a parasite eating its way out.

We were flung to the left, as I swerved around the remnants of a tall male infected who dove out in front of the car. I peered at the gas needle; it was sitting at half a tank. I wasn't sure how long it would last, especially with the crazy driving I had to do. Nor did I have any idea where I was going, so I was just burning gas until a plan formed itself.

Chloe had stopped her crying and was peering out the window. I slowed the car and eventually stopped.

Chloe turned to me. "Why did you stop? Are we goin' back?" Her voice was laced with a lethal dose of hope, making my next words even harder.

"No, we're going to find somewhere to hold up until I can figure out what to do. If we go back into that, we probably won't get back out. Did anyone ever mention a muster point?"

"A what?"

"Like a meet-up place if we were to get separated?"

No one had said anything to me, but maybe Chloe heard someone talking about going somewhere else.

"No," she wore a look of intense concentration. "Wait, I forgot. When you went on your supply run, we caught some words on the radio. The voice mentioned a safe place, we couldn't make it out too clearly, but I think they said somethin' like Hargrove?"

"Is that a town?"

"Dunno. It was real static-y."

I don't remember a town named Hargrove from the few times I glossed over the maps. Maybe it was a building? If it even was a safe haven.

"Did Zoe or Darren say anything about this Hargrove place?"

"Darren said it was probably a recordin'."

Then why hadn't we heard it before? There was no need to voice my doubt and get Chloe's hopes up. The sound of skin dragging along glass made me jump in my seat. I turned to see an infected with its jaw missing, banging at my window like he was bumming for change. The tendons that once held his jaw were now dangling freely, resembling discolored spaghetti.

I fished into my pocket and pulled out my extra magazine, replacing the empty one in my gun.

"Plug your ears," I commanded, and Chloe fists balled around her ears.

With the window rolled down just enough for the muzzle of the gun, I pulled the trigger. The infected's head whipped back. The smell of rot mixed with the scent of gun powder wafted through the window opening. My ears were ringing from the shot, like someone was banging wind chimes in my head to a bad version of *Beat It*.

Chloe was mouthing something to me, but I had no idea what she was trying to say. It took a good minute before I realized she wasn't mouthing words; she was actually speaking them.

"That was loud," I heard around the bells in my head.

I nodded, not sure if I would be able to speak without making my temples explode in pain. I started the car again, not having any idea of what the hell I was doing. It was like being back in my first year of university all over again, except I had another to care about besides myself this time around.

Chapter 28

We had been on the abandoned interstate for over an hour with no sign of anyone from our group. I was quickly running out of options as the gas gauge continued to count down like an executioner before he pulled the electric chair switch. The sun would eventually set, and I couldn't have us out here in the open, sleeping in the car. We needed to find a house or some place that we could temporarily secure.

Chloe spoke up. "Where we goin'?"

I took a deep breath. "I don't know."

She shot me a look like she couldn't contemplate my level of stupidity, "Well that's helpful."

You can't hit a child. You can't hit a child. "Then what does the all mighty Chloe suggest?" I retorted and realized I was arguing with a kid.

"Dunno, but just drivin' is stupid."

I clenched my jaw. "Okay, well how about we take the next exit?"

"And then do what?"

"Well we need to find a place to sleep and some food. We should keep the stuff I brought as emergency rations."

"And then what?"

I breathed through my nose. "I don't know."

"You say that a lot."

This was not going anywhere.

"Can you look in the glove box and see if John has a map in there?"

Chloe unlatched the box and started to rummage through the contents. "I don't see nothin'."

I propped open the center console. "See if there's anything in here."

"Nope."

"Crap."

I needed a map or something as a rough guide. John, and to a lesser extent Taylor, had attempted to teach me the ways of the map reader. I wasn't absolutely hopeless at it now.

"That sign says Gibson, 20 miles," Chloe pointed out.

"So I guess that's our first stop."

There were no signs of life on the interstate, which could be taken both ways. There were no signs of Ethan's truck either. I recognized the stretch of road from our recent supply run, and I prayed that we didn't run into the psychos from the police station. Duson was still a good two hours down the road, but they may be on the move. Thinking about them made me itch to turn off of the interstate.

After a bit, we went down the turnoff, a small town greeting us. The streets were as lifeless as the interstate and a measly few cars lined the road leading into town. The store fronts were closed up, a few windows smashed in along the avenue.

Nothing moved, except for the few roaming infected. All towns had become ghost towns. It was hard to believe almost three months ago this place would have been busy with life. I turned down a residential area, side-swiping an infected in a torn apron with a cat print. None of the houses we passed looked severely damaged, but it was hard to tell.

"What are we doin'?"

"We're going to find a house to secure for the night. Gather some supplies and find me a map."

"Then what?"

I hated when kids asked questions all the time. Especially when I didn't have an answer for them.

"Try to see what this Hargrove place is. Maybe it's a town or a building. It's kind of the only lead we have right now."

"Then we should get another radio, too."

"Good idea." Chloe smiled at my praise.

I had no idea how to go about this. Should I secure a house and leave her there while I went to find what we needed? Or should I bring her with me, in case something happened to her while I was gone? Neither choice was ideal.

We found ourselves in an older residential area. I pulled up to a house that was somewhere in the middle of the round cul-de-sac. There was an old Ford Taurus parked in the driveway. Judging from the grime that coated it, the vehicle had been there for a while. The house looked intact; no busted windows or boarding up. I turned off the engine and peered around us.

A straggling infected was slowly shuffling toward us. Chloe stared at me wide-eyed as the decayed thing got closer. I reached into the back for my bag and pulled out my new hunting knife.

"Stay here."

I took a deep breath to steel my nerves, and then exited the car. The door clicked softly behind me. I could hear the gurgling sound the infected was making; she was maybe twenty feet away. The knife was gripped tight in my stressed fist and once again I found myself missing my Berettas with the silencers attached.

The late afternoon sun was illuminating the infected from behind, so I had to squint to keep a steady eye on it. I cast my eyes downward, and they landed on the rake that was left abandoned on the neighbour's front yard. I jogged over to retrieve it, and the infected followed my movement. With the claw end held up, I started toward the oncoming infected. It reached for me at the exact moment I raised the rake like a bat and let it swing. The thing made a low, squealing sound as the metal pegs connected with its face. My arm shook with the force, but the infected was still flung to the ground.

The rake broke in two from the contact. Wood splinters flew all around me like confetti and I was left with a short spear. *Waste not, want not.* I twirled the broken handle so that the sharp edge was facing the ground. I stepped over the female infected and brought it down with all the strength I could muster. The broken end landed roughly where her right eye was, taking up the socket completely.

Her limbs stopped moving, and murky blood dribbled from the wound. I placed the back of my hand against my mouth, trying to block out the smell and keep myself from hurling. *Do I do something with the body?* I wasn't sure if it would attract other people or not. I grabbed the things' legs and dragged her toward the opposite houses. They had some bushes that lined property that were now badly overgrown. They would do for hiding a body.

Dear God, what has my life come to?

A freshly killed corpse would signal to other survivors that there were living people nearby and I didn't want that. I was huffing from the exertion when I returned to the car.

Chloe made a face as I opened the car door. "That was gross."

"You shouldn't have watched that." I was doing a terrible job babysitting.

"You never said to close my eyes."

"It was implied."

"What's that mean?"

I sighed. "Never mind. Just stay here while I scope out the house."

"Should I close my eyes?"

I shot her a look, "No, you need to keep an eye out. If anything comes, I want you to duck down and keep quiet."

She gulped and nodded.

"Pass me that bag, please."

Chloe rooted in the back seat and passed me the plastic bag with the ammo in it. I quickly reloaded my empty magazine and slipped out the one currently in my gun to top up. *I should have kept that rake.* I didn't want to have to use the gun because it would draw in the unwanted attention.

"I wasn't kidding. Stay here. And lock it after I close the door." I pointed at Chloe, ironically the way my mother used to do to me, so she knew I was serious.

"I will."

I closed the car door and heard the lock mechanism spring into place. I had the gun in my hand, as I tentatively approached the house. There was no movement inside; the curtains were left wide open. The porch stairs creaked under my feet as I approached the house. I peered in the big living room window. There was still no movement inside, so I tested the door and of course it was locked.

Going back down the stairs, I decided to try the back entrance. The grass was overgrown, and weeds had taken over the yard from the lack of maintenance. I unlatched the lock on the gate and stepped into the backyard. It was just as overgrown as the front. Children's toys were lying all over, and I had to step over a bike on the pathway.

I glanced around the fenced backyard before I stepped in any further. There were no infected, just a rusty swing set stood toward the back. The swings were moving slightly from the breeze. The house had sliding doors, so I tried them out. When they slid open, I let out a breath in relief; I didn't want to have to smash any windows.

The inside was musty and hot from being locked up for so long and not even having a window cracked. I stood still for a few moments to see if I heard anything rustling. Silence. I entered the kitchen and moved toward the front door with my gun still gripped in my hands. I flipped the deadbolt in case I needed to make a quick escape out front.

The main floor wrapped around the whole house, so I started there with my inspection. It was clear; next was upstairs. The old staircase groaned, as I walked up to the landing. I started with the rooms on the left and worked my way down. Sweat was running down my temples from the oppressive heat. We would have to open up some windows if we were going to stay the night.

There was no rotting smell, which was always a good sign. A body stuck in this heat would have stunk up the entire house. All the rooms were clear; I even made sure to check the closets. The main bedroom was in disarray, as if they had left in a hurry and there was a boy's room that was a complete pig sty.

I ran back down the stairs to grab Chloe from the car. "Come on," I said when I opened the back door to the car.

Together we lugged in the few bags we had, which wasn't much. I locked the door behind us and closed the curtains throughout the house. I decided to open some windows upstairs to let the breeze in. We plunked down the bags in the middle of the living room.

"Are we goin' to sleep here?" Chloe looked up at me.

"Yeah. Later I'll drag the couch in front of the door and push the table up against the back doors. Maybe we can drag a mattress down here so we can stay on the main floor."

"Are we goin' into town?"

"I think I should go by myself."

Chloe ran to me and grabbed my arm. "You can't leave me here by myself!" She looked like she was on the verge of tears again.

"Chloe, I can't be worrying about watching you when I need to watch for the infected," I tried to reason in the calmest voice I could muster.

"No!" Now she was crying.

I kneeled down to her level. "You will be safer here. I will make sure you're secure before I leave."

She shook her head defiantly. "Please don't."

My head was swimming with turmoil. Both choices were less than ideal. Chloe was scared, and what if something happened to me? Then she would be stuck here by herself. But then again if I brought her, something could happen to her. She sniffed and launched herself at me. I patted her head awkwardly as she clung to me.

"Okay, fine. But you have to stay right beside me and do whatever I say without hesitation. You think you can manage that?"

She nodded eagerly as she unlatched from me. This was going to be a long day.

Chapter 29

I rooted through the decorative bowl by the front door and found a set of keys that opened both the front and back doors and a spare key for the Taurus. During our exploration of the house, we found a decent amount of supplies. When the owners had left, they had only packed like they were going on a trip. Bad for them, good for us. Even the medical cabinet was still full, so I emptied the contents into one of our bags.

Chloe grimaced when she saw that the child living here was a boy. "Do I have to wear boy clothes?"

"Would you rather wear what you have on for who knows how long?"

I had it much worse. The lady of the house was very...old-fashioned. Her wardrobe reflected the closet of an old lady, not the thirty-something mother smiling in the family photos lining the walls. Looks like mom jeans must have been too risqué around these parts.

"You think you have it bad?" I turned to Chloe showing her the hideous floral dress with ruffles and all.

"That looks like somethin' my grandma would wear," she cracked a smile.

After some digging, I managed to find a couple of shirts that would have to do, but I refused to wear the long, ankle skirts she seemed to have an abundance of. They were a tripping hazard. The only thing of use I found in the boy's room was a sleek, aluminum bat.

I had spotted a general store on the main drag when we had entered the town, guessing it was about a five-minute drive from our hideout. It would be longer on foot and limit what we could get, but it would attract less unwanted attention than having the sound of an engine roaring through town. As long as I got a map, I didn't care how long it took.

We could use some more food to add to the dried and canned goods we had found in the house. There was a full flat of water bottles in the pantry, which was probably the best find so far, but I still wanted to get as much as I could get my hands on. There was no guarantee for food anymore, so we had to become hoarders. Also I wanted to see if there was a hardware store on the main drag so that I could see about some more guns and ammo.

"I miss Ethan," Chloe sniffed, bringing me out of planning mode.

"I miss him, too, and all the others."

Every other time I had lost Zoe, whether it was at the bar or on campus, I would just text her, and she'd immediately respond. Now, we no longer had that luxury. Even if the cell towers miraculously started working again, I'd be screwed since my cellphone had been in the backpack I'd lost at the police station.

I hoped Zoe was okay, safe with the others. This wasn't like when she would take off with a guy from the bar, and I'd worry about her becoming another body stuffed in a freezer; this time I really had no idea where to start looking. She was my last lifeline to my old world. *Please be alive. Please let them all be alive.*

"Do you think we'll find 'em?"

"I hope so."

"I told Ethan about the recordin' too, you know."

I perked up. That was the best news I had heard in a while.

"When did you tell him about it?" More importantly, why had he not mentioned it to me? Was I the only one who didn't get any information told to them? This irked me to no end.

"A few days ago when I remembered it. He said Darren was probably right about it bein' a recordin' and all."

"This is very good news."

"You think he'll go there?"

"I hope so. It's the only lead we all have. I just need to figure out what this Hargrove place is."

Chloe hopped up. "I saw a radio in the kitchen."

I listened to her run across the living room and pad around in the kitchen. Chloe returned with an old fashioned radio that had a bent, silver antenna sticking up.

"It runs on batteries," she announced. "See, no cord."

She held the thing up proudly then plunked it down on the coffee table. We gathered around as the room was filled with the hissing of the radio frequency. Slowly, she turned the channel dial. After a few minutes, it became apparent that no miracle recording would pop up and say, "Hey you, go to this address. Here are the directions."

Chloe scowled at the radio once the knob had reached its last channel. I sighed. Nothing was ever that easy.

"Looks like we're on our own. But do you remember what channel it was on when you heard it?"

"No. But I scanned through 'em like this last time."

That means it wasn't a recording, which meant someone was making the announcement, and you had to be alive to do that. Maybe there were lots of people there. Maybe there would be finally some order and even answers. I had to stop from getting too ahead of myself. Hope was a powerful thing, especially when it was crushed.

I wondered how far a radio signal could carry. Too bad I didn't have Google to ask. The chances are that whatever this Hargrove place was, it wasn't too far. I guess we shouldn't go barreling down the interstate too far away after all. I stood up suddenly.

"All right, let's get this trip over with."

Chloe nodded sternly and flicked off the radio. Stale silence filled the room once again. I made sure we had eaten and drank some water before we left, so we had the energy we needed. I was nervous putting my gun in the back of my waistband, like they always do in the movies, but I saw no other option. The safety was on. I made sure of that. Chloe had put on the Transformers backpack she found, and I had on the faded denim one I found in the closet by the front door. With my new aluminum bat in hand, we left the house through the backyard.

There was no gate leading to the back alley behind the house, so I placed a patio chair by the dark brown, solid fence to use to hop over. Then I tossed another chair on the other side, so we could get back up again. I helped Chloe over and down, then jumped myself. The ground was hard and unforgiving, making my ankles sting from the impact.

"You okay?" Chloe asked, concerned that I had already injured myself.

"I think I'll live. Now keep an eye out and stay right beside me."

I righted the plastic chair I had tossed over and pushed it up against the back of the fence. We started our walk down the dirt path that doubled as a back alley. If we kept going west, we would get back to the avenue that leads to Main Street. The breeze was rolling around stray garbage, making me tense from the noise of the rustling. Chloe was practically glued to my side, both of her hands knotted around the straps of her backpack.

I already regretted bringing her out with me.

I gripped my unused bat tight in my hand; the gun would have to be a last resort. Our feet scraped along the dirtied path, our breathing deep. Being out in the open like this made me feel naked and scared. I didn't like it.

I heard the rasping before I saw it. Chloe gasped and grabbed onto me. An infected was reaching toward us, a mixture of bodily fluids running down its face. The thing's ratty coat was snagged on a board that had dislodged from a fence. I led Chloe as far away from the grabbing hands as the alley would manage.

"Do we just leave it there?" Chloe asked, just barely above a whisper.

"It's stuck, no point in wasting time."

Finally, I spotted the paved road at the end of the alley. I peered out. There were two infected stumbling in the middle, aimlessly wandering.

"Stay right beside me," I said again for emphasis.

We took a right and jogged down the sidewalk; old habits die hard I guess. Both heads turned toward us and started in on our direction.

"They're comin'!" Chloe latched her hand onto my shirt, gripping the fabric.

"You have to let go, Chloe."

I had to pry her stiff fingers from my clothing. I couldn't have her weight holding me back if I had to take out those two in a hurry. She reluctantly let go, and the fabric was wrinkled from where she had held on. I grabbed her hand with my free one and dragged her along. There was no way I should waste time in dealing with those two.

We kept up a good pace and soon the two infected were just a figure on the horizon. They would undoubtedly catch up to us, but I would have to deal with that later. One more right turn and we would come to the street we needed. I pushed us up against the corner of the first building and peeked around it. The road was lined with shops on both sides; the angled parking in front was empty except for an old Chevy and a newer Buick.

I did a rough count and came up with eight visible infected. I'm sure there was more hiding all over. The general store was housed right in the middle on the left side of the street; the building was bigger than all the rest. It's pointed front sign stood up above the rest of the roofs. A hardware store was further down from us on the right side, luckily the side we were currently on. I turned back to Chloe.

"Here's what we're going to do. We're going to go to the hardware store first, then hit up the general store on our way back. We're going to follow this sidewalk and you're going to stay to my right."

All the infected seemed to be congregating to the left, leaving the right side clear for now. As soon as they heard us, that would change. So the route to the hardware store was the best opinion. Chloe nodded at my directions.

I took a deep breath, "All right, let's go."

We turned the corner, Chloe to my right so that I was on one side of her and the buildings were to her other side. Walking briskly, I had us hunch down so that we attracted as little attention as possible. Along our path there was an infected slumped up against one of the buildings, his legs blocking the side walk. I put out a hand to stop Chloe.

"Hold up."

I handed her the bat and unsheathed the hunting knife I had stuck in my pocket. The thing looked like it wasn't moving, as I approached it with caution. I glanced around, and it appeared that the other infected still hadn't clued into our presence, yet. Using the tip of my sheathed hunting knife, I poked the thing in its temple. The head slouched to the side, away from me. It was truly dead.

I motioned for Chloe to come to me, and she hurried over. I held her hand as she stepped over the unmoving legs and then I climbed over myself. She stared wide-eyed at the dead infected the whole time; I had to tug on her hand to get her moving again. We hurried along and reached the hardware store. I pulled on the silver handle and the door opened. I held it ajar and peered inside. The only light was coming in from the giant display windows, but it was enough to illuminate the small store.

I ushered Chloe in and closed it gingerly behind us.

"What's that smell?" Chloe grimaced as she covered her nose.

I scrunched up my own nose as the odor reached me. That could only be one thing. There was a dead body in here and it had been in here for a while.

"Stay right here," I pointed to the spot she was standing on.

I took back the bat from her and moved to the far left. I quickly peered down the four aisles made from metal grate shelves; it really was not a big store. It looked clear, so I had Chloe come over to me. The glass and wood sales counter lined the back wall and behind it was empty gun racks. *Shit.* The shelf that held the boxed ammo was almost picked clean as well.

There was a white door behind there labeled *Employees Only.* I lifted up the countertop that doubled as a door so we could get behind the counter. Various shells littered the floor; I could feel them under the sole of my shoes. The decaying smell was getting even stronger, and I had to lift the collar of my shirt over my nose. Chloe's eyes were watering from the smell. I held up my hand for her to stop.

"Stay behind the counter and yell if you see anything."

Judging from the intense smell, I had a hunch that something nasty was waiting for us behind that door. There was no way Chloe should see that. Once I made sure she was out of eye-shot, I went to turn the handle. The smell hit me like a physical thing. I turned to the side, unable to stop the contents of my stomach from coming up. Once I was done heaving, I straightened back up, desperately wanting mouthwash. Chloe was as far away as she could get while still behind the counter.

I breathed through my mouth, as I opened the door further, allowing in as much light as I could. Death was all that greeted me.

Chapter 30

Of all the things I had done. Of all the things I had seen. This was beyond the worst I could imagine. Just thinking about it hurt. *Is this what humanity has come to? Is this what we've been reduced to?* This sight would haunt me for the rest of my life. It wasn't an infected feeding on some poor sap. It wasn't a group of infected trapped back here. No, it was much worse.

Scrawled on the back wall in dried blood, blotted with fingerprints were the words, "And Like Him, We Too Shall Rise." In front of that, a scene pulled from the crime section of a newspaper looked back at me. Two small children were decaying on the ground, a hole adorning each of their foreheads. Next to them was the badly rotted body of a woman with a matching bullet wound, a Bible clutched in her dead hands. Across from them, slumped to the side, was a male figure with a fallen handgun at his side. The wall behind him was stained with blood and brain matter.

I stood there frozen, unable to move. *Why?* The only word echoing in my head.

"What is it?"

"Stay there!"

Whatever was in my voice had Chloe stop in her tracks. I quickly shut the door, wishing I could scrub the image from my brain. Nothing could prepare you for something like that. I rubbed at my eyes; maybe I could force the image out.

"What was it?"

"Drop it, Chloe."

And to my surprise, she did. I floundered for a moment, the shock throwing me off. I turned to the shelf and tried to distract myself by searching for 9mm ammo. I managed to find a box and a half, but all the guns were cleaned out.

Except for the handgun in there, my brain cruelly reminded me. There was no way I was going back in that room; it wasn't worth it. And I'm sure it would be considered bad luck using that gun. A shadow passed over us as an infected crossed in front of the display window.

"Hold still," I whispered.

We both froze hoping the thing would move on. It turned its head toward the window, tilting slightly, as if curious. With jerky movements, the infected continued on shuffling past the window. I swallowed loudly. We needed to cut our losses and get to the general store, which would mean taking out those infected.

Did I risk the gun for that? Or try to take them out melee style? With that many, a gun seemed like the easiest way to take them out. But that meant noise, so we would have to hurry in the store in case more infected showed up.

We left the counter behind and started back through the aisles. I handed Chloe the aluminum bat. It was light and not too big for her stature. I had spotted an axe on our way down the aisles, so I decided to upgrade. The axe was heavier but manageable. It would do more damage than the bat and that's all that mattered.

I couldn't wait to leave this building, I was desperate for it. I looked out the window and spotted the infected that had passed by. He was just slightly to the right of the building. I would have to take him out first.

"Chloe, I'm going to get you to hold the door open. If anything happens or an infected comes near you, you close it okay?"

"What about you?" She looked up at me with concerned eyes.

"I will be fine. I can outrun these few infected. If that happens, I will lead them away and come back, you understand?"

She nodded. I opened the door, and she gripped it tight to hold it open. The infected turned its head toward me and made a gurgling sound, as he approached. Its foot was bent at an odd angle, so he limped toward me rather slowly. I wound up the axe and let it swing, as I used my forward momentum to take it out. The blade landed soundlessly in the infected's neck. No blood spurted, and I could see the spinal column once I yanked the axe free.

With its arms still reaching for me, the infected fell backwards. I assumed the noises it was making meant it was angry, but I didn't give it time to get back up again. I placed my foot on its chest and brought the axe down. The head came clean off and rolled to the right of body. To make it even more grotesque, the head was still snapping away with what was left of its rotten teeth.

I flipped the axe in my hand and brought the blunt side down on the severed head. The forehead caved in like a cracked egg, and then the snapping sound stopped. I whipped the axe around, trying to dislodge some of the blood and skin from the blade.

The other roaming infected seemed oblivious to what just happened, which was fine with me. I pulled the handgun from my waistband and clicked off the safety. The infected were spread out, making for good target practice. But I needed my aim to be spot on, so that they didn't all start to come after me when I fired.

I propped the axe up against the tailgate of the old Chevy and started toward the nearest infected. Using both hands to steady my aim, I took the first shot. It rang true, and the infected dropped like a stone. Then all heads were turned to me. I took the next one, but I would have to move closer to get the rest.

They all started to shuffle toward me, and I walked to greet them. I felt like a crazy person, heading toward the danger rather than running from it. I also felt pretty stupid, as I basically ran around them in circles, picking them off one by one. Ten shots later, I was surrounded by slain bodies. My breathing was ragged from the exertion and adrenaline, my arms limp by my side. My chest heaved, as I peered down at my morbid handy work.

I looked like a sole survivor of a bomb blast, surrounded by all the fallen corpses. Chloe poked her head out of the doorway, and I waved her out. She ran to me faster than I would have thought possible. I gathered up my axe, and we silently headed to the general store.

"We have to make this fast. There was no way that noise wouldn't attract other infected in the town. Remember, we need to find a map."

I ejected the empty magazine and slipped in the full one. Cupping my hands around my eyes, I gazed into the general store bay window. There didn't seem to be any movement, but I could only see so far. As I opened the front door, the bell hanging above it chimed, signaling our entrance. *Stupid small town stores.* I gritted my teeth as my ears picked up the sound of movement coming from one of the furthest aisles.

Chloe was right behind me, gripping her bat like she was ready to swing. I just hope I wasn't too close when she did. I readied my axe as the sound got louder. Stepping toward the aisle, I could see a rather large, masculine infected wearing a shopkeeper's apron. It was torn and dirty, just like the rest of him. His beard was patchy around his emaciated face.

I heard Chloe gasp behind me. The thing regarded me with interest, almost like he was savoring his prey. It was eerie.

But I'd had enough of this. Enough of waiting to be attacked.

Letting out my own yell, I ran for him and swung with everything I had. The axe blade embedded in the infected's massive chest with a hollowed *thud,* and he let out a hiss as he was knocked back from the impact. The shelf behind him shook with the force and started to teeter.

Products on the shelf fell into the aisles, like they were abandoning ship. The axe was still imbedded in its chest, so I lifted up my foot and used him as leverage to yank the axe free. His arms tried to reach for me, but he was thrown further back from the momentum. This time the shelf decided to tip completely. I watched as the metal shelving toppled to the side, falling into the next one. I had started a chain reaction. All four shelves had fallen over, like dominos, except much louder.

I quickly turned back, worried that Chloe had been squished. She had made herself as small as possible and was wedged safely in the corner by the front door. I looked back to see the infected lying on top of a pile of products, beside the now angled shelf. It reached for me again, as if I would just come to him.

So I did just that.

I brought the axe down again and again. Thick, congealed blood sprinkled everywhere. Pieces of skin and cartilage were flying around, but I couldn't bring myself to stop. I kept swinging that axe, long after the infected had stopped moving.

Anger.

It's all your fault.

Frustration.

It's not fair.

Sadness.

We are all doomed.

With a strangled cry, I let it all loose on this infected. Faintly, the sound of the blade clanging against the linoleum floor reached my ears. By the time my arms stilled, I was out of breath from the effort. My arms burned from the sudden use of so much force. I had to lean a hand against the wall for support, as I caught my breath.

Catching a glimpse of my reflection in the beverage-cooler door made me cringe. Head to toe I was covered in blood and skin clumps. I wiped at the mess on my face, using my sleeve as a rag. When I say the infected was now in pieces, I meant it. He was splattered all over his store and wouldn't be getting back up again. It looked like a massacre and I was the butcher.

Chloe shouldn't have seen that. I couldn't bring myself to look at her. I felt like a monster.

Chapter 31

I swallowed nervously, as I turned to Chloe. Her stare said more than words ever could. She looked terrified of me; like she was worried I needed a next victim.

"It's clear now," was all I managed to croak out.

It took a few seconds before Chloe tore herself from her corner.

"I'm sorry you had to see that."

She looked at me for a second and then nodded. "I'll be fine."

I should really have given her more credit.

I managed to get a lot of the surface goop off, but my clothes were pretty much trash at this point. Still, I tried to get most of it off.

"Do you think we will be able to dig through this?" Chloe asked, as she bent down by some fallen goods.

"I don't think we have time for that. Just the essentials."

I continued down the clear aisle, aiming for the non-food items that looked like they were at the back of the store. I heard Chloe unzip her backpack and shove some stuff in.

"Stay close," I prompted and she ran to me as she slipped her pack on again.

The back of the store had some skylights, which was rather lucky considering the sun from the display windows didn't reach back here very well. The back shelves were out of the line of fire and were still upright.

The store place was pretty picked over. Gaping holes adorned the shelves where product should have been. I slipped off my backpack and started stuffing in soap and a few other hygiene items. Clearly I would need that tonight.

"Look!" Chloe exclaimed and I grabbed for my axe that I had set down.

She was pointing to a white metal spinning rack. Maps. And there were still some left. I hurried over and patted Chloe's head.

"Good job."

"Eww, you didn't get stuff in my hair did you?" She wiped at the top of her head.

"Now you can smell like me." I forced a small grin and her face scrunched up.

There was one map of Louisiana left and a couple of different local maps. And they were the laminated ones, too. I quickly stowed them safely into my backpack. Now, that meant we could grab what we wanted. They had a small pharmacy area that had been picked clean, but I scavenged some gauze, Benadryl and basically everything I could. To my surprise, they had some generic clothing as well. This really was a general store.

I found a grey hoodie, sweatpants and some V-neck T-shirts, which I rolled up and stuffed into my bulging bag. I guess I was going to stay looking like a university student for a little longer. I suppose when shit hit the fan almost three months ago, people weren't looking for clothes. We went back to the food area and grabbed what we could still reach. In less than ten minutes, we had gathered a collection of canned and packaged goods; nothing that would be considered particularly nutritious, though. I had spotted some of those reusable mesh bags and we each filled one to carry.

I needed to be able to swing into action if need be, and Chloe could only carry so much. I threw the bag over my shoulder, grunting at the extra weight. Chloe was able to wear her backpack and the bag with more ease. Dreading the next part, we crept back to the front of the store. New infected had appeared further down the main drag, right where we needed to go.

"Shit."

"What?"

"The infected have already started to migrate here."

There were only three that I could see, but I was willing to bet more were on their way. *How am I going to pull this off?*

"All right, you really have to stay by me this time."

"I've stayed by you the whole time," Chloe shot me a droll look.

Does nothing faze this kid?

I gave the bag on my shoulder one more heave for good measure and tore down the stupid silver bell above the door. The last thing we needed was literally for a dinner bell to ring. I bid this place fucking adieu and tore through the door. We kept up a brisk walk, not wanting to tire out in case we really did have to run. I directed us away from the few infected that started to stroll down the main road.

Rounding the corner of the building on the edge of the street once again, we ran into a group of infected. I immediately stopped and twirled to the side. Using the few seconds of confusion to my advantage, I grabbed the strap of Chloe's backpack, yanking her to me and basically pulling her around the infected. They started after us, some moving faster than the others.

"I think we're going to have to run some."

I picked up my pace, making sure Chloe was right beside me and could keep up. I spotted the alley entrance we needed just a bit down, but proving with my theory that the universe was out to get me, it was blocked with a good few infected. Basically there were infected in our way and behind us. The street was beginning to become saturated with them.

"Bailey, I'm scared," Chloe tearfully exclaimed.

Even she could see how screwed we were.

"We're almost at the alley."

I didn't have the time or the capacity to make meaningless reassurances at the moment. I jerked to a stop a few meters from the alley, planning on using my axe again. The bag I was carrying slid off my shoulder and scratched down my arm, leaving angry red welts in its wake. I suppose it was heavy enough to use as a weapon.

I tossed my axe toward the infected guarding the alley entrance and they peered down at it as it clanged to the ground.

"You just threw your weapon away!" Chloe screeched.

"No I didn't."

I ran to the infected and swung my heavy, filled to the brim bag at the first one. I had the odd urge to yell, "This is my purse," at them as I brandished the bag like a weapon. *Maybe I am starting to lose my mind.* The infected went flying into the other two and they all fell down in a mass of limbs. A few cans popped out the top, but I didn't bother retrieving them.

"Come on!" I yelled as bending to pick up the axe.

Chloe ran to me, her bags jerking up and down. The alley had more infected lying in wait for us and the others had started to catch up and were now pouring into alleyway after us. I used my axe to poke at the ones that got too close, having to only stop to take one out that was directly in front of us. I couldn't afford to get bogged down.

The house we were aiming for loomed in the distance.

"I see it!" Chloe huffed.

I had to crack open the skull of one female infected blocking the fence we needed. I thanked my past self for having the foresight to toss a chair over. My brain must have been working overtime. Using most of my reserve strength, I tossed my heavy bag over the pointed fence, then Chloe's.

"Hurry!" Chloe yelled.

I had to knock back an infected that had snuck up on me with the butt of my axe. Seeing no other option, I stomped my heel down on the middle of its skull when it hit the ground. A flash of a memory shot through my brain, reminding me of the time Darren did that and how disgusted I was.

Chloe climbed onto the chair and I gave her a boost. Her leg and arm latched over the ragged boards at the same time I was steam rolled by an infected. I heard her scream as I hit the ground, shoving at the body trying to tear into me. Drool and fowl breath hit me, but I was able to shove it to the side. I scrambled to pull the hunting knife from my pants.

By the time the knife was clear of the sheath, the infected had crawled back to me. I shoved it back and rolled on top of it, rearing up my arms to bring the knife down. It landed in the things mouth and went out through the back of its head. It gurgled for a bit and then stopped moving. I jumped up and saw that Chloe was no longer on the fence. She must have fallen to the other side.

I climbed up on the chair and threw my backpack and axe over. I don't know where the strength came from this time, but I was able to pull myself up enough with my arms that I could hook my leg over. My pants snagged on the pokey fence when I brought my other leg over, tearing right down the seam. This made me lose my balance, and I toppled the rest of the way down, landing on my side. Pain shot up my whole right side, especially in my elbow, which I had sticking out as I flailed down. I quit breathing as the pain made my eyes water. I had to force my lungs to start again, praying that nothing was broken.

Wheezing, I managed to sit up. New pain shot down my body. I was able to focus long enough to stand up and spot Chloe. Dragging my backpack onto my screaming shoulder, I went to usher her into the house.

"Bailey," she said weakly.

I looked down at her. She was clasping her left arm tightly. Bright, red blood was pouring from her arm, staining her clothes and dripping onto the overgrown grass.

Oh God.

Chapter 32

Her face was paler than I had ever seen it, she was probably in shock. I ran to her.

"Oh god, oh god," I started to panic.

I tried to lift up her right hand to see how bad it was, but as soon as I did, blood started to spurt anew. It looked bad – out of my realm bad. It was deeper than any cut I had ever gotten. That fucking, splintering fence must have sliced her arm open when she fell.

"Let's get inside," I had to really focus to keep the panic out of my voice.

"Am...am I goin' to be okay?" Chloe's eyes were glassy.

"Of course." I had no way of knowing that.

We left a bloody trail all the way to the sliding door. My hand slipped on the door handle from all the blood that coated it; I had to wipe it off on my already ruined pants. This was too much blood for an adult, let alone a small child. I flung open the door and sat her down on a kitchen chair. I started to pull open all the drawers searching for a towel. After I tried all of them, I finally opened the right one.

I forced Chloe's hand away and shoved the sunflower print tea towel on the bleeding wound.

"It hurts!" Chloe screamed, and I had never felt so powerless. She started to kick out her legs, and I had to jump to the side to avoid them. Blood was staining the towel at an alarming rate.

"I know it hurts Chloe, but you have to push on this as hard as possible okay? I'm going to run upstairs and grab something."

I ran off before she could protest. I flew up the stairs, into the little boy's room. He had to own a belt that I could use as a tourniquet. I threw open and rummaged through his dresser, clothes flying everywhere. I found a faux leather one that would work, so I ran back down the stairs in a flurry.

Chloe was now screaming and crying, the initial shock having worn off. She was like a banshee; her pain was palpable. "Make it stop!" Her face was now red from all the screaming.

She needed to stop yelling. We already had all those infected in the alley. No doubt they were banging and pushing on the fence trying to get in.

"I'm going to tie this around your arm okay? It will help stop the blood, so I can treat it."

I looped my arm under hers and latched the belt, tightening it just past the elbow.

"OW!" She flailed, but I tugged it as tight as it could go.

"I know it hurts Chloe, but this will stop the bleeding," I pleaded with her.

She weakly pushed and scratched at me, trying to get me to release the belt. But even as she was doing that, I could see that the blood flow was slowing when I lifted the tea towel.

"See it's working," I pointed out. "Now I need you to be really brave right now and hold this belt."

I realized she had more strength than most adults would, when she grabbed the end of the belt I was pulling on and started to tug.

"Good. Now we need antiseptic."

I ran to the living room where the stuff we grabbed from the medicine cabinet was currently sitting. There was a brown bottle of peroxide that I needed to find. Chloe was going to hate this even more. I made a mess of our bags as I rooted through them to grab the bottle. Once I got back to the kitchen, I took out the gauze we pilfered from the general store.

All this was going to do was disinfect the wound. It was deep enough that she needed stitches and there was no way I could administer them to a flailing child.

Superglue.

Darren's tidbit from when he patched up Ethan roared into my head. I had spotted a tube when I was going through the kitchen drawers. I went back to the various open drawers and found the rolled up tube of superglue. This would have to do. I took a deep breath, realizing I would more than likely have to hold her down.

"Chloe, I need you to lie on the floor."

"Why?" she demanded through tears and snot.

"I can't put the disinfectant on properly unless the arm is flat out," I lied through my teeth.

She looked at me hesitantly, so I tried to hurry her along. I helped her to the floor and she sprawled out. Every time I reached for the wound, she tried to move her arm away. Human instinct I guess, to avoid pain as much as possible.

"I need to hold the belt!" she tried to sit up, but I gently pushed her back down.

"Don't worry about that. I just need you to be brave, can you do that?"

She looked at me; tears were running down her face like a faucet.

"Just make it stop, please!"

I kneeled down beside her with all my supplies. "Now Chloe, I don't want to scare you or lie to you, but this will sting. The peroxide will kill any germs in the cut; we can't have it getting infected."

She tried to move away from me again. "Wait–"

Before she could finish, I placed my knee on her upper forearm to hold it in place and poured some of the clear liquid onto the wound. She thrashed wildly and screamed like I was the one who did it. I kept my hold on her arm with my knee and used my other hand to hold the lower part steady.

"PLEASE STOP! IT HURTS SO BAD!"

I had to try to block out her screaming and pleading for me to stop. It was hard. I felt like I was killing her, but it was for her own good.

The wound hissed and bubbled as the peroxide ate away the germs that had embedded themselves in there. I wiped away the white bubbles and blood with another clean towel I had grabbed. Then poured more peroxide directly into the wound this time. She kicked and jerked even harder, but I was stronger and used my weight to keep her arm in place.

The bleeding had slowed immensely, and I took that as a good sign. Her breathing was labored from all the fighting against me and screaming.

"Please... just stop," she tearfully pleaded.

I noticed the fight was leaving her. I felt like an abuser. The worst person in the world.

Finally, after another round of peroxide, the fizzing stopped and it no longer reacted to the wound. This was a guess on my part, but I think that meant the disinfectant had done its job. Now was time for the glue. I poured the peroxide on my fingers and scrubbed it in. I needed them to be sterile.

The lid was stuck to the top of the tube, so I had to use the towel for leverage to twist it off. The smell of vinegar reached my nose once the lid came off.

"Is it over?" She sounded so defeated.

"Almost. I just have to make sure the wound closes."

I dabbed a fair amount on my finger tip and spread it slightly on the edges of the wound.

"STOP!" Chloe started screaming and kicking again as I aggravated the sore wound.

Once I figured I got enough on there, I pinched the two sides of the cut together.

"DEAR GOD, MAKE IT STOP!" She was so loud, that I had to take feelings out of the equation.

I shoved my free hand over her mouth to smother her screams.

The look in her eyes said it all: Traitor.

She continued to jerk and scream against my hand, I could feel the vibrations against my palm. All the windows were open along with the back door and those things at the back fence didn't need to be spurred on. I released the wound and it didn't reopen. The glue had worked.

I took my hand off her mouth. "I'm just going to put some gauze around it, and it will be over."

"I hate you!" Chloe spat.

That hurt, twisting up my stomach in knots, but I had a job to do. I wrapped the gauze around a few times and tied it off. As soon as I removed my knee, Chloe shuffled away from me, cradling her bandaged arm. The collar of her shirt was stained with tears and her clothes were matted in her blood. I was a horrible protector. I should never have been here in the first place, should never have been in charge of another human being. I wasn't cut out for this.

I looked down at the mess I had made. The white tiles were stained with blood and peroxide. Dirty towels and opened supplies surrounded me. I had just held down a child while I attempted to treat a serious wound with zero experience. Chloe would have been better off with anyone else but me.

Chapter 33

Chloe huddled as far away from me as possible, like a kicked puppy. Even through her tears and sobs, she managed to shoot me a hateful glare. I swallowed past the lump in my throat and started to clean up the mess, trying to distract myself from what just happened. I left out all the supplies on the table; I would need to re-dress the wound tomorrow. Chloe shot up and ran into the living room. I heard her stomping as she ran up the stairs, away from me.

I didn't blame her. I had handled that poorly, but what else was I to do? I had no idea how to treat a wound of that magnitude, let alone on a kid that wouldn't hold still. I could sit here and try to justify my actions, but the truth was that I should never be responsible for a child. She got injured under my watch. My own side groaned in pain as I moved about. After all that, I was sure my elbow wasn't broken, just really sore and swollen.

The sun was going down fast, like it was in a hurry to get to its evening plans. I didn't hear banging on the sturdy wooden fence anymore, but there was still movement and moaning in the alley. Maybe the infected had forgotten why they were here in the first place or had just given up. Bottom line was that they were still out there. Right in our own backyard took on a whole new meaning.

I felt numb at this point, or felt too much; I couldn't tell the difference. My mind wasn't coping well with the events of this past day. I was running on autopilot, but unfortunately it wasn't a very good program. I felt the way you did when you came to the end of a particularly good book and now didn't know what to feel. Lost. Heartbroken. Empty.

I stumbled to the back doors. In the rush of everything, I had forgotten to close them. The setting sun shone through the spaces in the fence, making the yard appear stripped. Our bags were still lying on the grass, odd items thrown all around the mesh totes. I walked over and started to shove them back in, very aware of the sound of bodies moving slowly on the other side of the fence.

My task became harder, as my vision blurred. Tears were dropping onto my hands, like little liver spots, as I picked up the various cans and boxes. Pain bloomed in my chest. *What have I done?* I wanted to scream. I wanted to yell into the sky a slew of curse words in every language. I wanted to disappear. I gripped the can in my hand and wound my arm back to throw it like I was a pitcher for the MLB.

But I couldn't. Everything I did put us in danger. I lowered my arm in defeat, and then stood up; the bag I was holding flopped over to its side. I started lashing out at the air all around me, like I was a kid throwing a fit. In a way, that's exactly what I was. I needed to inflict pain, so that mine felt small in comparison. I wanted the world to know how shitty I felt.

I picked up my discarded axe and started to whack at the ground with it. Chunks of grass and dirt leapt like grasshoppers fleeing for their lives, from the uneven hole I was making. My body was starting to become heated from my spectacle; I must have looked like a raging lunatic. With a deep breath, I tried to center myself. I dropped the axe and dipped down to pick up the bags. With one in each hand, I walked back over to the house.

I threw the heavy totes inside and their contents rolled all over the floor like a glass of spilt milk. Except milk wouldn't have made that much noise. The infected started to scrape along the fence, alerted by the banging sound.

Fuck it. Let them devour me.

We were all doomed to be food for the worms sooner or later. Why not end it now? I could hear growling coming from the crowd; some had started to lightly bang on the fence. They didn't realize they were powerless to knock over their obstacle with their decaying arms like dried tree branches. But they were powerful enough to take down this world; the irony was almost too much.

Dead, infected people owned this place now. They marched into the streets like all armies before them, except they didn't discriminate. We were all fair game. All races, all colors, all genders. We were all equally screwed.

I slid down the rough outside paneling of the house, resting my head in my hands and wept.

Chapter 34

I managed to get my sobbing under control. The streaks of my tears were drying on my face, making the skin feel dehydrated. Once I shed my last tear for myself, I decided that was enough. Using the outside of the house as leverage, I pushed myself back to my feet and wandered back inside. My little episode had made the pain in my elbow come back with a vengeance and the side I had landed on screamed at me for my stupidity.

The kitchen was filling with shadows; later all we had to keep them at bay were the camping lanterns we found while searching the house. I wiped at my face, embarrassed by my behavior. Not only had I made a fool of myself, I got the infected all worked up right outside the fence. At least they seemed to have calmed down again for the time being. It seems like they have the memory of a goldfish.

I tiptoed back outside for my axe, which was now coated in blood and grass. Once back inside, I flipped the lock on the sliding doors and overturned the kitchen table up against them. If something or someone wanted inside, they would have to work for it. I made sure the front door was dead bolted and pushed the couch in front of it. The sound of the legs scraping across the hardwood floor echoed in the house. At least I didn't have to worry about repairing the damage.

Darkness was starting to set in, and it made me nervous. This would be the first night without the others. I didn't have them to depend on, I had only myself. I found I missed them dearly. We were our own family, looking out for one another. Yet they had abandoned me. Or was I the abandoner? I didn't want to believe that anyone had left anyone behind. Maybe things would have been different if I had stayed behind, maybe they would have turned out exactly the same. There was no way to tell now.

All I could do was hope that they were all alive. What mattered now was surviving and finding our dysfunctional little family.

Taylor smirked at me yet again, laughing to himself about my mishap. How was I to know you couldn't just smoke anything in the meat smoker? You could have smoked salmon, why not smoked trout? I hated the taste of fish and figured at least smoking it would make it edible.

We were all situated around the campfire, the flames blazing like an inferno. Stars had started to peek out through the receding day light, now dotting the sky above us. The cabin was currently airing out the burnt fish smell. If you thought fish smelt bad before, just wait until it started on fire. Ethan had managed to put out the flames before any damage was done to the smoker, which reminded me of a tall safe without the lock on the front.

"Is it useable?" I asked timidly.

Ethan chuckled, "It'll live to smoke another day."

Chloe cocked out her hip. "Why would you think puttin' trout in there on as high as it can go, would be a good idea?"

"You can smoke salmon can't you?" I said to Ethan.

"All right, enough. Nothin' we can do about it now 'cept let the place air out," Ethan interjected.

John and Ethan had gone out earlier to catch the fish; apparently there was a small lake and stream nearby that had a decent-sized fish population. Ethan said normally you wouldn't have been able to take home so many, but there was no fish and wildlife police left to complain. We didn't have to worry about making a run into the city for poles and gear because there was already some stashed in the cabin. We were damn lucky to have run into Ethan; he had pretty much everything we needed out here.

They had a grill set up on top of the fire pit, roasting the rest of the fish. I guess I won't be able to get myself out of eating this.

"Looks like you're not getting out of it this time," Zoe grinned, knowing full well how much I disliked fish.

"Well, I tried."

"I didn't know fish could catch on fire like that," Darren said.

I sighed; I was never going to hear the end of this.

"Hey, you gotta break a few eggs before you can make an omelet, right?" John winked at me, his eyes full of mirth.

"If my clothes stink, you'll be washin' them," Taylor quipped.

"That'll be the day," I snorted. "Maybe they will be the next thing to start on fire."

Chuckles rang out around the camp fire, all while the disgusting fish continued to sizzle.

I smiled at the random memory. I found it strange how you started to recall all the arbitrary memories when you're growing despondent. It's not the bad stuff, but rather the things that remind you what you're living to fight for. We had been through so much that there was no way I was giving up now. I started to feel hopeful.

We will find them.

I started to clean up the mess I had made in the living room when I had torn through the bags looking for the peroxide. Heading back into the kitchen, I went to grab my backpack to sort out. As I rummaged through my backpack, some items fell to the floor, the pink Benadryl package among them.

There was no way Chloe was going get any sleep tonight, not with what had happened and all the pain she must be in. I rooted through the kitchen cabinets for an opaque glass, and then twisted the top off of a water bottle. Using the blunt end of a butter knife, I crushed up two of the small, pink tablets. I mixed the powder with the water, hoping she would just drink it and get some much needed sleep. I grabbed a couple of granola bars as well as some over-the-counter painkillers.

I walked quietly up the stairs, like when I used to tiptoe into the house after going out to the bar. I found Chloe lying on the boy's bed with her back to me. She was sniffing softly.

"Chloe, I know you're mad right now, but you need to eat and drink something," I said, my voice barely above a whisper.

She ignored me, so I just remained in the doorway. Eventually she turned to me, glaring the whole time. As she sat up, she put out her hand for the items. I passed her the glass and she started to chug the contents as I opened the bars for her. With her arm out of commission, she would need some help.

Chloe passed me back the almost empty glass and tore into the first granola bar. After everything that happened, I'm surprised I wasn't just as famished.

"Here, I brought you something for the pain."

She eyed me warily as she chewed her second bar. I passed her two of the white pills and the glass back. She was smart enough to see that she needed the pills and took them without hesitation. She rolled away from me, back to lying on the bed.

I guess I had been dismissed. I hoped she would eventually see that what I did was for her own good. Although, that didn't look like it would be anytime soon. Maybe if she could forgive me, I could forgive myself.

I went down the hall into the main bedroom to find something to sleep in. The husband's large shirts would do. I grabbed a clean white one and the comforter from the bed and headed back downstairs. Even though I badly needed sleep, I would still have to be on alert. I would hear better if I was on the main floor.

I also needed to wash up somehow. You never realize how dependent you are on everyday things until they are forcefully taken from you. I didn't think the shower would work in the house and there was no well like Ethan's cabin. When I was cleaning up our supplies, I remembered the wipes we had scavenged from the store.

It took a whole 12-pack of wipes, but I was able to get the grime off of my skin. I placed my ruined clothes in a plastic bag and threw them in the kitchen garbage. I could smell the heavy baby powder scent clinging to me, but it beat the smell of rotten meat any day.

I lit up the lantern, and the soft glow brightened the room. I made up my bed on the couch, which currently doubled as a brace against the door. Setting out my weapons within reach, I laid down. My stomach growled, finally catching up to all the exertion from today.

I gnawed on a granola bar and some trail mix to appease the hunger. I would kill for some fresh food, but canned peaches would have to do. Luckily we had found a can opener in one of the kitchen drawers, otherwise the canned food would have been useless. I would undoubtedly have butchered the can if I tried to use my hunting knife. After I had stuffed my face, I wobbled back to the couch, dimming the light on the lantern.

Weariness was in my bones. My body was exhausted, and my mind wasn't in the best shape either. *Didn't people say things always look better in the morning?* Somehow, I doubted that would be the case tonight. But as soon as I closed my eyes, sleep took me.

I woke to the sun pouring through the off-white lace curtains. They didn't do a very good job of blocking the light out and they were hideous to boot. I had no idea what time it was, but judging from the stiffness of my body, I had laid in this one position for hours. Everything popped and cracked as I sat up; I felt like I had aged twenty years.

I had meant to go check on Chloe before I fell asleep, so I headed upstairs first. I found her breathing deeply, still fast asleep in the boy's Transformer sheets. Apparently he had been a fan. I went to the bathroom and examined myself in the mirror. My elbow and a good chunk of my right arm were bruised, as was my side. The elbow was also slightly swollen.

I peered at the tub and tried the faucet just to see what would happen. The pipes groaned in the walls, but water started to pour from the tap. It was rusty at first, but cleared after a few seconds. They must still have had water in the tank. I laughed out loud as I plugged the drain and let the tub fill up a bit. The water was freezing since there was no power to heat it up, but it was better than nothing. I turned the tap off, not wanting to waste one drop.

I went down the stairs as fast as my creaky limbs would allow. Snatching up the soap and shampoo, I went back up to my frosty bath. Bathing in my books was a necessity, not an option. The water was only up to my ankles, but that was all I needed. My toes and fingers were almost blue by the time I had cleaned myself off and my teeth were chattering. I toweled off, not bothered in the least. Cold was something I could deal with, especially if it meant I could wash up.

A cleaner reflection looked back at me from the mirror. This was much better. I let the water out and left the supplies there for Chloe to use later. Once back downstairs, I unfolded the maps.

After a good thirty minutes, I tossed the map I had been looking at to the floor in frustration. Nothing was giving hints as to what this Hargrove place was. It wasn't a main building, it wasn't a suburb, it wasn't a park, and it wasn't on there. It wasn't even a fucking street name. How was I supposed to find it?

I felt useless without the Internet. This place might as well have been across the country for all it was worth. With an angry sigh, I returned to the maps. I scanned a local one, a red medical cross icon catching my eye. According to the map, there was a medical center just off of Main Street. This was one of those small towns where everything was either on Main

Street or just off of it. Chloe would need some antibiotics to keep an infection at bay.

It looked like I was making another run into town before we left this place.

Chapter 35

My body really didn't like the idea of moving, but I had no choice. An infection wouldn't just wait for me to get off my ass. Memories of the hospital came flooding back to me, making me even more hesitant. What are the chances the medical center wouldn't be picked over? *Is it worth it?* That was a selfish question. Of course, I had to go.

Now I had to decide if I should walk again or take a vehicle. I had found the spare key to the Taurus sitting in the drive way and could afford to damage that one. It would attract attention, but I didn't think my body was in any shape to be running away from hordes now. And I would get there faster. The alleyway behind the house was still littered with infected, so I would have to leave out the front door. This meant taking the longer way to where I needed to go.

Vehicle it was. I just hoped the owners had left enough gas in it. I began packing for my scavenging trip. I emptied out my backpack and straightened up our supplies. There was a fair sized mound of bags and items taking up room in the living area. If I monitored the provisions, we could easily make them last two weeks. But the question was, do we stay here expecting a miracle to drop into our laps or hit the road? I had no clue where to even start looking for this Hargrove place, and the chances of running into it while driving aimlessly were pretty much nil.

Hopelessness began to haunt me once again. It seemed like it was a constant battle. Not just to keep ourselves from the infected, but to keep ourselves from giving up. It was easy to give up once hope was lost. I wasn't used to making the hard decisions. Before all this shit happened, hard decisions never came up in my old life.

And as much as Ethan was not happy about it, John had made most of our hard decisions. John was a natural leader and the most mature of us, so it was easy to let him steer things. I mean we all had a say in matters, but he had this way about him that made you feel like he knew exactly what he was doing. Maybe I would have been better off right now if we hadn't let John slide into that role so easily.

Not that any of that mattered now. John wasn't here to tell me what the right path was; I had to figure that out for myself. And it made me want to pull my hair out. How John had not gone bald was a mystery.

The sound of shuffling upstairs pulled me from my thoughts. It looks like Chloe was awake. I heard the stairs creak, as she descended down them. She was rubbing at her eyes still yawning from sleep, courtesy of the allergy medication. I picked up a water bottle, twisted off the cap and passed it to her. She took it from me and sat down by all the supplies, rooting through for something to eat. Silent the whole time.

I let her get some food down before I started to talk.

"Chloe, I need to redress your arm."

She froze mid-chew. I glanced away awkwardly, not sure of where I should even be looking.

"It will be quick, I promise."

She didn't say anything, instead gave a little nod and remained seated. I went to the kitchen to grab the peroxide and gauze. She eyed me warily, as I kneeled beside her. She held her arm as far away from her body as possible, as if she didn't want me any closer. I tried to act like it didn't affect me. I tried to handle this like an adult, but it was difficult. I wanted to plead with her that I did it for her own good and that her wound was treated because of me. I wanted to beg for her forgiveness and to stop hating me, but I didn't.

I carefully removed the old, soiled bandage. The wound was an angry shade of red, and I could see the hardened superglue on the surface. The veins that ran from the gash were a lot more visible than before, making it look like thin tentacles slithering from the wound. That couldn't be good. She really did need those antibiotics. I poured some peroxide on the wound, and Chloe hissed in a breath from the contact. Once I cleared off the liquid oozing from the cut, I rewrapped her arm with clean gauze.

"I'm running back into town."

Her head whipped around to look at me.

"According to the map, there's a medical center in town, and I need to get you some antibiotics. You're going to stay here with the doors locked. I shouldn't be very long since I'm going to take a car this time."

She didn't say anything in return; she just stared at the floor and started to pick at a snag in her pants. I could tell she wanted to say something, but she stubbornly remained silent. I passed her a couple of generic painkillers, and she swallowed them in a hurry.

I went back to my preparation. Sitting on the couch, I refilled the magazines for my gun. There weren't very many bullets remaining in the box, and since the hardware store was a bust, I didn't know where else to get ammo from. All I needed were regular 9mm bullets, but even that was asking a lot now. I made sure I had my hunting knife and my axe. I really wished I still had my belt with the holsters to place the gun and my knife on. But it was currently residing back where the cabin was, having left it there in all the commotion.

We could try for a run to John's gun shop.

That thought honestly hadn't occurred to me until then, and I felt stupid for taking that long to come to that conclusion. Maybe they all went back there, too. Although, they would have needed to commandeer another vehicle since the truck was more than likely taken by Darren, and we currently had the car. It was the only place besides the cabin that we had all been to before.

I quickly pulled out the larger scale map of Louisiana and started to look for the area outside of New Orleans where John's shop was located. Taylor had circled it on our old map before and I knew it was just off of a main road that ran outside of the city, through a small suburb area. I scrambled around for a pen and circled roughly where Taylor had before. I had to basically carve into the laminated surface.

If I could just get myself to the outskirts by backtracking from the interstate to the suburbs, I was confident I could locate the store. There was that gas station and grocery store we had stopped at that stood out. If I found that, I could find the store. I finally had a concrete plan and it felt invigorating. My brain had finally kicked into gear. I felt like I should share my plan, since I wasn't the only one it affected.

"Chloe, I just had an idea."

She was already looking my way since she'd been watching me as I flew into motion, scanning the map.

"Once I go get some supplies from the medical center, I think we should try to go back to John's gun shop."

Chloe still refused to talk, but I could tell from her expression she thought this was a good idea too. Even if they weren't there, we could grab some much needed ammo and guns. She nodded and continued to pop trail mix into her mouth. Her hands were filthy, reminding me that there was still some water to wash up in.

"So it turns out there is still some water in the tank here. It'll be freezing, but you should go take a bath. I left soap and shampoo up there."

Without a word, she stood up and headed upstairs. I heard the groaning of the pipes a few minutes later. I was glad she listened. I would have to redo her wrappings again, but at least she wouldn't be covered in germs to feed the infection.

Once my weapons were in order, I stuffed a couple of water bottles and some quick food in my backpack, along with a flashlight we had found. I rescanned the local map, trying to memorize the route. I had to take a grand total of two left turns to get to the street I needed. The medical center was off of the main street, but there were residential houses still to one side of it. It almost seemed like someone converted an old house into the center.

Again, I wondered what the chances were that the place hadn't been picked clean. The rest of the town was still in pretty good shape, as far as buildings went anyways. The Main Street stores still had most of their windows intact and other than the major items like bullets and perishables, the stores were not completely empty.

I looked down at the keys to the house and the Taurus that were lying on the floor beside me. I was not mechanically inclined in any way, shape or form and I kept my fingers crossed that the car started without issue. I didn't want to potentially damage John's Mazda; we needed that one to run.

I got up and peeked out the front window, pulling the hideous curtains to the side. The street had a few roamers. One was dressed in a torn jogging suit, and for some reason the image of a zombie speed walking club popped into my head. I really was starting to question my sanity, but at this point, who wouldn't? After everything I had witnessed, I was surprised I wasn't rocking myself back and forth in a corner. *One day maybe.* Right now I had a goal to focus on which seemed to keep the lurking insanity at bay.

It took some effort, but my sore body was able to move the couch away from the front door. With my axe in hand, I closed the door behind me. I would need to take out the few infected before I left, for Chloe's safety. My limbs creaked in harmony with the porch stairs. There was nothing I wanted more at the moment than to soak in a hot tub.

One decayed head turned to me with a hiss and started its trek toward me. Once it got close enough, I brought the axe down, and the infected's head split open like a tree trunk. I quickly yanked the axe free from the fallen dead weight. The one in the track suit was now coming toward me, ironically a bit faster than the rest. Maybe she was in better shape as a human than the others. I swiped out my foot and the thing landed on the driveway hard. I heard the sound of a bone cracking and her right arm was now bent underneath her at an odd angle.

She reached up, intent on grabbing anything she could get her gnarled left hand on. I placed my foot down on her left arm to hold it down and clubbed her in the head with the flat side of the axe blade, like I was hammering a nail into a coffin. Despite my body's protest, I took out the remaining two. I looked around at the fallen infected. I sighed, knowing what I had to do next.

I started to drag the bodies to where I had hidden the last one. By the time I was done, there was quite the pile, but the overgrown bushes still managed to hide them. I walked back to the house, my elbow giving off heat it was so sore. I peered up into the bright, blue sky. It gave no indication of the horrors we were faced with, in fact it seemed almost serene. You would think with all that had happened that the sky would be a constant mass of dark clouds to reflect the abysmal form of life we were now forced to live. But no, it instead mocked us with its ocean blue hues; I was almost resentful.

With the keys in hand, I started the Taurus. I had to try a few times as the neglected engine tried to start. It roared to life on the third attempt and I watched the gas needle land on the full line. At least it had gas. When I was done with it, I would need to siphon the gasoline out for the Mazda. I turned on the windshield wipers to clean off the dusty mess. Chemical cleaner and dirt ran down the sides, and I could finally see out of the glass. Leaving it running, I went back inside and found Chloe sitting on the couch. I grabbed my backpack and weapons.

"Lock the door once I leave and keep your head down."

She didn't reply, and I shut the front door behind me.

Chapter 36

I got into the car and tossed my bag on the seat beside me along with my trusty axe. With one last look, I made sure the area around the house was clear. Nothing moved, so I hit reverse and left the neighborhood behind me. The street that connected to the cul-de-sac had barely any infected on it. Most of them must have been congregating in the alley behind the house we were squatting in.

There were a few wanderers on the road; I made a point to hit them. Pushing down on the gas petal, the Taurus lurched forward with infected in the crosshairs. A feminine-shaped one hit the right corner and spun like a top down to the tarmac. The next one hit the grill and bounced up, cracking the windshield on the passenger side. I watched in the rearview mirror as he landed in a crumpled mass on the hard ground.

A strange face peered back at me through my reflection. Her smirk was cruel and hollow. It scared me. I tore my eyes from the mirror and back to the road; there would be no more of that. This car was disposable to me, but I still needed it to get back. And encouraging crazy behavior could only lead to something worse. I was fully aware that it looked like I was coming unhinged. I wonder if most people who go crazy know they're insane? A question for the ages, I guess.

So I swerved to avoid the others in my way. I took my last left and found myself on the road that ran behind Main Street. Houses lined the boulevard, and I counted until I hit the fourth one in. That should be the medical center. There was a sign posted above the door that said, "Gibson Medical Center. All are welcome." No cars were parked outside, which was a good thing. Last thing I needed was to fight someone for the supplies inside. I parked and got out, with my backpack and weapons in tow.

An infected shuffled toward me from the front lawn, his face was...well...missing a part. A baseball sized chunk of the left side was gone. I could see through the cheek and into the mouth. Also the left eye was almost torn out of the socket. I had no idea if his face had been eaten or blown off with a gun. I used my axe to take it out of its misery. Again, I found myself dragging a body, this time disposing of it behind one of the neighboring white picket fences. *You know, there's a joke in there somewhere.*

Maybe that thing was here for some treatment or at least had tried to get some before he turned. This made me wary of what I would find in the medical center. I cautiously walked up to the front steps. Whoever owned this building had renovated it completely. The front door was one of those push open glass ones that you found in all the shops. There was also a metal gate pulled out on the inside for added security. It looked like the front door was a bust.

I should have known it wouldn't be that easy. The gate created a diamond pattern with the light, coating the front lobby in shadows. It had a reception desk and waiting room chairs lining the walls. There was a hallway that I couldn't see very far down toward the back. I started walking down the side of the building, looking to find another point of entry.

The backyard was like an extension of the waiting room. Instead of grass, the yard was covered in cement and had a bunch of tables and chairs. One of the canary yellow seats was occupied. A rather fat infected man was sitting in one. I tip-toed over to the unmoving mass and poked it with the end of my axe. Its bloodshot eyes snapped open and he lunged for me, moving faster than I thought possible. I scrambled back and tripped over an uneven slab of cement. The thing landed half on top of me and I struggled to push his heavy form off.

He snapped his teeth and gurgled, all while trying to claw at me. I pushed the handle of axe along the things neck, keeping his teeth away from me. My elbow protested the whole way, but I was able to muster enough strength to keep pushing the axe away until my arms were fully extended. Slowly, the infected rolled off of me and with a final shove, I bucked it to the side. I rolled as soon as I was clear and yanked out my hunting knife.

Had this been another time, I would have probably laughed at the fat infected as he struggled to get himself up, his bloated stomach creating an obstacle. I brought the knife down on the top of its head and it sunk down to ground. I wrenched the knife out of the infected's skull and wiped it off of his ripped dress shirt. It always seemed so insulting in movies when the killer would clean their weapon on the victims' clothes. Now it seemed more practical than cold.

I sheathed my knife and stretched out my elbow, trying to get rid of the stiffness that was setting in along with the pain. Another door blocked my entry. There was a heavy set padlock on the outside. I raised my axe and brought it down on the hasp staple. One side of metal piece detached from the wooden door frame and hung loosely. I tried the door knob, but I already knew that would be locked too.

I wedged the axe blade in between the door and frame as much as I could and started to pry it open. I was grunting from the exertion, the creaking sound of the frame spurring me on. After a few seconds the door slid open as the piece in the door frame came loose. I grabbed the door and yanked it all the way open. The smell hit me first. The place had been locked up tight and it looked like I was the first one to try to break in, so why would it smell like rotting bodies in here?

The light from the front didn't reach the back hallway, so I had to pull out my flashlight. The beam of light illuminated the dust motes flying in the air. It looked like I was the first one in here in a while. I closed the door behind me as much as I could. The long hallway was surrounded with doors, some open, some closed. I peered in the opened ones. They were the standard examination room with a chair and patient table in them. I tried the door labeled *Lab*, but it was locked. My elbow was begging me to stop using force, so I went in search of the keys.

Various medical posters lined the walls, stressing the importance of safe sex and getting your prostate checked. I made it all the way back to the front waiting room, which was still empty. The old floor creaked in one spot, the wood beginning to rot. I heard a bang come from below. I froze and swallowed. There was that cloying smell of rot, yet everything up here seemed clear.

Snooping through the receptionist desk, I found various labeled keys in the desk drawer. I scooped up the one that was for the lab and grabbed the basement one as well. The lab door opened with a click and I shone my flashlight in before entering. It was clear of bodies. Shelves lined the room and a locked cabinet at the back caught my attention. It was made of glass and I could see the pill bottles just sitting in there.

Using the end of my axe, I broke the glass doors, looking away as I smashed the glass. I read through all the labels and grabbed the ones that ended in the suffixes -mycin or -cillin. I knew enough that those were antibiotics. After throwing my stash into the backpack, I looked around for more supplies to scavenge. Sterile, stainless steel tools littered the place and gave me the urge to shiver. They always reminded me of horror movies.

A louder bang caught my attention. I shouldered my backpack again, the pills rattling like a child's toy. The noise had come from downstairs, and I headed back to the door labelled *Stairs*. It opened without a key, and I was faced with a looming set of stairs leading further down. I beamed my light in and saw another door at the bottom of the landing. The smell was tenfold down here.

Morbid curiosity was getting the better of me. I knew I should just leave now that I got what I came for, but part of me wanted to know what the hell was down there. I knew it would be nothing good, just like what we found in the hardware store. Using my axe, I propped open the door at the top of the stairs then started down. There was a rattling sound that was getting louder as my footfalls echoed in the confined space.

I stilled my breathing and put my ear up against the door. The rattling sound was coming from inside somewhere. The key fit in the lock perfectly, but my hand froze. Did I really want to see what was down here?

Then I heard a voice say, "Well, isn't this a coincidence?"

My heart stopped in my chest.

Chapter 37

I turned around slowly, dread like a lead ball in my stomach. At the top of the stairs stood Riley. He had a look on his face that I couldn't quite classify as a smile. *How did he find me?*

The pink tip of his tongue ran over the bottom of his teeth. "Well, I can't say this isn't a surprise, running into you like this. I thought we had seen the last of you."

"Are you following us?"

"Well, well. I thought you were a mute," he smirked. "You didn't say a word last time."

"Forced imprisonment does that to a person." I glared back.

His grin spread further across his face. "You left me with quite the souvenir, you know." His hand came to rest on the spot where my knife had sunk in. "I can't say I've ever let someone get the better of me before. Took ten stitches and a bottle of Captain Morgan to set me right."

What do I do? What do I do? Should I shoot at him? I was trapped at the bottom of the stairs with the unknown on the other side of the door. He'd more than likely return fire, and I was a sitting duck down here. I desperately wished that whatever was on the other side was an improvement. I turned the knob and dashed inside as I pulled out the keys. I fumbled with the lock on the inside, making sure they couldn't get it. Heavy footfalls sounded down the stairs.

"You're only going to make this harder on yourself," he said. "I just want to talk."

I'm sure all killers say that to their victims. It was pitch black down here and foul, damp air clawed at my nostrils. I dragged the flashlight from my backpack and clicked it on. I heard the chains rattle before I saw the bodies. A skeletal infected reared toward me, and I stumbled back until I hit the wall. It was yanked to a stop a few feet from me. With its arms outstretched, it scratched at the air between us.

I blinked a few times, my eyes adjusting to the sight and my heart rate starting to return to normal. A metal collar was fastened around the infected's neck, a chain running from it to the wall. Two other infected were chained up, but they didn't seem to have as long of a reach. One was not even moving, lying still in a pool of filth.

Okay, so this isn't an improvement. I needed to get out of here. I shone my flashlight around, trying to spot an escape route. Muffled voices were on the other side of the door; Riley must not have been alone. Then the banging started. They were ramming the door trying to get in. The two mobile infected now had all their attention focused on the smashing sound.

Using the wall as my guide I shuffled along, getting further out of their reach. The beam of light landed on a small, boarded up window. It was one of those tiny basement windows that basically served no purpose other than to make it feel less like a dungeon. Good thing I had lost weight in the last few months, I could probably squeeze through it now. I shuffled over, the infected still rapt upon the banging. It reminded me of when my brother used to taunt our neighbor's Rottweiler by banging on the fence. I ran into something hard at waist level and shone the light down. A mobile hospital bed laid in my way. The sheets were stained in blood, and a pair of handcuffs dangled from the bars.

I gulped audibly as I maneuvered around it, careful not to step into the infected's chain radius. They still weren't paying attention to me. I mean I was being extremely cautious with not making noise or sudden movements, but fresh meat had to be calling to them. I had never been so close to an infected and been so slow. Usually I was running from them. It was like I no longer held their interest once I wasn't making noise or making noticeable movements in their sight range.

Now was not the time to question it. I stuck the end of the flashlight into my mouth and tried to pry away the boards. They weren't nailed on, just placed against the glass. Daylight spilt through the small opening, providing a little bit of vision. Now I could see the basement more clearly.

There was a heavy, industrial door toward the back that looked like it headed into a small room. It seemed very out of place for a doctor's clinic. The walls were covered in smooth tiles, making it look more like a shower room than a basement. Hospital beds were scattered all over the room, tables with trays of tools beside them.

The gleam of stainless steel scalpels and scissors were reflected back at me. Maybe they had used this as an operation room? *Or for something worse?* The way the infected were chained up led me to believe the latter. And what the hell would they need the meat locker-looking room for? *The shit I get myself into...*

The banging increased tenfold, spurring me on to use the butt of the flashlight to smash the glass. Still using the flashlight, I cleared off the rest of the jagged pieces. I shoved my jingling backpack through the opening, but I couldn't reach it fully. I needed something to gain ground with. Whipping my head around, my eyes landed on the hospital bed I ran into. With a heft, I rolled it toward the window. The wheels squealed from lack of use, and one of the infected turned toward me. I stood as still as I could, waiting for it to go back to clawing uselessly in the direction of the door.

Once it grew tired of staring at me, I wheeled the bed the rest of the way. The door flew open at the same time I planted a foot on the bed. Riley, and the man I recognized as Conner, burst into the room momentarily caught off guard by the infected waiting to devour them.

"Holy shit!" Conner yelled as he slid to a stop.

Unfortunately for him, he entered the room first in a sprint and was unable to stop in time. The infected with the longest chain latched onto him and took a massive chunk out of his arm. Conner's scream bounced off the walls, encouraging the other infected.

Riley pulled out his gun.

"No man, don't!"

The gun flash briefly lit up the dim basement. Conner dropped like a stone, the hole in his head still smoking. The infected fell down with him, tearing into any part it could get to. Riley's head snapped in my direction, and I scrambled to get out, having wasted precious time watching the whole scene, hoping Riley would meet his end too. No such luck.

I had my arms and head through the opening, my legs flailing to try and get purchase. I felt a hand wrap around my ankle and yank. My arms scraped along the window frame, and I landed face first on the disgusting hospital bed. Then with another forceful pull, my face met the cold cement. I could taste blood in my mouth, my teeth having sliced open my tongue.

Riley tsked. "You just cost me another good team member." Roughly, he grabbed my upper arms and turned me over. "You're going to pay for that."

I spit the blood welling in my mouth at him. He made an angry grunt, and a hand flew to his face to wipe the blood off. I kicked out my leg, and it landed just to the right of his groin.

"Bitch!"

Using his brief moment of distraction, I scrambled onto all fours and got up. He was right behind me, having recovered fast. Riley tackled me to the ground; my hands flew out, instinctively grabbing at anything and a tray of tools clattered to the ground with us. The sound of the stainless steel hitting the cement rained down all around us.

I used the tray still gripped in my hand to smash Riley's face. He grabbed my wrist, pried the useless weapon from my hand and threw it away. It rattled like a tin sheet, as it sailed away from us. I fought to punch and hit him, but Riley managed to gather my wrists in his hands.

"Keep fighting me. I like it." He was out of breath from our wrestling.

"Fuck you!" I yelled straight into his face, blood and spit mixing with my harsh exclamation.

"You would like that wouldn't you?" His grin didn't reach his eyes, they were dark and dead. He might as well have been an infected for all I saw in there. "But that's not what this is about. Revenge. Once I kill you, I'll find the rest of your group and kill them too."

To emphasize his point, his hands moved from my wrists to my neck. My oxygen was cut off abruptly, and I clawed at the hands now squeezing the life out of me. The pressure on my neck was beyond painful, and I kicked out my legs, desperate to get air. Black dots began to line my vision.

"Fighting will only make it last longer."

The coldness in Riley's eyes was replaced with sick amusement. He liked killing. This world didn't ruin his life; it set him free. He had killed before and would keep doing it. What if he did find my friends? What if he found Chloe? I removed my nails from the hand wrapped around my neck and felt around the floor near me, looking for anything that could be a weapon. I didn't have much time. I was fading; blackness invaded the edges of my vision, like termites eating away wood.

My hand wrapped around the hilt of one of the dropped tools and with my last remaining strength I brought my arm up in a wide arc. The sharp edge of whatever tool I had grabbed embedded itself in Riley's neck. His eyes went wide in shock, and his hands flew to his neck.

Cool, blessed air reached my starved lungs and I heaved in deep breaths. My eyes watered, and my throat burned like I had never felt before. It was like acid-coated the inside of my throat and air was water being poured onto it. Riley was pale and clutching at the handle protruding from his neck. Blood poured from the wound like a faucet turned to max. It looked like I had stabbed him with a scalpel.

He collapsed to the ground, his mouth open and flapping like a gaping fish on land. I hauled myself to shaky feet and reached into my waistband. I loomed over him, the gun aimed right for his forehead. Once he saw the gun in my hand, he reached up. Whether it was to plead for his life or beg for it to be quick, I will never know, because I pulled the trigger.

He won in the end. Now I was a monster, too.

Epilogue

I don't remember much of the drive back to the house. Hell, I don't even remember how I got out of the medical center. It was like a time skip. One minute I was standing over a dead body, the next I was parked, sitting in the front seat of the Taurus with my backpack in the passenger's side.

I had killed a living person, but I was glad Riley was gone. Something like peace settled over me. I stared into the rearview mirror, prodding at my red neck. Bruising was already starting to mar my skin. I tried to speak, but a squeak was all that escaped. Swallowing hurt like a bitch, but was still working correctly.

There was one less threat in the world and that had to count for something. It was cut and dry case of self-defense, and no one could hold that against me.

Was it self-defense? I could have easily gotten away while Riley squirmed on the floor in his own blood. He eventually would have died from blood loss anyways. At least, that's what I told myself. But that wasn't the only reason.

I wanted to do it. I wanted to see with my own eyes that he had died. And I did.

I walked from the driveway to the house, looking no more alive than the mountains of infected I had killed. I felt subhuman. Stopping, I dropped my backpack to the ground. The front door seemed to be getting further and further away. My mind was starting to play tricks on me. My subconscious was none-to-subtly telling me not to go in.

I was not ready to play human, at least not so soon after. Maybe I should have stayed away. It was faint, but I still heard the sound of the deadbolt being flipped. The door opened to reveal the little concerned face of Chloe. I peered back at her, not saying anything, not daring to move. She looked at me, her eyes taking in the damage I had sustained and the backpack resting at my feet.

She threw open the door and tore down the steps. She ran into me full force. Her arms wrapped around my middle and I could tell she was sobbing.

"You came back!" she cried, hugging me tightly.

I placed a hand on her head. I wanted to tell her that of course I did, but my voice wasn't cooperating at the moment. She looked up at me, and I pointed to my neck so she would know why I couldn't speak. She didn't need to know that my reluctance to speak was not only due to physical limitations.

"You're hurt."

I gave her a meager smile and thumbs up to let her know I would be fine. She released me and placed her small hand in mine, determination set in her features.

"Don't worry. We'll find 'em."

Bonus Chapter

New Orleans, Three months earlier

Zoe was facing me, her mouth going a mile a minute. I couldn't hear her over the roar of the crowd and music. Horns were blasting nearby and I, by some means, ended up with more than one metallic bead necklace. This was odd because I was less risqué than Zoe, who had actually *earned* her beads. One drunken frat guy tried to lift up my shirt, but that ended when I kneed him in the groin. I don't think he appreciated the grin on my face.

Zoe quickly dragged me away from the scene; the guy's friends were hollering and dying of laughter at their fallen comrade. She tried to chastise me for not playing nice, but the effect was ruined by the pulsing dance music.

"You know, we're supposed to be living out our last moments of university life before we have to head into the drudgery of real life," she screamed over the noise.

"So? That doesn't equate to be accosted," I shot back.

Zoe rolled her eyes and downed the rest of her drink.

"Live a little! Come on, let's get some shots!"

Oh God, once the shots started I was a goner—but what the hell. I let her drag me over to the nearest drink stand and shove a countless number of shots my way. She was flirting with the drink server when my pocket started to vibrate. *What the...? Oh right, my phone.* I pulled my cellphone from my pocket, a text message popping up on the screen from my mother. *Condoms or do I have to show you the book again?*

Oh god, not the book! My mother was a doctor to her core, even when it came to her children. I remember the sex talk she gave me when I was a preteen; it included the dreaded book. I had nightmares after that. It showcased a bunch of information and pictures of various STDs. It was technically a textbook, but dear god it was awful. Those poor med students.

I tried to put it from my mind as another alert popped up on my screen. This one from CNN about another confirmed case of a new strain of the flu virus or whatever it was; I just sort if skimmed it. This was like the fifth article in the last few hours. If they kept this up, people would start to freak out. Oddly enough, this one stated that the sick individuals were harming others. Someone from the CDC was speculating that the high-grade fever was causing the erratic behavior. I guess I would just have to keep an eye out for anyone who looked sickly.

The phone slid back into my pocket, and I threw back another shot, this time some Jose Cuervo. Zoe nodded her head toward the biggest mass of people and we squeezed ourselves into the mosh pit of partiers. Despite my earlier reluctance, I actually enjoyed myself. It was easy to get lost in the overbearing music and dance, until you threw up your overpriced drinks. Well, maybe not that last part.

We had been having a good time until the music near us cut and someone yelled, "Cops!" over the fray. People panicked and started to disperse. There were a lot of underaged kids here and some pretty high people, so I guess that was reason enough to run. Zoe shrugged at me and pointed her thumb to the other stage down the street. I nodded, and we walked with the crowd to the other area. Police were running toward us, heading to where we had just come from telling people to move along. *I wonder if cops were contractually forced to say that?*

I looked back, curiosity getting the better of me, but I couldn't see anything over the horde of people migrating to a cop free zone. There were a group of guys walking beside us chatting about it.

"Dude, there was blood everywhere."

"I've never seen so many cops at once before."

"Please, your family is like the poster child for the TV show *Cops*."

"Fuck you, Darren!"

"There's always one douchebag who has to bring a knife."

"Naw man, that's the thing. He didn't have a weapon, he used his *teeth*."

Huh, I guess some people just can't handle their alcohol.

About the Author

N. D. Iverson is a writer living in Alberta, Canada, trying to find her niche in the world. She has a Bachelor of Commerce degree – which she is still trying to find a practical application for. *This Would Be Paradise* is her first book and will not be her last. You can count on that. For more information, please visit her website at http://www.ndiverson.weebly.com.

Want to be the first to hear about sequels, new releases, and discounts?
Join her mailing list! http://eepurl.com/brHXVf

Thank you for reading!

Dear Reader,

I hope you enjoyed the first installment in my Zombie Novel Series *This Would Be Paradise*. I've had many readers ask me: "What is the next chapter in Bailey and Chloe's adventure?" and "Will they ever find their group again?" Well, I say stay tuned because the next exciting arc in their story will be coming in This Would Be Paradise Book 2.

As an author I love to hear what readers think after reading my novel. Some people rooted for Taylor and Bailey to be together, while others rooted for Ethan and Bailey to be together. Some people could identify with Bailey on a personal level, while others better identified with Zoe. So please feel free to tell me what you thought after reading the book, what you loved, even what you hated. I'd love to hear from you. You can contact me through my website here: http://ndiverson.weebly.com/contact.html.

Finally, I would like to ask a favor. If you're so inclined, I'd love a review of *This Would Be Paradise*. As a self-published author, Amazon and other eBook site reviews are my bread and butter. You the reader have the power to make or break a book. If you have the time, you can find my books to review on Amazon, Nook, Kobo, iTunes, and Goodreads.

Thank you so much for reading *This Would Be Paradise*.
In gratitude,

N. D. Iverson

Book 2

This Would Be Paradise: Book 2 is now available at all eBook retailers!